THE REMOVED

THE REMOVED

BRANDON HOBSON

WHEELER PUBLISHING
A part of Gale, a Cengage Company

LIBRARY OF CONGRESS CIP DATA ON FILE.
CATALOGUING IN PUBLICATION FOR THIS BOOK
IS AVAILABLE FROM THE LIBRARY OF CONGRESS.

ISBN-13: 978-1-4328-8946-3 (hardcover alk. paper)

Published in 2021 by arrangement with Ecco, an imprint of HarperCollins Publishers

Printed in Mexico
Print Number: 01   Print Year: 2021

In memory of my uncles, Bob and Leon Briggs, who spirit-walked across water to visit me during the writing of this book.

(ᎯᏍᏇ ᎤᏔᏪᏉ ᎯᏍᎫ)

Our moans were night crawlers under the weight of removal.

— Diane Glancy,
Pushing the Bear

PROLOGUE:
RAY-RAY ECHOTA

September 5
Quah, Oklahoma

The day before he died, in the remote town of Quah, Oklahoma, Ray-Ray Echota rode his motorcycle down the empty stretch of highway, blowing past rain puddles and trees, a strong wind pressing against his body. He was fifteen years old. Workers along the side of the road wore orange vests and white hard hats. They didn't pay any attention to him as he flew past them, hunched forward working the throttle. He rode for the pureness of the thrill and for the isolation of riding alone in an area where few police officers ever patrolled. Clouds hung low and pale before him as he rode home past fields and old buildings, heading east into the hills, landscape and sky blending into the horizon.

That night he did impersonations at home to entertain his parents. While Ernest and

Maria watched their police drama on TV, Ray-Ray staggered into the living room wearing dark sunglasses and waving a cane around, pretending he was blind. He stood in front of them, blocking their view of the TV, and spoke in his best French accent: "Care to help an old blind man, monsieur? I am in need of assistance."

"Funny," Maria said. "Isn't he funny, Ernest?"

"I'm trying to watch my show," Ernest said.

"But monsieur," Ray-Ray said.

Ernest leaned forward and watched Ray-Ray as he removed his sunglasses and went through his usual impersonations: Pee-wee Herman, Marlon Brando's Vito Corleone, even Ernest's friend Otto, who told old Cherokee stories drunk:

"Listen, Chooch," Ray-Ray said in Otto's low drunken voice. He pretended to smoke an imaginary cigarette. "You know the story of Tsala, who was killed for refusing to leave the land? Let's go get another whiskey."

"Not bad," Ernest said. "We'll probably see him tomorrow at the Cherokee National Holiday."

The following day, September 6, marked the anniversary of the 1839 signing of the Constitution of the Cherokee Nation in

Oklahoma. Ernest spoke with an unfamiliar excitement in his voice about the date's importance. "This is a very important day for all of us, since it marks the Trail, so we should honor it." September 6 usually fell close to Labor Day weekend and brought people from all over the country to Oklahoma. The Echotas planned to spend the entire weekend watching stickball games, attending powwows, pageants, and art shows.

Outside, a storm was heading west instead of east. A soft rain pattered against the window, the beginning of a thunderstorm. The night was cool. The house smelled of fried catfish from dinner, which they had eaten on TV trays there in the living room.

"Did you finish your homework?" Maria asked Ray-Ray.

"The paper is done. A-plus with smiley face. I bid you all good night. Ave atque vale."

"What?"

"It's Latin for hail and farewell. Ave atque vale."

"Sure, sure," Maria said. "Now go play with your little brother."

Edgar, the youngest sibling, was sitting on a blanket playing quietly with Legos in the corner of the room, as he often did. Ray-

11

Ray limped over to him, dragging his leg like a wounded soldier, and collapsed. He began helping Edgar stack Legos together.

When Ray-Ray was younger he had fallen out of the tree in their backyard, breaking his leg in three places. He'd spent a few days in the hospital, where he told the nurse he had learned to levitate like the false prophet Simon Magus.

"I flew up in the air forty, fifty feet and then fell," he said. "That explains the broken leg."

The nurse looked at Ernest and Maria, confused.

"My son has an active imagination," Ernest kept saying, which was true. Ray-Ray always carried with him a notebook in which he scribbled song lyrics and sketched strange creatures, beasts with fire shooting from their eyes and tongues hanging from their mouths, chubby old men with pig snouts instead of noses, and Uktena and Tlanuwa, the mythic hawks who carried away babies. Ernest and Maria encouraged his artistry, his drawings and impersonations, and also loved how he enjoyed searching outside near the lake for animal bones, bird bones, and feathers to make necklaces. How he wore certain shirts he said were for healing. How he was fascinated

12

by the sky and would go lie down and watch the stars at night. How he mowed lawns and cleaned roof gutters for two summers until he earned enough money to buy his own 250cc Nighthawk, the motorcycle he would ride to the mall in Tulsa on September 6, the day he was shot by a police officer.

Sonja, who was sixteen and the eldest sibling, was eccentric in her own way too, retreating to her room every day after school and staying there all night, rarely coming out. Sensitive to the strange intimacy of family conversations, she preferred solitude. On this night, she was in her bedroom writing long letters to boys at school and listening to Joy Division. She would later wonder why she hadn't been in the living room spending time with Ray-Ray. If only I'd been a better sister, she often thought.

The night of September 5, his last night alive, Ray-Ray lay next to his younger brother Edgar on the floor with the Legos. "We should build a castle," he said. "It could be beautiful, brother."

"I'm building a monster," Edgar told him excitedly. He held up his Lego creature and roared.

"Little brother," Ray-Ray said, "there are enough monsters in this world."

■ ■ ■ ■

PRESENT DAY

■ ■ ■ ■

PRESENT DAY

MARIA ECHOTA

September 1
Near Quah, Oklahoma
At sunset the locusts flew, a whole swarm of them, disappearing into the darkening sky. They buzzed each night, moving through wind and trees, devouring crops and destroying gardens. The sky was pink and blue on the horizon. Another unusually rainy season had caused weeds to sprout up everywhere, so we were seeing more locusts, more insects.

"When was the last time it snowed?" Ernest asked.

My husband was in the early stages of Alzheimer's. He was seventy-four but looked young for his age. He still kept his gray hair long in a ponytail, still had his same laugh and sense of humor, though he was getting more and more confused. We had known about the Alzheimer's for almost a year, and of course these things never get easier with

17

time. He grew frustrated easily. He would forget little things like why he'd walked into a room. Whenever he did this, he would look down at the floor and struggle to understand. I would find him rummaging through the garage, and when I asked him what he was looking for, he couldn't tell me. He was growing considerably worse.

"I'm turning into tawodi," he said. "*Tawodi* means hawk in Cherokee."

We were sitting on our back deck, where Ernest liked to look for geese flying over the lake. I watched him lean forward, squinting.

"I'll eat locusts and honey like John the Baptist," he said.

"Ernest," I said quietly.

"I see a sailboat out there. I see smoke or fog, maybe a spirit."

"There is no spirit out there," I told him.

He reclined back in his chair, still looking.

"Ernest," I said, "tomorrow Wyatt is coming. Did you remember?"

He was thinking.

"The foster boy," I said. "I have Ray-Ray's old room ready for him."

"You already mentioned it before."

"He'll be here tomorrow," I said. "Remember?"

"Wyatt, sure," Ernest said. "Stop asking me if I remember."

18

"I wanted to make sure."

"I got it."

The call had come a few days earlier from Indian Family Services. It was Bernice, a former coworker of mine. I had retired from social work a year earlier. Bernice said they needed an emergency foster placement for a twelve-year-old Cherokee boy. Would Ernest and I be able to take him in temporarily?

"You're our only available Cherokee family," Bernice said. "His dad's in jail, mom left the state. Right now he's at an aunt's, but she's in bad health. We're trying to contact grandparents."

When I told Ernest, I was surprised he agreed. We had never fostered before. "He can mow the grass," Ernest said. "He can play checkers. Catch fish."

We could see the lake behind our house, and a small amber pond down past where the road ended was also visible. Most people liked to go fishing at the lake, but Ernest preferred the pond, which he said was always a decent place to fish, full of catfish and largemouth bass. There were fewer people there, and bullfrogs and yellow-striped ribbon snakes lived in the water. He had been talking about fishing a lot more.

Ernest shivered in his sweater, even though

it was still warm. "Time to go inside," he said, getting up from his chair.

"I'll be right in," I told him.

He slid open the screen door and stepped inside. I leaned forward and looked out over the yard. Red and yellow leaves were scattered everywhere on the sloping ground. Evenings were quiet and still. Some mornings I sat on that deck and watched a red-tailed hawk return to its same nesting tree while red-winged blackbirds gathered at the birdhouse. Every now and then several cedar waxwings would land on a branch, apple-blossom petals in their beaks, and sit there watching me.

In the distance, tonight, a fog settled over the lake, and I could sense the presence of something gathering there.

We lived on a winding dirt road by Lake Tenkiller in a hardwood forest of persimmon, oak, and hickory trees near the Cookson Hills. Many years ago, the Cherokees came to this area during the Trail of Tears to build a nation. They developed a tribal government, constructed buildings and schools, and invented a syllabary. Ernest and I both grew up in Quah. When we were newly married, he built a back deck onto our house, overlooking the slope of trees

20

down to the edge of the water.

It was in this place that we raised our three children. Here, in our house made of rock and brick, with its slanted roof and chimney full of spirits. Here, where we slept under the blue light of the moon in the dark sky, waking sometimes to see a deer at the edge of the yard. I remember seeing a family of deer gather down the hill near the water. And how sad our daughter Sonja was when they never returned, and how Ray-Ray promised they would return one day. Sonja was only a teenager. After Ray-Ray died, she sat watching for a deer all winter, but we never saw them again. "It's deer season," she said. "Maybe they died, too. Maybe someone shot them and dragged their bodies away in their truck." I pictured their bodies hanging somewhere, and all that blood dripping. We sat on the back deck, and I prayed for deer to return and for Sonja to heal. We soon saw other deer along the road, but Sonja was still unhappy. "It's not the same family," she said. "I can tell. This deer is different. The deer that came to our house are dead."

Fifteen years earlier, on September 6, our son Ray-Ray rode his motorcycle to a mall where he evidently got into an altercation with two other guys. Someone fired a gun, and Ray-Ray was shot in the chest by a police officer. The police officer heard a gunshot and instinctively fired at the Indian kid. Afterward, when the police officer gave his statement to the press, he swore he thought Ray-Ray had been the one who shot the gun, but it had been a white kid. The officer was temporarily placed on administrative leave. After months of investigation, the police department declared that the officer's behavior was justified in the shooting, so it never went to trial.

Everything changed in me after that.

How do you lose a child to gun violence and expect to return to a normal way of life? This was the question I struggled with the most. My son was a victim. The officer who shot him — now retired — lived in our town, and there were many sleepless nights when I wanted to drive to his house and kill him myself. I wanted to hit him as hard as I could, so that he could feel pain. Yes, yes, I have always known grief is difficult and that forgiveness takes many years. I still haven't learned to completely forgive. I could only put it in the will of the Great Spirit. Ernest handled it better than me; he was able to get himself together and go back to work at the railroad after a month or so. A doctor prescribed Xanax for me, and then for a long time all I did was sleep. Every day I sat in a chair by the window.

My sister Irene came and stayed with us to help out, especially with Sonja and Edgar. In the midst of my depression, Irene dragged me to a Methodist church service one Sunday, where I heard the Doxology for the first time. After that I kept hearing the phrase in my head: "Praise God from whom all blessings flow," over and over. When I got home, I wrote it down in my notebook. My therapist encouraged me to journal as much as possible. I once wrote, *I no longer am afraid of dying. If I die in my sleep, I am fine with that.* Another time I wrote, *I feel so guilty for wanting to die when I have Sonja and Edgar who so desperately need me. I feel like a terrible person.* But the Doxology kept returning to me. Thinking about it was so comforting, I found my journaling didn't return to such a dark place.

Ernest kept his mind busy by focusing on Sonja and Edgar, being a good father. He took them out to movies, to parks, anything he could do to get them out of the house while I stayed in my chair, depressed. Only in the past few years have we finally started acknowledging the anniversary of Ray-Ray's death. Now, every September 6 we build a small bonfire, and each of us shares a memory. Ernest and I decided it would be a good way to get the family together, because we were never all together anymore.

Around six in the evening, I heated up a leftover casserole for supper. Ernest and I ate on trays in front of the TV, watching a show on unsolved crimes. Ernest kept pointing the remote and adjusting the volume up and down.

"Maybe the foster kid can fix the TV," he said.

"Well, there's nothing wrong with the TV."

"I think it's the volume."

"The volume is fine."

"What do we do? Sit here and take it?"

I saw the frustration in his face, looking at the remote. He was obsessed with the colored buttons and their functions, the menus on the screen. The remote made him nervous. I thought of the years in the past when we had sat in the same chairs in front of the TV, eating supper contentedly. How different he looked now, giving such a confused gaze, a confirmation that things were declining quickly. While he continued to stare intently at the remote, I heard Sonja come in through the front door. She lived just down the road in a small house and had been coming over more often now that

Ernest was getting worse.

He looked up at her when she stepped into the room, and for a moment I wondered whether he even recognized her. She walked over to him and put her hand along his back, rubbing in a light circular motion. "How are you, Papa?"

"I don't know. Goddamn remote."

Her face grew solemn, as if she realized the severity of his illness. We were all speechless for a moment while I stared at her. Sonja, at thirty-one, strongly resembled my sister Irene when she was younger, though they were nothing alike. My sister had always been demure, reserved, conservative. Sonja stayed out late nights. I worried about her and the younger men she dated, some of whom attended the college in Quah. I wanted her to settle down; Ernest and I both did, but the more we brought it up, the more she withdrew from us.

"There's a guy I want to meet," she finally said.

"A new guy?" I said. "What does he do?"

"He's a musician," she said. "I'm going to see him play tonight at a bar near campus. Tonight I'm going to talk to him. I'm finally going to meet him. I've thought about it for weeks."

"A musician? What's his real job?"

25

"I haven't even met him yet."

"Well, how old is he?"

"I don't know. Twenty-three?"

I didn't say anything. I got up, and Sonja followed me, helping me take the dishes into the kitchen. I turned on the water in the sink and rinsed the plates, then handed them to Sonja to put in the dishwasher.

"Did you talk to Edgar about Ray-Ray's anniversary next week?" she asked.

"I was busy helping Irene at the powwow all weekend, but yesterday I tried calling him, and he hasn't called me back."

"Me either," she said. "I'm concerned."

"I am, too," I said. "It's been too long. It's been weeks."

"He might be embarrassed," she said.

We'd had an intervention with Edgar six months earlier. He had been living with his girlfriend, Desiree, in New Mexico and got hooked on meth. He'd stolen money from Desiree and from us. Before the intervention, he had visited and said he needed money to pay for an alternator replacement on his car, plus repairs for an oil leak. Ernest loaned him over $400 in cash. He'd already dropped forty pounds in weight, so we were on edge. Sonja thought he was doing cocaine, too. Edgar was only twenty-one, my youngest baby. The thought of his

26

drug use had nauseated me. I could hardly eat. A month later Desiree had called and said she had to bail him out of jail for breaking into a car.

Ernest, Sonja, and I had driven to Albuquerque to confront him. We arrived at the rental house he shared with Desiree, who was waiting for us on the front porch when we pulled into the drive. Edgar was taking a nap on the couch. When we walked in, he woke with a start and sat up. He didn't say anything, but he looked terrified. I think he knew what was happening. I sensed that Desiree had already said something to him, and that he expected us. We all sat down at the kitchen table with him and told him we were worried, his drug use out of control, he was slowly killing himself, and we didn't want to watch him die.

"You have to realize the harm you're doing to yourself," I told him. "We want you to get help before it's too late."

I thought the intervention had worked. He broke down, told us he would go to rehab as long as we paid for it. Sonja had already found a residential treatment center in Tulsa, where he agreed to check himself in the following week, but he never went. We couldn't force him to go, and his relationship with Desiree was falling apart. We had spoken to him a few times on the phone, but he mostly kept his distance from us, which surely meant he was still using. I prayed he would come home.

In the kitchen I wiped my hands on a dish towel and turned to Sonja. "Do you think there's any chance he'll show up next week?"

"He knows it's important to us," she said.

"You think so?"

"I mean, I think so."

"Tell him it's important to Ray-Ray," I said.

That night Ernest woke me from sleep. He was standing beside the bed with his hand on mine. I felt the coldness of his hand and sat up.

"What is it?" I said.

"There's a noise," he said. "It's coming from somewhere outside. I have to go outside and check."

"What kind of noise?"

"I don't know, a hard knock. A clanging. I heard it outside. I have to go check."

He started for the door. I didn't want him going alone, so I put on my slippers and followed him down the hall into the kitchen, where he peeked out the window. He turned on the back porch light, unlocked the door, and stepped out. I waited by the door, watching from the window while he looked around. He walked to the side of the house, then to the middle of the backyard. He stood still for a moment, as if he'd forgotten something. Then he headed to the shed, and I saw the light come on in there.

I opened the back door and walked to the shed. Once, a few years back, we kept birdfeed in large sacks out there, but that had caused a problem with mice. That was the winter Ernest was hospitalized for pneumonia, and every day when I returned home from the hospital, I found another dead mouse in a trap. We never went into the shed anymore.

"I'm looking for the rocks Edgar was talking about," Ernest said.

"What rocks?" I said.

"The colored rocks. I think he said green or red rocks."

"When?"

He hesitated, confused, so I waited for him to finish. He kept looking around. The shelves were mostly filled with old paint cans and tools. There was an old basketball trophy in the corner of the shed. Ernest picked it up and held it so that I could get a good look at it. "Edgar's trophy," he said. "Basketball from junior high. When was it?"

Things were getting more difficult at night, much worse than during the day. Sleep problems, the confusion of dreams. He had always been a deep sleeper and heavy dreamer. We used to tell each other about our dreams, laughing at the absurdity, the surreal humor, even back when the kids were still young. But now it was too difficult to watch him mumble on about things he created in his mind — hearing noises, looking for figurines.

He stared at the trophy, looking sad. It was as if he understood how confused he was. Maybe he realized the foolishness of his actions, waking up in the middle of the night and dragging us both outside to the shed. But I let him have his time.

He said, "I guess he's gone, Maria."

I waited for him to look at me.

He said, "I wish he'd come home."

"Me, too," I said. "Let's go back to bed."

That night, unable to fall asleep, I sat at the dining room table with my notebook. I journaled intermittently, which had always helped ease my mind:

The bonfire is in five days. I have so much I need to do to prepare for it, but I worry Ernest can't handle it anymore. I want Edgar here. I don't want to lose him like we lost Ray-Ray.

I considered the complexities of time, how slowly and how quickly it moves. Fifteen sad years had passed since Ray-Ray died. We had started having the bonfire on the tenth anniversary of his death, and for the past five years it had become a way for us to get together and be honest with one another and focus on the importance of our family, our land. Even though Ernest and I had both grown up near here, I never felt such a strong connection to the land around us until we started doing the bonfires. But with Ernest's declining Alzheimer's over the past year, I feared this would be the last bonfire. Our very first bonfire, which was Ernest's idea, he and Edgar went out to gather firewood together. They came back laughing about something Edgar had seen, a stick or twig he had mistaken for a snake, which had made him drop the firewood and run. Ernest kept laughing about that, I remember. And as we stood around the bonfire, reflecting on what we were thankful for, Ernest had said: "I'm thankful we can laugh even in times of sadness." This was our gift to Ray-Ray, our way of understanding and making healing and sadness feel eminently right.

This is my hope, I wrote in my journal that first year, *that the bonfire will continue as a memorial for Ray-Ray and to mourn for others who pass away in the years to come.*

Edgar had made it to the bonfire every year, and since the intervention had failed, I hoped this year's bonfire would be one more chance to help him back on the right path. I wouldn't give up on him. I was consumed by an emptiness I tried to fill however I could: through prayer, meditation, journaling. For the first time in many years, I struggled to sleep at night, worried about Edgar and Ernest. At such times I always felt that an epiphany was about to come to me, but I was never able to put my finger on it. One night some months earlier, thinking Ernest had quit breathing in his sleep, I turned over in bed to see that he was in fact awake, staring up at the ceiling with the fear of someone who had been struck repeatedly across the face. "I dreamed about dead people," he whispered, immediately closing his eyes and falling back asleep. The next morning Ernest had no memory of it, but the moment haunted me.

When I did manage to sleep, I often dreamed about Ray-Ray as a young child, maybe five or six years old. I never dreamed of him as a teenager, even though he was fifteen when he passed. In these dreams he would be missing, and I couldn't find him. Ernest and I would show up at a gymnasium to pick him up, and he wouldn't be there. Or we would be at a crowded park somewhere, searching for him. Those dreams were the hardest.

I had another recurring dream, about a man carrying an owl. I wondered who he was, this stranger. He was silent and kind, offering me beads or a piece of warm bread, a cup of dark wine to drink. There was nothing romantic or attractive about this, and certainly nothing suggestive about my feelings toward him. If anything, he appeared as a traveling monk, maybe a spiritual man, dressed in ragged clothes and holding the owl on his arm.

"It sounds like you're dreaming about Skili," Irene once told me. "He's a ghost or bad spirit. He brings bad news."

But I didn't tell anyone about my dreams of Ray-Ray appearing in the form of a bird. When I woke and sat outside on the back deck in the mornings, sometimes a bird would fly near and land in the grass, cock its head as if watching me. It made me miss him terribly.

Sitting at the dining room table, I closed

my notebook and turned off the light. I felt my way in the dark down the hall to our bedroom and got back into bed. My mind was alive, racing with thoughts as usual. Tomorrow the foster boy, Wyatt, would be coming into our home, this house made of strong brick and rock. This house able to withstand bad weather and furious winds throughout the years, with its stable roof and walls and plaster that tightened when the earth moved. This house, our house, that creaked and ticked with the passing of time, welcoming the voices of strangers and the company of spirits whose laughter lifted like smoke through the chimney. I wondered how such a place remained firm, intact, solid, throughout its years of soaking up all the crying and pain, the laughter and longing, all the memories birthed from my swollen belly.

EDGAR ECHOTA

Rae and I ate in silence. Actually her name
was Desiree, but I called her Rae, like my
brother's name. We were living in a cheap
rental house with dirty windows and bugs
behind the refrigerator and in the bathroom.
I needed help. My drug supply was low. I
knew I was spiraling into a meth addiction,
and I took oxycodone, too, or whatever I
could get. Everyone knew what was happening to me, how horrible I'd started to
look and how bad my addiction was becoming. Doing pills had started as a way for me
to avoid feeling miserable all the time, but
the more I used, the more depressed I
became. It was a fucking nightmare. I was
only twenty-one and already at a dead end.
Rae was about to leave me. I knew I was
getting worse because I could look anyone
in the face, even her, and tell a long,

elaborate lie. It made me feel awful, even though I knew I was a terrible liar anyway.

We stared into our plates, moving pasta around with our forks, pausing every so often to drink cheap wine from plastic cups. We barely ate anything. Light slanted in through the windows, pulsing particles of dust. The house ached with a sense of dread for me — I could feel it everywhere, on our street, or in every New Mexico town surrounding us. I wondered whether something bad was about to happen to me. I pictured other people like me, fuckups getting high and avoiding their own loved ones, looking out their windows with longing and terror, afraid of their lives falling apart. Thinking this made me feel better.

It was like this night after night. I had followed Rae to art school a year earlier, back when I still felt hopeful about our relationship and my future. I kept my drug use a secret for months, meeting people in the park or smoking when Rae was gone and I was in the house alone. It didn't take long for Rae to notice that I was becoming overly thin, developing tooth decay and skin sores.

At the table I had a sudden coughing fit, bringing a napkin to my mouth, which made Rae stand up and take her plate to the kitchen sink. I heard the water from the faucet come on, then the grind of the garbage disposal. Her silence was a presence designed to put me on edge, a way of communication to reinforce what I feared would happen soon: that she would leave for good. Once Rae left, I knew I would be truly alone, since I had been pulling away from my family for months. Ever since they showed up for the intervention, I had been promising to go to rehab, and I wanted to go because I knew how much sadness and worry I had caused them. But I couldn't bring myself to check in, and now I was way too embarrassed to go back home and face them.

I set my fork down and watched Rae rinse dishes in the kitchen.

"Put on Ornette Coleman," she called out to me. "The record we were listening to last night."

I downed my cup of wine and went over to the turntable to put on the album. I put the needle on the record and, as the music played, picked up the album cover and looked at it. Rae once said Ornette Coleman was the spitting image of her dad, who had been a jazz drummer himself. Maybe that was why she wanted to listen to it. Her dad had introduced her to free jazz in New Orleans, where Rae spent summers growing up. He died when she was a teenager. When we first met, we had bonded over our experience losing a family member. Death brought us together, that's what we always joked.

I sat on the couch and listened to the frantic shrill of the trumpet, the wild cymbals and drums. Listening to jazz revved me. I could drum my hands on my lap for entire songs, long periods of time, which was something I did almost every time we listened to music. I could imitate Charlie Watts, Stewart Copeland. That drummer from Cheap Trick with the cigarette hanging from his mouth. Rae hated when I did this. She stepped out onto the back porch to smoke and talk on the phone. I never knew who she was talking to. I wanted to care more than I did, but our relationship had become so routine and dull that I never felt the desire to ask. When she came back into the house, she told me my mom had called her.

"What did she want?"

"I'm tired of making excuses for you," she said. "Call her yourself. The anniversary is coming up."

"I plan on going," I said, but I didn't know if I wanted to go home or not. I knew Rae was pulling away from me. I wondered whether she was cheating on me, although she had never actually given me any reason to be suspicious. All she wanted, I think, was some sort of physical tenderness from me, or maybe a sign of empathy, which I never gave her. I knew deep down it was my fault she was pulling away, but I almost wanted her to for some reason. I couldn't understand why I would want to punish myself.

I looked up and saw that she was standing with her hand on her hip, giving me a look like she couldn't understand anything I was saying.

"I don't know," I said.

She stopped herself from speaking, looking annoyed, then turned and went back into the kitchen, which made me want a hit from the pipe. I did not feel guilty or ashamed of this, of course, because the way I saw it, getting high could make me feel better the same way antidepressants helped people, even though it wasn't doing anything anymore except making me feel worse. I understood, too, that I needed to get better so I could be a better boyfriend to Rae. I'd worked on a ranch with my friend Eddie for a while, which was good for me, but at the end of summer the work ran out and I had to get a job I hated at a hardware store.

They let me go after missing too many days. Now I couldn't get motivated to find more work. Rae worked at an art gallery and was able to handle the bills, and I felt guilty about not being more interested in helping out.

While Rae was in the kitchen I stepped into the bedroom, quickly pulled off my T-shirt, and got the pipe from my dresser. A hit or two from the pipe always revived me. When Rae came into the bedroom, I was already smoking.

"What the fuck are you doing?" she said.

I was hunched over my pipe, taking another hit.

"What the fuck, Edgar?"

I finished one more hit, and when I turned to her, she was already gone. I set the pipe down carefully on my dresser, then went to the screen door and saw her pulling out of the drive in her Mazda, talking on her phone. She was always talking on her cell phone. I didn't have a cell phone anymore. Or maybe I did and never used it. At the screen door, just then, I suddenly felt the urge to go after her.

Here's what I did: I rushed out of the house into the cold air, shirtless. Across the street, a teenage girl was kicking a soccer ball in the yard, and she stopped to look at me. Rae glanced at me and sped away. I stood in the middle of the street and scratched at my arm. The girl turned away when I looked at her. Then she picked up the soccer ball and went into her house. My arm was itching terribly. I saw that it was bleeding from where I had scratched so hard. When I walked back into the house, Ornette's trumpet was blowing like wild laughter.

I went into my room and put on a hoodie and sat on the edge of the bed. I thought of Rae and me in the beginning, when we stayed in bed all day. We spent many days like that, too lazy to get out of bed, which was one of the reasons we felt so attached to each other: we saw it as connecting spiritually, emotionally. I fed her soup, carried the dishes to the kitchen. I brushed her hair, then hugged her waist in bed and fell asleep with my head in her lap. We smoked weed and listened to music. Those were good days, and I knew it would never be like that again.

Now, sitting in the house alone, I was fidgety and agitated. How many nights had I sat there in the past, waiting for her to return? I pulled my hood over my head and walked back out the front door. I figured I would go meet my friend Jessie, who often sold jewelry in the park nearby, and maybe hang out with him so that I wouldn't sit around the house being depressed or angry about Rae. I walked quickly down our street, hurrying past the corner gas station with the green roof, past the small Assembly of God church with its motto JESUS IS HERE on the sign out front. Then I broke into a run down the street, crossing over to the park. My heart was racing when I arrived, and I felt immeasurably sad.

It was near sunset, and the park was mostly empty. There was no sign of Jessie. I walked to a bench and sat. I felt like a goddamn loser, wanting to get high. Someone would show up, this was what I thought, but nobody showed and I couldn't sit around.

Out of the corner of my eye I saw a bird, a red fowl, strutting like a rooster. I stared at it a moment. Spreading its wings, it saw me and started to charge, as some will do. I turned and ran away through the park. I ran until I couldn't see it anymore. It was almost dark now, and when I crossed the street, I heard motorcycles coming. I kept walking in a hurry, and the cycles got louder, and when I stopped to catch my breath I turned and saw people riding past me, like a blaring windstorm, a whole line of loud motorcycles with rumbling pipes and red taillights.

Several months earlier, Jessie had given me a small red fowl in the park. It was harmless and small enough to hold in my hands. The fowl was partially red with spots of orange, a rounded chest, and a sharp beak. I lifted it and said, "What's your name? I'll name you Red Fowl," and Jessie and his girlfriend Shawnee laughed.

They had their own fowl. The people around the park kept fowls and brought them to the park for exercise, feedings, sharing them with anyone who wanted to see them. Right there, I made the decision: the fowl was mine. I would feed it and watch it grow into something bigger, a rooster or larger fowl, whatever it was. The fowl cocked its head and looked around. I could see its little chest breathing. I put my hand on its chest and felt the tiny heart, the pulsing beat, rhythmic. The fowl was alive. I put it in my jacket pocket to keep it warm and safe. The fowl kept still then, never moving. When I put my finger in the pocket I felt the bird nibble, which tickled a little, but it was never painful. It never scratched at me or tried to get out of my pocket all night. I felt an overall sense of acceptance with it, as

43

if it needed me and I needed it. It's strange to articulate the feeling for me, but the others in the park felt the same way about theirs. Fowl, fowl, fowl.

Jessie, Shawnee, and I walked past the park and along the road that runs beside the highway until we got to Jessie's house, where music was blaring and a party was going on.

"It's a party to celebrate nothing and everything," I said. "It's a party to celebrate my new fowl, this bird."

"We were already here," Jessie said. "We just went outside to give you the fowl. Be careful with it, though. Someone brought it here to my house. My own fowl's so big now I can't even carry it around like I used to. It scratches my skin. Claws at my mouth. I've heard it will knock out teeth if I'm not careful, so I have to keep my eye on it."

"I have to watch it for him," Shawnee said. "I'm the one who keeps it tame."

"Mine won't be that cruel," I said. "I won't feed it so much. I'll let it nibble at my finger and peck on me as it grows, but I won't let it get out of control. Not this fowl."

"That's what everyone says," Shawnee told me. "That's why I never took a fowl. Jessie offers one to me, but I haven't ever taken it. Just look at Jessie's fowl. The thing is so big it lives out back in a coop and shrieks in the morning and at night. It wakes him up shrieking. You have to feed it or it'll attack you. I googled that shit once. Those fowls become aggressive and will charge you, and if you walk away or turn your back, it'll attack. Fucking all around Albuquerque."

Jessie was chewing on a straw. "You have to raise your arms and flap them so that it thinks you're a bigger creature than it, and you gotta hope it goes passive."

"My fowl won't attack me," I told them.

"Be careful with it. If you're not careful with the fowl, it will want to be fed all the time and become angry."

I took the fowl out and looked at it. Its beak was tiny, and it seemed to almost smile at me. What kind of fowl smiles? But mine did — or at least that was the way I saw it.

"Come inside," Jessie said, but I declined. I wanted to enjoy the fowl myself, not share it with others. Others inside the party would want to see my fowl.

"No way am I going inside," I said, and laughed a little. "I'm taking this fowl home."

"Good luck," they both said.

I unlocked my bicycle from his porch and rode it back home, where I would have to hide the fowl from Rae. She wouldn't like the fowl, never. I steered my bike with one hand so I could check on the fowl in my jacket pocket. Its eyes were glowing in the dark as it looked up at me, smiling. I had a happy fowl, and it made me happy. It was fine right there in my pocket, with me protecting it, already grooming it. The fowl wasn't trying to hurt me or make any noise at all. The fowl was so nice.

When I got back to the house, I hid the fowl in the bedroom in my dresser drawer so Rae wouldn't find it. I told it good night and looked at it. The fowl had no odor whatsoever. It never made a sound, just breathed its chest in and out, breathing heavily for a tiny thing.

That night I wasn't able to sleep because I kept thinking about the fowl. I took it out of the dresser drawer while Rae slept and stayed up all night in the living room with it, looking at it and touching it and letting it nibble and peck in my hand. I had no appetite and the thought of food made me feel sick to my stomach.

The most fun thing about the fowl was feeding it, and like most things, it grew quickly and became bigger, but it began to smell bad and shit and vomit in the house. The fowl was too big to hide from Rae, so I had to carry it with me to the park and leave it there. It tried to follow me, and when I picked it up and threw it, I must've injured it, because then I saw the fowl drag itself across the ground toward me. I ran away from it that night. I kept hiding from the fowl anytime I saw it in the park, but it always saw me and ended up back at my house, which frightened Rae and caused us to fight.

The only way I could get rid of the fowl was to ignore it. Eventually it went away, but never for good. Sometimes it returned, and whenever I saw it, I felt a pull at my heart to want to pick it up and hold it. I could never fully rid myself of the fowl, and there was something I loved about it, no matter how disgusting or how elated it made me feel.

When I got home, Rae was still gone. I called her cell but got her voice mail. "It's me," I said. "Where are you?" I hung up. I couldn't figure out if I was mad or sad. I didn't know whether to be angry at myself or at Rae for ignoring my call. In the kitchen I drank the last of the wine. I looked through drawers for a pack of cigarettes but couldn't find anything. Then I went into our bedroom, packed a duffel bag, and left.

I drove my shitty low-slung Oldsmobile to

47

the El Cortez Motel. It was the motel where Rae and I used to stay sometimes, pretending we were somewhere far away. I wanted to call her on the motel phone and try to get her to come stay with me. The motel's VACANCY sign flashed pink out front. Inside, I was certain the motel clerk recognized me. He chewed on a toothpick and wore a patch over one eye. His hands looked like my dad's, dry and cracked with stubby fingers. Behind the front desk, the sign on the door read: MAN GER. All the motel doors opened to the empty parking lot. Nearby, a desolate highway stretched west through the plains.

"The door says manger," I said. "Away in a manger."

The clerk handed me the key to room 121 but never looked at me.

I walked down the row of doors until I got to my room, opened, and went inside. It smelled of old cigarette smoke and cleaner. I immediately went to the phone, which was the old rotary kind. I called Rae's cell, and she answered.

"I'm at the El Cortez Motel," I said.

"Why? Go back home."

"Drive over here," I said. "I'm sorry I smoked. It was because my mom called you. Drive over here."

She was silent a moment. "No, you need

to go home. You lied again. I told you I was leaving if you kept smoking that shit."

"Please come to the motel."

"My God, Edgar, I can't even talk to you right now. I'm staying at Jessica's tonight."

She hung up, and I immediately called back. It went to her voice mail. I called again, and the same thing. I was a little high. I'd brought along a small duffel bag containing a bottle of a few oxycodone pills, aspirin, a tape recorder, a few cans of beer, and Rae's broken sunglasses I had doctored with black tape. These were all the things I needed for the night. I took the sunglasses out and squeezed the tape on the handle to make sure it hadn't loosened. I put them on a moment, then took them off and set them on the desk beside the bed.

I wanted to talk to someone. A roadside motel like the El Cortez was not a good place to feel lonely. The room was a mirror image of all the other rooms, the center of nothingness, dim and warm despite the air conditioner blowing. It felt like an isolated presence, welcoming me. But I liked the room dark — no light entered from the drawn curtains, which were green. The lamp threw a jagged and intimidating shadow across the pale wall, and the carpet, partially stained, was avocado.

In the room I sat on the edge of the bed, looking up at the ceiling. Something in my head was expanding, I felt, trying to force its way out. My skull felt heavy when I kept my head tilted back, looking up. This was how things went — first the head, then the stomach. When I saw my reflection in the mirror across the room, I wondered whether people saw me differently. I'd lost some weight.

In the bathroom I took an oxycodone and drank a cup of water. The only thing I had in my pocket other than my wallet was my turquoise snakeskin lighter, which was a gift from Rae. I imagined her here with me. I thought of her watching me play chess in the park against one of the druggies, daring me to lose. She kept me on edge, a dominant and unpredictable force. I started to feel sick to my stomach.

I turned on the TV. A movie was on, showing a man walking through the desert. I stared into the TV. The man was walking and walking, going nowhere. Where was he going? I wondered. A drifter, a wanderer, in search of something important. This must be real life, I thought. Searching for something, trying to move forward. Looking for meaning or happiness. The commercials were all in Spanish.

When a commercial came on, I peeked out the peephole and saw the parking lot outside. I could see desert dust blowing around in the wind. I looked back up at the ceiling and felt a sense of transparency and isolation, a sense of longing, a dampening of the soul. The room smelled like all the other motel rooms. Above the bed hung a framed watercolor of a farmhouse painted in browns and reds. A field surrounding the farmhouse was dull green, with nothing else around, only empty pasture. The farmhouse looked vacant, too, with a broken-down pickup truck beside it. No sign of life anywhere. I wondered who lived there and then who painted it, and for what purpose. On a different wall, the only other picture in the room, was another watercolor, a painting of an old wooden fence with barbed wire. A dreary sky in the background. A barbed-wire fence. I wondered why a fence, such a lifeless and dull thing, seemingly in the middle of nowhere. A fence, used to enclose territory. It was as if the motel was emphasizing its loneliness.

The room darkened as I sat in silence. This was how I liked to spend late afternoons, it occurred to me, sitting in a room as it darkened. Letting the darkness spill over me and the room. I opened a beer from my duffel bag and played the tape on my recorder, hearing my own voice. I heard myself say, "I looked for the Great Spirit today." I heard myself laugh through my teeth, but I wanted to hear someone else's voice, by circumstance, unfiltered and cautious.

I stopped the tape and called a random number. A woman answered. "Hello?" she kept saying. I hung up on her. The next number I called was a business. The guy who answered said, "Maintenance."

"I want to talk, if it's all right with you," I said.

"What?"

"Where do you work? I just want to talk."

He hung up.

I called a number that registered a busy signal. I found it strange and rhythmic, an alert of sorts. The sound put me at ease, helped me feel better. I became aware of my surroundings, of the dim motel room with the green curtains and pale walls. Maybe there were no colors in the room. In my mind I see black and white, something out of a French film. I liked watching the room dim on its own, listening to the hum of the air conditioner blowing.

I called my friend Jessie, but he didn't answer. Then I called Byrd, an old friend I hadn't spoken to in several months. He'd crashed his Harley on a highway just outside Tulsa and managed to survive with a concussion and stitches in his tongue. "I grew my hair out," he told me. "Now everyone thinks I'm Neil Young. The guy at the diner keeps asking me what happened to Crazy Horse. What happened to the Stray Gators, he says. Sing 'Yonder Stands the Sinner.' Sing 'Cinnamon Girl.' Where are you?"

"New Mexico."

"Come back to Oklahoma. You need somewhere to stay? You can stay with us, kid. I got an extra mattress in the basement. I got *Rubber Soul* on vinyl. I got *Exile on Main Street*."

"My man Keith Richards."

"Hey, Lucille's sister's in town with her kids, so I gotta go. Try to lay off the shit, brother."

"I miss you, Byrd."

He had already hung up. I found myself waiting for someone to pick back up, but the line went dead. I turned on the lamp and called Sonja, who was half asleep when she answered.

"Is everything okay?" she said. "Where are you?"

"Albuquerque."

"Is everything okay?"

53

"Rae left me, and I just wanted to talk," I said.

"Well, I'm sorry, but don't use it as an excuse to use meth. Are you coming home for the bonfire?"

"Maybe. I don't know."

"Everyone wants to see you. I want to see you, and so do Mom and Papa. They keep asking me about it, and I tell them I don't know."

"I don't know."

"I hope you come home," she said.

After I hung up, I didn't feel like calling anyone else. I thought again of Rae, and how we could heal each other through language. We could say words and reach an understanding. We could touch each other's face and say one organic word. Sometimes we never spoke. We once spent an entire afternoon embracing in the park.

Darkness spread around me. After a long while I got out of bed and took a beer with me into the bathroom, where I filled the tub with warm water. I removed all my clothes and stepped into the tub. I wanted time in isolation, quiet, but there was laughter coming from the next room, voices talking. My body felt warm and heavy in the water. The heaviness was an abstraction, I felt, a part of some equation convoluted by the presence of the room. Be aware of your surroundings, Rae used to say. Be aware, cautious, observant of time and place. I'd dealt with too many dealers who could hurt me. She didn't want to see me beaten up over drugs. She was right.

I popped open a can of beer and reclined in the tub, thinking of the times she and I splashed around in the tub in a different motel bathroom, maybe at the Route 66 Motel or the Knights Inn, a mirror image of this room. A bathroom with the same tile full of squares, part of the equation to entrap me. Motel bathrooms all look the same, I told myself. I thought of Rae, of us splashing around one hot July afternoon during a dust storm that sanded over the windows. We listened to the Mexican radio station and drank Mexican beer. We paid the housekeeping to stay away, immersing ourselves in our own bodies, in each other, for six days.

In the tub I counted the tiles from ceiling to floor, around the room. It became a sort of game, counting vertically by row, then horizontally, eight, fifteen, then twenty, thirty-four. I kept losing track. The tiles over the sink were smaller and of a different color — pink rather than light blue. Pink, the color of skin and flesh, the color of body parts, tongue. By the time I finished my beer I had counted over a hundred square tiles, not counting the partial tiles that stopped at the edge of the tub. They were not half tiles, maybe a quarter of a tile. The numbers were confusing, and I couldn't figure out the pattern, but I thought of it as a game. I had a strange and intense vision of being stuck in an elevator as a child, gripping my mother's hand. A hard jolt from a cable or faulty electrical circuit. A woman crying out. A loud ringing alarm from somewhere. I felt the loss of air, no oxygen, the room shrinking. Closing my eyes, gripping my mother's hand. My mother bringing me closer against her. The doors finally opening.

In the tub I let myself slide down into the water until my head was underwater and I was staring directly up at the trembling ceiling. I blinked underwater. I felt my eyes burning and saw only blurred whiteness above, everything shaking. I saw myself falling backward. I realized then I was drowning, being held under water by some force beneath me. The heaviness of my body made it difficult to sit up, but I managed to gain enough strength to lean forward and gasp as I came out of the water like some horrific beast, sputtering as I steadied myself in the tub. I leaned forward and pulled the plug to drain the water.

Slowly, I stepped out of the tub and watched the water drain as it made a loud sucking noise. I got dressed and went through my bag for a cigarette. The room felt much dimmer than before. I looked to the curtain and saw part of it trembling from the blowing air conditioner. On TV, an old movie showed a crippled boy taking his first steps. I sat on the edge of the bed and watched. The boy's mother fell to her knees. A crowd of people surrounded the boy. There was no sound. I changed the channel with the remote and saw a movie with De Niro, the young, tough De Niro, sitting in a dingy apartment, writing in a notebook. De Niro, talking to himself, strapping a gun to his arm and ankle. Pointing a pistol at his reflection in the mirror.

I spoke into the tape recorder. I said, "Because I didn't mean to hurt anyone." I said, "I'm sorry I got high." I talked for a while about what I loved about Rae, pretending I was being interviewed by the brother I barely remembered. I said, "Ray-Ray and Rae."

By sunrise I had spoken thousands of words into the recorder. At the window beside the door, I peeked out the curtains and looked up at the morning sky. I could see the open land past the parking lot, dust swirling in the wind. I could see the motel sign, the pink VACANCY flashing. A hawk swooped down and landed on the sign. From my bag I took out the oxycodone pill bottle, tilting the last few pills into my hand, and swallowed them with a beer.

I put on Rae's broken sunglasses and lay down in bed to try to sleep. A surge of pain went right to my head, and I saw myself projected forward into the darkness, an eccentric and intense sensation. Outside the window, I saw my ancestors walking and falling. Some were crawling. I saw the soft, yellow light on the horizon. I saw the rain lifting from earth to sky.

SONJA ECHOTA

I secretly watched Vin Hoff for months before I ever met him. I'm not kidding. This was not love — let me be clear on that, though I had an immediate attraction to him. The attraction was really quite strong. There was also the fact that Vin was in his early twenties, and I was thirty-one. I have always liked younger men.

The public library downtown where I worked had a comfortable shaded area beside the south entrance where I parked my bicycle. After work, sometimes, I sat on the steps by the entrance and observed Vin playing with his son in their yard across the street. I'm aware how strange it looks for a woman to ride a bicycle to work, but I never liked to drive. I was, in fact, the only woman who parked a bicycle at the library. All the other bicycles belonged to kids.

Vin looked rough around the edges, drove both a car and a motorcycle, and was a single dad. I loved hearing the sound of his laughter. He was a musician who played guitar in a David Bowie tribute band downtown at the Branch, a local bar near the university in town. He was broad-shouldered, with the short, unkempt hair of a fashionable young man. He looked young in a sort of James Dean way, usually dressed in blue jeans and T-shirts.

His son was a boy of seven or eight named Luka. I learned this one afternoon as I watched Vin and Luka play from the library steps. "Luka, Luka!" Vin would say. Luka flapped his arms like a bird. He ran across the lawn and fell down. He jumped and pointed to the sky. I watched from afar and clapped for him. Overhead, clouds darkened from an approaching storm. When it started raining, Vin and Luka went inside, but I stood under the awning of the library, waiting for the rain to let up, thinking they might come back. I pulled out my sack lunch and ate cold pasta from a plastic container. I stomped on the ants with my old black boots. The people who came in and out of the library must've thought I was homeless.

For months I watched them and never saw

the boy's mother. Vin and Luka came and went frequently. When they weren't home, I sat on the steps playing on my phone or reading the novels of Colette, which I had checked out from the library. With every passing week I grew more comfortable with what I was doing, sitting on the steps and reading and watching this younger man and his son.

The first time I was close to Vin was when he took Luka for a walk and I followed them a few blocks to a diner on Main Street. Inside the diner I stood behind them in line, so close I could see the creases on the back of Vin's neck. Luka wore a red T-shirt and blue jeans. His arms were well-tanned, his hands small. He had light-brown hair trimmed short on the sides. Had I actually reached out and touched him that day, tapped him on the back with a finger or nudged him on the shoulder, had I met them in that moment, I wonder if things would've been different. As it was, though, the waitress seated them at a small table near the window, and I didn't have any money, so I left.

Another time I rode my bicycle to the liquor store, and by coincidence, Vin was there. He was buying a bottle of wine. He paid with cash and said something that made the girl at the register laugh. Did he know her, I wondered, and what exactly did he say to her? I turned away so he couldn't see my face. After he left, I asked the girl at the counter what he had said, and she looked confused. "Do you know him?" I asked.

"A little," she said. "He comes in every now and then. I think his name is Vin."

"I know his name," I said, and left. But the truth was that I didn't know his name, and now I did, so I was quite happy.

When I was young, Papa told me to watch out for boys. They're like snakes, he said. They will creep up on you and trick you when you're vulnerable. My mother laughed at Papa anytime he said things like this, and I didn't believe him. Once there was a boy I liked in school who didn't like me back. His name was Thomas and we were in sixth grade. I sat behind him and stared at the back of his head. I liked something about the way his hair was unkempt, the way he slouched in his desk, the sneakers he wore. His blue jeans, his collared shirts. His small, delicate hands. I remember thinking I wanted to go swimming with him, envisioning us playing in a pool somewhere, splashing around. We would wrestle and I would dunk him and hold him underwater. He would spring up out of the water and kiss me. It was a fantasy I enjoyed. At school, some of the boys liked to say that Thomas had once peed in the bed during a sleep-over. One day they were laughing about it. Thomas was trying not to cry, but I could see his eyes fill with tears. He was so cute it didn't matter to me whether he cried at school or peed the bed in sixth grade. But he never paid any attention to me. One day I approached him on the playground, grabbed his finger, and twisted his hand. I felt sure that if I could just get him to talk to me, he would like me. Thomas pulled his hand away and yelled at me to stop. He looked at me with this sad look, and I started laughing, happy I got his attention. Then he walked away and never talked to me again.

On my day off, I rode my bicycle to the library. Even when I wasn't working, I would often come in to use the computer, since I didn't have one at home and mainly used my phone online. At the computer I watched a video of a tiny coconut octopus underwater, enclosing itself in a clamshell. The tiny octopus moved slowly across the floor of the ocean, unraveling its tentacles around the clam and climbing into it before closing it.

"The shells serve as a shelter for these octopuses off the coast of Indonesia," the narrator said.

I watched the video over and over. I don't know why I was so captivated. It might've been the gracefulness with which the octopus enclosed itself, the way it moved so slowly, so certain of its goal. In a way I found it soothing, almost meditative. I wanted to believe that my goals were as important and necessary as this task seemed for the octopus. Why did it need shelter at that moment? Was there a predator lurking nearby, or did it simply feel the need for privacy and isolation, the way we humans need our privacy?

When I got off the computer, I headed downstairs to the basement and saw an old Native man, probably in his seventies or so. He wore a sleeveless shirt and baggy pants and had a cane with him. His hair was mostly gray and hung down to his waist. He was filling up his thermos at the water fountain. Something about him caused me to stop; perhaps it was that he looked a little like my grandfather, but this man had scars on his cheek, and I found myself staring at them.

"A bear cub scratched me a few weeks back," he said, noticing me. "I was in the Rockies when I saw the bear. It looked peaceful, harmless, calling for me to reach out for it, to help it. But when I bent over to pick it up, it slashed me across the face. I didn't get angry. What good is anger? What good is vengeance?"

"You look like my grandpa," I said. "He lived to be one hundred and three."

His gaze was intense. "My brother always wanted to live to be one hundred. The other day I visited him at the cemetery on the hill."

"I have a brother there, too."

"Buried?"

"Yes."

He finished filling his thermos and turned to me. "I saw a young man walking around by himself. Maybe it was your brother's ghost."

He laughed at himself, took a drink from his thermos. But his face held a sadness, somewhere between longing and pain.

"I'm Sonja," I said.

"Wado, Sonja," he said. He nodded and wished me a good day, limping away with his cane.

I watched him disappear among the shelves of books, thinking how odd the

65

encounter was, but that was always happening to me. My whole life I've felt I had strange encounters with people, so much so that in school I once made a list of strangers who came up and talked to me or asked me random questions. Maybe there was something important this man possessed in his spirit, manifested for me, but what message was he bringing?

I went outside and sat and waited for Vin to come out. They almost always came outside around this time. I wanted to finally meet him, and I considered, in a moment of excitement, crossing the street and going right up to the door and ringing the bell. Soon enough, though, Vin and Luka came out. They started walking down the block, so I followed them down Main Street to the fall art festival downtown. The festival was on a blocked-off street full of tents and booths, crowds of people, a stage with some teenage girl playing an acoustic guitar and singing a country-and-western song. Poor girl, she wasn't a very good singer, and not many were paying attention to her. Vin and Luka walked ahead of me, stopping to buy snow cones. They walked from tent to tent, Vin holding Luka's hand. I trailed far enough behind that I wouldn't be conspicuous, but close enough that I could see them when they stopped at a craft table. I walked past them, shielding my face behind others, then stopped at the next tent and browsed watercolor prints from a local Cherokee artist, an older man wearing a bandanna. I ran my hand over bracelets and necklaces and saw him glance at me. I bought a threaded turquoise bracelet and stepped away. At the craft table, Vin was looking at his phone while a woman helped Luka make something with colored paper. I wanted to be that woman, to kneel down and help Luka make crafts and color on paper. After a few minutes I left and went home.

I lived in a small house down the road from my parents. I was glad I lived close to them, since Papa was seventy-four and in the early stages of Alzheimer's. For weeks he had been paranoid about someone watching their house. One night he sat on the deck for three hours, keeping a lookout for a burglar, until he finally fell asleep. I hated seeing him this way.

He never said much to me, even before the Alzheimer's. Truthfully, we hardly ever talked at all. I wouldn't say he ignored me, but he was more interested in Edgar, especially after Ray-Ray died. With me, he liked to just sit on his deck in silence and look out at the lake, the moonlight reflecting in the water. He always told me to pay attention to nature because it was usually crying out to us. We watched squirrels run across the grass. We listened to cicadas. Leaves fell from the trees and played in the wind like pale birds.

I decided to introduce myself to Vin that night. I was at the Branch, where I had seen him perform several times. This night I felt bolder for some reason.

I sat at the bar and had a few glasses of Tempranillo while his band played their set. Vin sang only a couple of songs and mostly played electric guitar in the band. I would say they were of average talent, though the college kids enjoyed them. When they finished their set, I felt an urge to assert my presence, to make myself visible to him. I am a woman with shrewd eyes and a slender chin, and I felt confident that Vin would like me once he met me. I didn't mind being older than guys I dated. The French writer Colette was in her forties when she was rumored to have had a sexual affair with her sixteen-year-old stepson. How magnificent she was, a woman who wrote so beautifully about sexual energy and desire, a woman I very much wanted to be like. I wished I could be like her without worry of being judged.

Vin sat at the bar with another young guy who was maybe in his early twenties. Sitting at the other end of the bar, I stared at Vin until he noticed. I waited for him to respond to my smile, to see whether he would react. Sure enough, he smiled and said something to the guy sitting beside him. His friend glanced at me and then quickly looked into his glass and took a drink. Vin kept looking over at me every so often. I can say now that if our attraction began anywhere, it was right then.

For a moment I studied Vin, my throat dry and my body taut with anxiety among all the smoke and people around me. I couldn't say exactly how I was feeling, though I knew I felt a strange combination of confidence and slight airlessness. This is how you attract a stranger. This is how you show you're interested, how you smile and look him intensely in the eyes. How many times had this worked in the past? My instinctive response to his smile was to mouth *Hi,* but instead I turned to the bartender and cupped my mouth like I was sharing a secret. I wanted it to look like I was whispering something, but I really just ordered another glass of wine. I knew Vin was watching, and when I glanced back at him, he was still looking at me.

He began talking to a girl with red-blond hair, clearly someone he didn't know. How many twentysomething girls approached him after his sets onstage, how many introduced themselves, introduced their friends, pretended they had met him before? I glared at him again, this time with a more serious expression, until he caught my eye and took a drink. The girl was talking to her friend, and they both laughed like schoolgirls. I thought of them texting each other in their anatomy class while their homely professor groaned on about skeletal and reproductive systems. I got a pen from my purse and began writing on a cocktail napkin: *Vin likes to be stared at. He requires a lot of attention, like a little boy.*

When I finished writing, I looked up and there he was. I turned on my barstool to face him and met his eyes. "Hi," he said. Or maybe he said, "Who are you?" Or maybe, "My name is Vin." Well, whatever he said, the music was pulsating around us, and I felt as if we were enveloped in silence. It happens like that, the gravity of the moment. He had this sad presence about him that reminded me of Elliott Smith, such a brooding, youthful soul, and I thought how strange it was that he could remind me of so many different famous people. I thought of how Colette described the men in her books in such ardent, sexual detail, so full of passion. How she focused on her own pleasure. Oh, to be so selfish! I desired Vin in the same way.

I handed him the napkin, and as he read it he smiled, or maybe he smirked, so I said I liked his set and told him he was really handsome, and he glanced away for a moment, looking embarrassed.

"I'm Colette," I told him.

"Colette," he said. "I like that."

"You like my name?"

He held this really intense gaze. I don't know if he was trying to be sexy, but he didn't need to try hard with me.

"Colette," he said.

It was simple, really.

Outside, he put my bicycle in the trunk of his car and drove me home with the car radio off and the windows down. We saw smoke in the distance from a fire on the other side of the lake, and to tease him I leaned in close to him and whispered: "Listen to the fire. What do you hear? It's telling you something. Do you hear it?"

The fire excited me. Yes, all that smoke and heat rising to the dark sky. Once we arrived at my house, we entered through the back door. I turned on the light, pulled off my boots, and Vin followed me into the kitchen for wine. As I reached for the glasses in the cabinet, I felt his hands on my waist. I let him feel me as I bent forward against the kitchen counter so that my hair fell in front of me. He moved in, kissed my neck. I turned and he kissed me. I bit his lip, pulled away. I kissed him again and put my hand against his jeans. I knelt down, unfastened his belt. Then his hands were in my hair, and I thought about the wildfires outside and all the smoke billowing into the dark night.

TSALA

My beloved son: time among the dead is mysterious. Time among the dead does not exist the way humans experience it during life. Time may be felt: U-di-tle-gi, u-hyv-dla!

Look to the sky, and there we are, soaring like hawks, circling in the air. We are the birds appearing like a string of red berries against the clouds. We are all around, the deities to cover every expansive body of land. We are bathed in rainwater, flying together. We are a sparkle of blue light inside rocks, the swift rising of smoke and dust, forming the hazy outlines of bodies.

We are speakers of the dead, the drifters and messengers, the old and the young, lurking in the shadows of tall trees at night, passing through the walls of abandoned buildings and houses, concrete structures, stone walls and bridges. We are the ones watching from underwater, rising up like mist, spreading like a rainstorm, over fields and gardens and courtyards, flying over towers and rooftops and through the arched doorways of old buildings with spider cracks in their walls. We reveal ourselves to those who will look. It has been said we are illusions, nightmares and dreams, the disturbing and tense apparitions of the mind. We are always restless, carrying the dreams of children and the elderly, the tired and sick, the poor, the wounded. The removed.

In 1838, the firing squad killed you before they killed me. Your mother adorned us in gold and jewelry and buried us. You must know that adornment is as important in death as in life, so they made it known that we were beautiful, even absent of our spirits. An elder had once taught me not to be afraid of death because there is no death — there is only a change of worlds.

I refused to migrate west on the Trail, and that is why we died. I refused because it was not fair treatment, and I was willing to sacrifice my life for you, our family, and our people. Yes, I know an old man has a mouth full of thunder. So does an old spirit.

Before you were born, I helped Dragging Canoe and his son take the fleshy side of enemy scalps and paint them red and tie

74

them to poles for the scalp dances. We imitated the Europeans who invaded us by dancing a foolish, awkward stomp to show their clumsiness. More importantly, the dance healed us by weakening the other races who were responsible for harm or sickness. It was also used to heal the sick for our own people.

At one of these dances I met a man named Dasi'giya'gi whose war medicine was an uktena's shedded skin and burned turtle shell, which he used to smear on his face and body for protection from enemies. He had never been wounded because of wearing this war medicine, as strong as yellowroot. He warned me of the seventh hell we were living in, and soon I had dreams of the blood and destruction. Dragging Canoe told me, "You will be a visionary with prophetic gifts. You must learn to understand this." He then told me the story of the young prophet:

Story of the Boy with Prophetic Visions

The boy dreamed of words written on the leaves that he could not read. In his dream he stood beside the gristmill his father built for grinding corn and watched the leaves play in the wind. As he followed the leaves, he saw Nun-Yunu-Wi, the Stone Beings, who gave him a reddish-brown rock. They told him to break the rock and use the red color to paint his face to hunt. When he woke, his father was ill and not able to hunt for food that day, so the boy painted his face red and went out into the cold day to hunt.

The boy shot a doe and ran to it. When he got to the dead doe, he saw leaves covering its body. The leaves were blue, and one of the leaves was fluttering as if from a breeze. He picked up the blue leaf and saw letters that formed a message telling him to warn people of the coming soldiers. This message upset him greatly, and as he dragged the doe by its legs, he grew so angry he slipped and fell, knocking his head on a rock that left him unconscious.

Visions came to him then. He saw people walking wearily through the snow. On and on they trudged, hunched forward in the wind through a storm. He saw people falling to their knees, dying in the rain. He saw guards with their rifles and the scowls on their faces, and he felt the misery sweep over everyone like a cold wind. He saw the terror and brutality and heard the crying of infants and children.

He saw the transformation of a corn stalk

into a beautiful woman whose drops of blood in the ground shook the earth and blossomed into a beautiful tree. Then he climbed the tree and saw, in the distance, the soldiers coming from far away. They were bringing oxcarts and wagons, and dust around them rose and formed into an image of a giant snake in the sky. He watched the snake cough dust so that soon enough he wasn't able to see the soldiers or the snake anymore, just an enormous billow of red dust in the sky, growing larger and larger.

When the boy woke, he saw that the doe next to him was still breathing. He looked deep into the doe's eyes, which were large and brown and watery. And the doe spoke: "Go and tell your people about your visions. Warn them about the coming soldiers, the cold winter, and the approaching suffering and death. I will see you soon."

Then the doe stopped breathing, with her eyes still open.

Beside the doe was another blue leaf fluttering in the breeze. The boy picked it up and saw the message: he would die soon, too.

He lay beside the doe, crying out in sadness and anger until he wasn't able to cry anymore. Then he slept for two days straight. He did not dream during this long sleep, and when he woke, he saw that the doe beside him had gone.

He walked all the way back to the village, where he warned everyone of the soldiers: "They will force us from our land!" he said. "A cold winter full of death is coming."

"We're afraid to tell people by the river," they said. "The Great Leech of Tlanyusi'yi is there and is eating people who go fishing. They disappear and never return. How do we warn them?"

The river was frightening for many people. There was a rock to walk across the water, like a bridge. People stood on the rock and fished in the river, until they noticed a long red snake that kept itself rolled into a ball. Whenever it sensed the presence of a human, the red snake unrolled itself and leapt out of the water onto the rock, then dragged the people into the water and ate their faces. Their bodies were found drowned along the bank with their eyes and noses eaten from their faces. One person said these dead people had no tongues.

"It is not my time of dying, even if I had dreams," the boy said. He set off for the river, happily singing a song:

Tlanu' si' gune' ga digi'gage
Dakwa' nitlaste' sfi!
I will tie red leech skins
On my legs for garters!

But when he got to the rock, nobody was there. He looked down and saw the water began to boil and foam. This is the account told to us by the spirits who watched from nearby.

The boy became unable to move from fear. "You won't kill me!" he shouted.

And the leech leapt up and carried him down underwater, and he was never seen again.

Beloved, we knew the soldiers were coming before they ever arrived. Our people knew long before, thanks to the prophecies. It was a time of fear, but we would never let fear bury us.

MARIA

September 2

In the morning I drove to the youth shelter to read to the children, since Wyatt wasn't supposed to arrive until the afternoon. The kids who stayed there had either been kicked out of foster homes or were waiting to be placed in a foster home. I'd been visiting there regularly since I retired. I always liked helping children. This was my career, in social work, finding justice in a world where it felt like there was no justice. I wanted to save everybody, especially children and families on the verge of losing everything. I wanted them to have a chance to succeed.

For sixteen years I was a social worker for the tribe, working with children and at-risk youth. I liked working with deprived children. I transported them to various foster home placements, youth shelters, or treatment centers, which often took a long time.

The trips could take two or three hours, so I told them stories about Cherokee myths, or other times I made up my own stories. I told them about my own family, my Cherokee ancestors who suffered on the Trail of Tears after Andrew Jackson forced thousands to leave their land. Some hid in the mountains, others died. The ones who survived barely made it, suffering through measles and whooping cough, walking in the brutal cold of winter, their cries drowned by the bitter wind. They were women walking hunched forward with blankets over their shoulders. They were men carrying children. They were on their knees, dying from pneumonia. My ancestors made it to Indian Territory, to Oklahoma, where they tried to start over. When I was growing up, my elders taught me about real history, about the removal, when many schools didn't talk much about it.

As a social worker, I watched children cower into their siblings, afraid of all the caseworkers. I watched them spit and call everyone evil monsters. I listened to them moan and wail in fear. The youngest kids were the most trusting. Our office had toys and treats for them during the hours they spent in our building. They had a TV, dolls, stuffed animals, crayons, building blocks.

They had books and handheld video games. The older siblings gave dirty looks and held on to their younger siblings, didn't trust the workers, never smiled.

"We want to help you," I told them. "We won't hurt you. We'll find a safe place for you. Everything will be better now."

At the youth shelter, I read stories from books about Cherokee culture and healing. Afterward I asked them, "What is healing?"

"When you don't feel like killing yourself," a girl named Amber said. She was twelve or thirteen, with light-brown hair cropped short. Her face and body were thin, but her pale-blue T-shirt and jeans were baggy. She sat forward with her elbows resting on her knees, listening to me.

"That's right," I told her. "You don't want to hurt yourself, you're healing. You're getting better. Maybe you start talking to a counselor or a doctor, too. But many years ago the Cherokees used nature for healing."

I read aloud: " 'All the trees and shrubs and plants of the earth were used to cure sickness.' " I stopped here and held up the book to show a photograph of a yellow flower, then continued: " 'The black-eyed Susan plant contains a liquid that cures earaches.' " A boy, maybe ten or eleven, raised his hand. He was small, sitting cross-legged on the floor. His hair hung in his eyes.

"My brother got a black eye," he said. "His name is Jack. He has medicine for his face."

"Did you know," I told him, "that some people put liquid from the black-eyed Susan plant in their tea and drank it?"

"Did it help their black eyes?"

"I'm not sure, but it helped them feel better. It was good for snakebites."

I held up another page with a photograph. "This is the catgut plant," I said. "The Cherokees believed that if you mixed the bark in water, it would make you strong."

Amber was really listening to me, leaning forward and concentrating. I told them a story about a young boy who was shorter than all the other boys in his school. "The boy isn't able to play sports," I told them. "He's too small to reach the monkey bars on the playground. None of the boys like him, so he spends all his time on the playground jumping rope and being friends with the girls. At home, his father makes him drink the catgut bark mixed into his tea, and soon the boy grows, gets stronger, and by the end of the school year he's stronger and taller than every boy in his class. Now all the boys want him to play sports with them, but he refuses unless they allow the girls to play too."

"Why?" Amber asked.

"At first the boys refuse," I said. "They don't want girls to play. Meanwhile, one of the girls who is Cherokee also has been drinking the catgut plant in her tea and challenges all the boys to arm wrestling. She beats every one of them, so the boys let everyone play. Boys against girls — guess who wins?"

"The girls?"

"That's right."

She gave a smile. Marty, one of the young part-time library helpers, came over and told me he could never get them to pay attention for very long. "And you make them interested in plants," he said. "How do you do it?"

"This is my passion," I said. "It has always been my passion."

On the drive home I stopped at the market to buy a carton of ice cream for Wyatt's visit. Outside the store I happened to see an elderly woman, standing stooped over with an afghan around her shoulders. I stopped to examine the stitches and folds in her afghan.

"It's beautiful," I said, touching the end drooping from her shoulder.

She smiled, taking my hand into hers. Surprisingly, her hands were warmer than mine. She rubbed my hand with hers, and for a moment I felt as though I had met her before.

"You're very nice to stop and say so," she said. "I'm from far away. My son is pulling the car around, and we're going to comfort a family whose child died."

I was saddened by her then, knowing she was senile. The car pulled up and a young man got out and came over to us. He had dark hair and looked Native. He smiled and said hello, then took the woman by the arm and helped her to the car.

"Take care," I said.

I waited for the young man to help her into the passenger's seat, where she strapped on her seat belt. She turned and looked back at me as they pulled away.

I had the house fully prepared for Wyatt to arrive: Ray-Ray's bedroom was clean, and the fishing gear was ready in the garage. On the back deck, Ernest appeared confused, his eyes dark and complicated. We had never fostered before, and I wondered if he was nervous. Wyatt was twelve, it occurred to me suddenly, a few years younger than Ray-Ray had been when he died. I hadn't realized until I saw Ernest sitting on the back deck, looking so tense. He was rubbing his brow with his hand, closing his eyes every few seconds and then opening them and taking in a deep breath.

I stood looking out at the water, which was calm for a day in September. "Everything's all set for Wyatt," I told him.

He looked up at me, and I wondered whether he even remembered.

"Wyatt?" he said.

"He'll be here in a few hours."

"What's his name?" he said, looking away and then back at me.

I sat next to him and touched his arm. "The foster boy's name is Wyatt. He'll be staying with us a few days. Bernice said it will likely be until the court hearing on Friday."

He cleared his throat and nodded. "Oh."

"We're a temporary placement for him."

"I got it," he said.

We sat quietly for a few minutes, looking out over the sloping ground to the trees and water. "I have a good feeling," I said, maybe more to myself than to Ernest. "We're the only Cherokee family available for him right now. It's us or the shelter."

I thought of Ernest before his mind started to decline, the way he carried on conversations, always laughter about something. I wondered why he didn't, or couldn't, laugh anymore. Was nothing funny? No memory, thought, or quick-witted joke on TV ever made him laugh anymore.

After a moment I went back inside to the kitchen table and called Irene. "I'm hesitant about the foster boy and Ernest," I told my sister. "The Alzheimer's feels worse every day. I don't know. I don't want him to get too confused in front of Wyatt. And I don't want to deal with the stress if Wyatt gets in trouble at school this week. It's stressful for a foster child to stay in a temporary placement."

"Stop worrying," Irene said.

I sat quietly looking out the window. My notebook was on the table where I had left it. I picked it up and opened it. I wrote:

If I could make the bonfire

and then . . .

If you only

But nothing else came. I felt my thoughts were interrupted, blocked. I had a deep longing to express something, but I couldn't place what it was.

Wyatt arrived around six in the evening by way of Bernice. They stood inside the front door, and Bernice introduced us. "Wyatt," she said, "this is Maria. She's retired. She used to work with me in the office."

Wyatt was all smiles, wearing a newsboy cap and baggy jeans. He blushed a little, removing his cap and shaking my hand.

"Very nice to meet you," I said.

"We've got everything in his bag," Bernice said. "The hearing's on Friday at one thirty. We'll meet in the courthouse lobby."

She gave Wyatt a small hug before leaving. He wasn't resistant to the hug, nor embarrassed. After she left, his gaze sharpened and he smiled in a familiar way. The look in his eyes was deepened by his silence, shy and boyish. He seemed awkward, waiting for me to tell him what to do. "I have your room ready," I said. "Do you want me to show it to you?"

I realized Ernest had walked into the room and stood with his hands in his pockets, looking at Wyatt.

"This is my husband, Ernest," I told Wyatt.

Ernest stepped in closer and extended his

hand, which Wyatt shook. Neither of them said anything, but they looked at each other. Then Wyatt picked up his suitcase and followed me down the hall to Ray-Ray's old bedroom, where he set some of his things on the bed and looked around the room. Ernest lingered in the hallway.

"This is it," I said. "I hope you like it."

He turned to me and smiled, still silent. He put his suitcase down and sat on the edge of the bed. His bangs were in his eyes, and he had to comb his hair back with his fingers so he could see us better. He was small for his age, I thought, though maybe it just seemed that way because of how he was sitting on the edge of the bed. When was the last time we had seen a child in Ray-Ray's room anyway?

Bernice had mentioned Wyatt was shy. I showed him the extra pillows and blankets in the closet. I wanted to ensure he felt safe. "Any specific requests?" I asked, hoping he might speak up. "A night-light? The door open at night? Anything you need, please ask."

He nodded, deep in thought. Then he opened his suitcase and began unpacking while I watched from the doorway. He seemed perfectly comfortable, but I knew this was routine for him, having stayed in other foster homes. He removed his clothes from his suitcase and folded them neatly before placing them in the dresser. Socks and underwear in the top drawer, T-shirts in the middle, pants in the bottom drawer. He hung up a tweed jacket and collared dress shirts.

"Wyatt," I said, "we'll go get supper ready. You're welcome to stay in here, or you can come into the living room and watch TV if you like."

He looked distressed, so I sat on the edge of the bed. He sat next to me. His head leaned forward, and he was on the verge of tears. He was not acting like a teenager, that was certain, and I assumed he was emotionally immature, and guarded, maybe closer to a ten-year-old boy. I placed my hand on his back and rubbed lightly.

"I'll go in the other room," Ernest said from the doorway.

I nodded, and as he left, I asked Wyatt if there was anything I could do to make him feel comfortable.

He shook his head, but I couldn't see his face under his hair.

"You don't have to talk," I told him. "You don't have to do anything you don't want to do. This is your room. It's a safe place, I promise you."

I rubbed his back for a moment longer while he sat there, leaning forward. Then I got up and started for the door. That was when he spoke up: "I'm okay," he said.

I turned and looked at him, but he was still sitting forward. "That's good," I said.

"I can do impersonations," he said. "Maybe I'll do one later."

"Impersonations?"

"I can do a Frenchman, monsieur," he said. "I can do Peewee Herman."

I won't deny he reminded me of Ray-Ray, even from the beginning. I was surprised by the feeling in my stomach, a pang that made me shiver, a taste of sweetness in my mouth despite not having eaten anything. I had a strange feeling all evening that Wyatt possessed a number of familiar traits. I wondered if it was simply because they were nearly the same age.

In the kitchen I made supper. I put some chicken in the Crock-Pot, opened a can of green beans. I turned on the stove and poured the green beans into a saucepan. The kitchen was a place for thinking, where my time was my own. I thought about what an odd coincidence it was that Wyatt said he could do impersonations of a Frenchman and Pee-wee Herman. I remembered how Ray-Ray was such a quiet little boy until he started junior high, and his personality blossomed. He was happiest and the most animated around us at home, doing his impersonations, singing, talking about music and movies he loved. He tried to make us laugh, and he succeeded. He was very different from Sonja and Edgar, who were both more reserved, more introverted. As Ray-Ray got older, he tried to be tough around his friends, often sarcastic, too, even at home.

Cooking supper, it was still strange to think that the whole family might never be together again. It was such a struggle to get Edgar back home — the last time we had seen him was at his intervention the previous spring. In his absence I felt weak with worry. I prayed to the Great Spirit silently. I prayed for comfort for Edgar and Sonja right there in the kitchen. I prayed for Ernest. I prayed for Wyatt to feel comfortable in our home.

In the living room, Ernest was trying to figure out the TV remote. This was part of his confusion, forgetting what buttons change from cable to video, what channels play sports or twenty-four-hour news. He could remember his birth date but couldn't remember how the remote worked. He remembered who was president when he was a kid but forgot the name of his hometown.

"What channel's the local news?" he asked, pointing the remote at the TV.

"Time for supper," I told him.

"Well," he said. "I'm wondering about the Thunder game tonight. Maybe the boy and I can watch it together."

"Let's go eat," I told him.

He followed me to the table, where we found Wyatt already seated. He didn't look up as we entered but only stared at the table, as if deep in thought. I wondered whether he was sad or afraid or just shy.

Ernest helped me set the table, and when I brought the food out, I had to let him know it was fine to go ahead and help himself. We ate quietly for a while, our forks clinking against our plates. I asked Wyatt if he liked school.

"I love it," he said without looking up, and I wondered whether he was being sarcastic.

"Really?" I said. "That's rare, I think. Liking school? What grade are you in?"

"Ninth."

"Lots of friends?"

Now he looked up, and I saw something change in his face. Maybe it was my interest in talking to him, or maybe it was the thought of someone he knew, but he smiled a little and set his fork down. And Ernest, too, set his fork down. When I turned to look at Ernest, I recognized a look I hadn't seen in so long; it was a look of confusion and wonder.

"I love people," he said, in a voice not quite his own. "I'm in drama at school. I like to act. My drama teacher is a really cool dude. He rides a motorcycle. I'd love to get a motorcycle someday."

Ernest stabbed his chicken with his fork. I wondered whether he would react to Wyatt's motorcycle comment, but he didn't appear to be listening. "Motorcycles can be dangerous," I told him. "Our son had one for a while, but we never liked it. Get a car when you're old enough to drive."

He bit his lip. I wasn't sure if he agreed or what he was thinking, but he remained quiet.

"Wyatt told me he does impersonations," I said to Ernest. "He said he does a Frenchman."

"A what?" Ernest said. "A Frenchman? You do impersonations, son?"

Wyatt leaned forward over his plate and glared at Ernest. "That is correct, monsieur," he said in a French accent. "I can speak like Inspector Clouseau, monsieur.

Tell me, what is it you do?"

Ernest brought a bite of chicken to his mouth and looked at Wyatt. I saw his face turn, and wondered if he caught the similarity to Ray-Ray's impersonations.

"I've been all over the world," Ernest said. "I was like a tawodi, a hawk. I traveled to Germany, Mexico, Canada. I've been to the West Coast and all the way up to Bangor, Maine. I was born in 'thirty-nine."

"Trippy," Wyatt said, nodding. "The good old days. The radio days. Some great music back then, eh?"

Ernest looked confused.

"Hey," Wyatt said, "I'll be right back, cool?"

He excused himself from the table, and I started taking the dishes into the kitchen. I rinsed them off in the sink and put them in the dishwasher. Back in the living room, Wyatt was showing Ernest a stack of records.

"My friends all like Scandinavian death metal," Wyatt was saying. "It's garbage, all modern music. I say to them, 'You kids need to appreciate good music.' "

"What do they say?" Ernest asked.

"Nothing. I tell them to remember the roots. Muddy Waters, I say. Give me vintage jazz. Give me big band. Give me blues."

Ernest took his hands out of his pockets. "And Sinatra?"

Wyatt puffed on an imaginary cigarette. "He swings, daddio. My favorite swinger."

He was really warming up to us, becoming more talkative and comfortable, which was entertaining.

"I like your saddle shoes," Ernest told him.

"Were you in the big war, sir?"

"The big war?"

"World War II."

Ernest paused. "I was born in 'thirty-nine. I was too young."

"What about Vietnam?"

"Vietnam? No, I was stationed overseas in Europe."

"I want to hear all about it," Wyatt said. "I want to hear everything."

I was surprised at how quickly Ernest answered the questions, all from memory. Maybe I shouldn't have been, since that was such a big part of Ernest's life, but it was so long ago, and he rarely, if ever, mentioned it anymore. I felt a surge of hope.

For a while I listened to the two of them talk about old movies — *Rio Bravo, The 39 Steps, East of Eden.* They talked more about music. Wyatt said he had alphabetized his records by artist, including a set of old 45s, all of which he'd either found in record stores or antique shops or been given by grandparents. He mentioned some names that sounded familiar: Ella Fitzgerald, Dean Martin, Count Basie — the list went on. I found it all so strange, this obsession with these old records, and wondered why they were so important to him that he needed to show them to us.

"You like the oldies, cha-cha-cha?" he asked Ernest. "What about the hard stuff? The Jesus Lizard?"

"What the heck are you saying?" Ernest said.

"Rancid? Skunk Anansie?"

"What?"

"Okay, Pops, maybe mellow is your taste. I have Elliott Smith."

Ernest stared at the album covers while Wyatt unpacked a spiral notebook that had all the records listed by artist, album, year, and record label, an entire catalogue he'd spent hours on, claiming he wanted to be a serious collector of vintage music.

"I only keep my top eight with me," Wyatt said. "I have forty-three records total. The rest are at my aunt's house in Kansas. She enrolled me in dance lessons last year, and I had to practice the Charleston with her while my cousins watched. They're all squares."

Ernest burst into laughter. It was the first time in months I had heard him laugh.

Ernest turned and looked at me, his eyes wide. "Is the record player working?" he asked. "Let's give this a listen. What do you think?"

He handed me a Dean Martin album. For the first time in many years, I turned on the turntable, blew the dust from it, then removed the record from the sleeve and put it on the turntable. I put the needle on the record and heard the scratching sounds I hadn't heard in many years. The music began playing.

We listened to it for a moment, the horns and piano. It made me think of Italian restaurants from many years ago.

Wyatt said, "Would you dance with me, Mr. Echota?"

Ernest looked at me possibly for help. I laughed a little.

"Dance?" Ernest said to him. "Right now?"

"Yes, sir."

"I'm old, son."

"Age means nothing. I just want to dance with you, sir."

"We're both males."

"That doesn't matter."

"I'm in bad health," Ernest said. "My

back is sore. I'm sure my colon is ruptured."

Wyatt looked at me, then began browsing through his records, rearranging them, showing them to Ernest, then organizing them in his sack. It was Wyatt's vehemence, I think, that brought Ernest to fall into a type of trance, staring at the boy.

When it was time for bed, I didn't need to tell Wyatt to brush his teeth. In the bathroom he removed his toothbrush and toothpaste and brushed. He even flossed, leaning as far as he could over the bathroom sink to study his gums and teeth in the mirror, rinsing and gargling with mouthwash, closing the medicine cabinet when he finished.

"I've learned to be fastidious about my hygiene," he said. "I'll need to be up by seven to get ready for school."

"I'll make you breakfast," I told him.

I bid him good night as he closed his bedroom door. Then for a moment I stood in the hallway, listening at the door. I heard the squeak of the bed. I heard him move around under the covers. Then I stepped lightly down the hall and into our bedroom.

Ernest was standing at the window beside our bed, looking outside. I saw his shadowy reflection and asked him what he was looking at, but he didn't respond. I put on my nightgown and got into bed while he continued to gaze out the window.

"Ernest," I said, and he leaned forward and put his hands on the window. His face was close to the glass, as if he saw something.

"Ernest," I said again. "What is it?"

"I had some moccasins when we were first married," he said. "Do you remember them? My father made them for me before he passed."

"You remember the moccasins?"

He half-smiled into the window, and I felt like a miracle was occurring. Something had jarred his memory. I could barely breathe in my astonishment.

"That boy gives me a good feeling," Ernest said. "That boy, Wyatt. It's Ray-Ray."

His words overwhelmed me. I sat up and turned to him. "What are you talking about, Ernest?"

"It's Ray-Ray," he said again, still staring out the window. "He's come home."

EDGAR

September 2
The Darkening Land
In the early-morning fog I left the motel room and took a train to the Darkening Land. I kept hearing Sonja's voice over and over: *Come home, Edgar. Mom and Papa want to see you, Edgar. What the hell are you doing, Edgar.* I wasn't going home though, at least not now. I didn't want them to worry about me, and if I called them, they would worry. They would harass me about not going to rehab. Then they would threaten to drive back out and have another intervention, which I didn't want. I thought I could handle everything on my own. I wanted them to feel proud of me, not ashamed, so I thought I could find a job and show them I was doing okay. Maybe I wouldn't go home to the bonfire, or maybe I would. All I knew was that I needed to leave Albuquerque for a while.

101

Everyone I saw on the train looked dead, but I knew they were all sleeping. I saw their bodies slumped, mouths open. Outside the world flew by. I wasn't able to see anything except fog. In the window I saw my smoky reflection. I leaned against the cold glass and tried to sleep. A man a few rows in front of me stood from his seat. His spine was badly crooked, and he bent forward, craning his neck to look back at me. I noticed that his eyes were bulging, and blood trickled from the side of his head. "The suffering, the suffering!" he yelled, coughing dust and smoke.

Another man and presumably his wife were in a seat across from me. The man was sleeping, and I could see mosquitoes covering the man's face. Just then he woke, swatted them away, and blew his nose into a handkerchief. "I don't feel well," he told his wife.

"You're pale," she said. "You have no color. Your face is empty and dead."

"I don't feel well," he kept saying.

He was so ashen and eaten by sickness, it was impossible to tell how old he was. By the time we pulled into the station, I wasn't feeling well either. At some point during the trip I had developed a headache in my right temple. The longer I was on the train, the worse I felt. I had the taste of battery acid in my mouth. I sat and waited while others got their bags and exited. I had my own bag, which I slung over my shoulder as I walked off the train.

Attempts to call Rae from the station proved pointless. I couldn't get a signal on my phone. The station was empty and dim, with no windows open and only a janitor sweeping the floor. Above us, a light buzzed and flickered. As I headed for the door, I recognized, surprisingly, a guy named Jackson who was a friend from childhood. He had thinning blond hair and wore glasses that magnified his eyes. He squinted at me, and for a minute I wondered if he recognized me.

"Edgar," he said. He pointed at me, the way we pointed at each other as a gesture of greeting back in school. I approached him, and we shook hands.

"What are you doing here?" he asked.

"I don't know," I said, and he laughed.

"You don't know? Well, finally, somebody from back home is here."

"I got on a train," I said. "I was in Albuquerque and needed to get out. I don't know. I left, and here I am."

"You look different, Chief. We used to call you Chief, remember? Everyone goes

103

through a metamorphosis, I guess. We change appearance, don't we?"

"My hair's gotten longer since the last time you saw me," I said.

"It was always long, Chief. I probably look sick from all this heavy air. The sun never comes out here."

He invited me to stay with him. I agreed, and we walked to his car, a battered thing smelling of rotting food and cigarette smoke.

I knew Jackson in high school, back when he was a misfit. Maybe we were both misfits. For a while we would shoot hoops together. He couldn't jump very well, sat on the bench. In ninth grade I was one of the taller kids and could touch the rim. I could shoot a fadeaway jumper and decent baseline shot, but by my sophomore year I'd injured my shoulder during a game and was done for good. People said I could've gotten a college scholarship in basketball or football. I was a good cornerback in football until that shoulder injury. The coach, a white man, compared me to Jim Thorpe. "You even look like him," he used to say. I made three interceptions in one game, but after that injury I quit all sports, no matter how much people encouraged me.

"Remember when I got suspended for

bringing my twenty-two to school?" Jackson asked on the drive.

"Who brings a rifle to school? Fucking nutcase."

Jackson was still proud of that. I always thought he was criminally insane, but others called him a genius.

In the car, he wanted to hear about what I'd been up to. I told him about Rae and how she left me. "I don't know if she's kicking me out of the house or what."

"You're here now, Chief."

"I guess so."

"I got a job for you. You're Sac and Fox tribe, right?"

"Cherokee."

"I was thinking you were Sac and Fox, like Jim Thorpe. What difference does it make?"

I looked at him, unsure what he meant by that.

"We can get around all that," he said. "I mean, we have this software in development you can help us with. It's a sports game."

Jackson jerked the steering wheel, swerving to miss something in the road. The sudden jerk jarred me, and I held the dashboard. "Goddamn," he said.

"What was that?" I asked.

"Wolf, I think. Or bobcat."

105

I felt a sudden and overwhelming fear. Where was I? We drove down a street with little traffic. The world was gray-blue, with snowy fog. Bare trees without leaves lined both sides of the road, though it wasn't winter. The houses we passed were all older wood-frame houses, with porches and maples and oak trees in yards. I noticed a sign: BEWARE OF AIR QUALITY.

"Where are we," I said.

"The Darkening Land."

"Stop saying that. I mean the name of the town."

"It's the Darkening Land," he said again. "Don't worry. Are you worrying? Do you need to go to the hospital, Chief?"

"What are you talking about?"

"The hospitals here are failures. People can't breathe here. There's coughing and disease. I've been through six surgeries to correct a broken rib with too much pain. They gave me hardly any pain meds. I wanted the good shit, morphine or fentanyl. The doctors ended up removing the rib while I watched."

I looked at him.

"I was stabbed in a public toilet," he continued. "I won't tell you the details. It was a restroom in a park. I thought the guy wanted sex, but he stabbed and robbed me.

Turns out he was a skinhead."

"You got pain pills at your house?" I asked.

"I wish."

While holding the steering wheel with one hand, he pulled up his shirt with his other and showed me. I saw a mass of scars on his side. He didn't want to talk about it further and quickly changed the subject. "People keep themselves entertained in weird ways around here. They play all kinds of games around town. Gaming consoles aren't keeping them satisfied anymore. But with real-life games, you don't know what's real and what isn't. Kids are spending twelve, fifteen hours a day playing. Adults, too."

"What do you mean, real-life games?"

"The new games are augmented reality. That's what we're working on developing right now for the game: holograms. Images. What's real and what isn't. Structure and chaos. You can be a big help, especially with the sports game."

"Where the fuck are we?" I said again, more to myself than to Jackson. I had a metallic taste in my mouth. I was still nauseated, and the road was in bad shape, full of potholes, jarring the car every time we drove over one.

"The images are a distraction," Jackson

107

went on. "People find real-life games more interactive. They get people out of their homes and communicate more in society. Remember those zombie campus games college students used to play?"

"No."

"Some students were zombies and some were humans, and they went around trying to shoot each other. It's like that here, but everywhere, with more people. We'll have to get used to it. Nothing we can do about it, Chief."

I questioned everything he was telling me. I wondered if he'd become a compulsive liar or if he was trying to make me paranoid; either way, something was off about him.

He glanced at me, then turned up the radio, but there was no music. There was static, only static.

Twenty minutes later we pulled into his place, a small brick house with a front porch and flickering yellow porch light. The yard was in need of being mowed, part weeds, and wet from humidity or rain. The air felt heavy as I got my bag from the trunk.

I decided right then I wouldn't stay long. I felt as though I was in some alternate universe. It reminded me of the black-and-white horror movies Papa used to watch before we had cable TV. His yard was washed out, and everything felt distorted, hazy with movement. I saw the ancient tree in his yard with cracked tree bark that resembled the faces of the dead. I saw insects crawling all over the bark. The insects buzzed, twitching their antennae.

I followed Jackson into his rotting house and asked for water to drink. The living room was warm and bare, with a few paintings on the wall of tanks and aircraft. I noticed model airplanes around the room — on the TV, on shelves, and one in pieces on the dining room table, which Jackson pointed at as we walked past. He said he was working on airplane models and other projects for his work involving holograms.

He showed me my room in the back, with a single bed and small TV and a window that looked out at the backyard. A desk fan was on, humming quietly. I put my bags on the bed and lay down.

"I'll be back with a glass of water," Jackson said.

I kicked off my shoes and closed my eyes. When I opened them, he was there again, standing over me with the glass.

"I'm glad you're here," he said. He sat on the edge of the bed. "All the emptiness and isolation is crippling around here. I feel

109

empty inside with no one to talk to. The place drains me of joy. Every day is gray, like Sunday — you know the song. But you'll get used to it."

I didn't know what he was talking about.

"I mean you'll get used to feeling sad," he said. "I used to sit in this torn booth at the Regal Café downtown and drink coffee and try to meet people, but nobody wanted to talk to me. One night I was there at three in the morning, and a man and woman sitting across from me kept looking over and whispering. I caught a glimpse of my reflection in the napkin dispenser, and I looked goddamn pathetic. My eyes were bloodshot from lack of sleep, I was unshaven, I looked like I was in pain. Everyone kept glancing in my direction. A construction worker sitting at the counter made eye contact with me and then looked away, shaking his head. It was terrible."

I didn't respond. He sniffed hard, then took a deep breath.

"It was like this before, though, sort of. From an early age I didn't like my face. Remember my uncle, who raised me? He always made dumb remarks about it."

I didn't remember, but I nodded anyway and took another drink.

"He sat in his stupid wooden rocking chair

every night, drinking and smoking cigarettes. He wore glasses and mumbled to himself. I remember nights in bed, how I imagined myself escaping while he slept beside me, snoring like a goddamn bear. Every so often he had seizures. I'm glad they found him murdered in his bed."

He apologized. It occurred to me how badly Jackson needed someone to talk to, even first thing in the morning. He changed the subject and began talking about his life with his ex-lover, their arguments about money and having other lovers. I listened to every strange story. I rarely spoke, nodding to confirm I understood what he was talking about. He stared past me as he reeled in sad memories. There were parties and drugs. He grew tired of people.

"You still shoot hoops?" I asked, changing the subject.

"Too out of shape. Plus I never liked it much. You were a great athlete for a while. You were the next Jim Thorpe. You even looked like him. Still do."

"I guess I lost interest."

"I was awful," he said. "I came off the bench in the semifinals at the huge fucking Mabee Center and blew it. I shot an air ball from the baseline. I missed a layup. I head-faked left and airballed a hook shot."

We were both quiet.

"Speaking of Jim Thorpe, I need to tell you about this software I'm working on," he said, "It's game development. A sports game, really simple. Everyone loves sports games these days. In this game, you can play sports with Jim Thorpe. You challenge him and compete in basketball one-on-one, hitting at the plate in baseball, tackling and throwing passes in football. The game's called *Thorpe 3D.*" He went on to talk in great length about a projector-like device that emitted a hologram of Jim Thorpe. The hologram could have whole conversations, apparently. Jackson said he could make new holograms from any image found on the web. The possibilities were endless.

"Holograms," I said.

"Yeah, they're basically lasers that produce high-frequency pulses," he said. "They're images that talk and listen to you. We're working on the voice-activation software at the moment. I'll show you it soon. It's downstairs in the basement. The images are incredibly real-looking. You can shoot hoops with them, throw a football."

"But you can't touch them?"

"The lasers burn your skin, which is a problem. A friend of mine burned his face trying to strangle a hologram. He was a retired prison guard from the federal reformatory. Anyway, right now I'm working on making holograms of other Indians. I could use your help. When you play three versus three against Jim Thorpe, you need other avatars. I can study your features."

"You need other Indians," I said. "This is what you want my help with? Because I'm Native?"

"Pretty much," he said. He laughed, coughing dust.

That night I was unable to fall asleep, too warm, unclear exactly where I was. I had my cell phone, but it wasn't registering a location. I tried to meditate and concentrate on something peaceful: an open field at dusk, an ocean, a cloudless sky. I needed peace. I didn't want to think about Rae or my family. I didn't want to think about anything. I stepped into the hall bathroom and closed the door behind me, locking it. The mirror was smudged. When I turned on the faucet, rusty water splattered out, gurgling in the pipes. I knocked on the faucet a few times with the butt of my hand, but the pipe kept gurgling. The walls were light green and ticked. I felt certain I was being paranoid, but strange houses always made me uneasy at first.

Back in my bedroom, though, I heard barking outside and looked out the window. In the fog outside I saw hounds rummaging around, tearing into garbage. One of the hounds ran off with a small animal in its mouth. The others were fighting, growling and barking at each other, their eyes yellow in the night. I saw the red fowl strut right past them, its head cocked. How did it follow me here? The fowl walked slowly, pecking at the ground. The wind moaned through the cracks in the windowsill. I saw dark trees with drooping branches out there. I saw black vultures hanging in the moonlit sky.

SONJA

September 2

When Ray-Ray was still alive, in the summers we used to ride our bikes out to the river and swim. We splashed and wrestled in the water. I was only one grade ahead of him. We got along really well, and because he was my little brother, he was very protective of me. I remember once a group of boys from his school showed up when we were swimming in a shallow area. Some of the boys started teasing him about me, telling him I was pretty.

"Hey, look at that hot ass," they said. "Hey, Ray-Ray! Your sister easy?"

"Shut up, fuckers," he called to them. "You guys wish she would even talk to you."

"Faggot," one of them said.

I thought it was all harmless, at least at first, but then Ray-Ray ended up getting mad and fighting one of the boys. I watched the whole thing until the other boys broke it up.

"I hate them," Ray-Ray told me later, but he wouldn't tell me why. I just assumed it was because they were harassing him. I wasn't as social as he was. I was quiet, mostly an introvert in high school, and other kids knew I was unpopular. Maybe my being quiet and unpopular bothered him. I wish I knew. We were a private family. Papa gave me comfort by telling me to let people think what they want. Let bad people be bad people, he told me.

The day after our encounter, Vin called, but I let it go to my voice mail. He left a message saying he had been thinking about me and wanted to know whether I would like to have coffee with him in downtown Quah at the Roasted Bean. It was noon. I waited an hour to return his call, partly to give the impression that I was busier than I actually was and partly to show that I was not checking my phone so often, waiting for him to call. When he answered, he asked if we could meet for coffee while Luka was in school, or was I too busy? So I agreed to meet him at the Roasted Bean in an hour.

When I saw him there, I pretended to act happy, and the first thing he did was apologize for acting a little "out of it," he said, or

116

maybe he said "out of touch," or maybe "out of town." He said he was taking Benadryl due to all the rain stirring up his allergies. He bought me a chai tea and himself a mocha, ordering for both of us; I found it strange that he ordered for me.

"My dad's really sick," he said.

"Oh, really?" I said, and my attention sharpened. "Sick how?"

"He's on chemo. He has lung cancer, and they're bringing in hospice to care for him at his house. It's so sad to watch him have to go through this."

"You're close to your dad?" I asked.

"We're closer now than ever. He's kept to himself since he retired. He lives out in the woods north of town."

"He doesn't come into town much, huh?"

"No, why do you ask?"

"I know more about your family than you think." He gave me an uncertain look, so I laughed it off and told him I was joking.

"Does chemo really even help?" I asked quietly into my cup. "Doesn't it just kill people eventually?"

"It depends."

"Well," I said, "I'm Cherokee, and we live forever, you know."

"I was thinking you were Hispanic. I mean, I knew you were part something,

117

something, but I wasn't sure."

"I'm something," I said.

He laughed, oddly, and I sensed a part of him I didn't care for. Why he'd said it that way: *something.* We walked down the sidewalk, past the little shops selling university paraphernalia, past the tattoo shop and the flower shop and the Thai restaurant where Papa liked to eat. We crossed the street, and I took his arm, feeling his energy as we walked. We strolled over to the alley between Muskogee and Shawnee, passing a dumpster behind Morgan's Bakery, and came to the back entrance of a local club where Vin played every so often. We stopped walking here, and he pushed me against the red brick of the building and kissed me hard. I embraced him, running my fingers through his hair. I let him touch me, run his hands over my body. We kissed for a while. I reached down to feel that he was hard and grabbed him, telling him I wanted him to take me right there. He said we could go to his house.

"I want you *here,*" I told him, right there in the alley, and he pulled back somewhat aggressively, telling me it wasn't safe, people walked down the alley all the time.

I laughed at him.

"What's so funny?" he said. "We can't do

118

it here, people will see."

"So what if we get caught? Someone may watch us and get off, or take a picture and post it online. Who cares?"

I dug in my purse for a cigarette and looked at him.

"Let's just go to my house," he said again. His car was parked down the street from the Roasted Bean. During the walk back, I didn't take his arm. I wondered what had happened and why he was suddenly so stressed, or if it was something else entirely that had created such a strange shift. He drove us to his house and parked in the drive. From here I could see the iron-fenced backyard, his back porch with its lawn chairs and table. I had seen none of this from the library. Outside, somewhere nearby, I heard an owl in broad daylight. I asked Vin whether he heard it, too, but he said he didn't. We stopped by the back porch and waited to listen, but the bird didn't call again. Vin asked if I was sure it was an owl. Maybe it was a car horn far away, he suggested. Or maybe a different bird or a bobcat. But I told him I know when I hear an owl. It worried me because Papa taught me that owls can be messengers of bad news. Papa had told me old Cherokee stories of dead people turning into owls and bringing warnings to people. When I said this to Vin, he said he found superstitions fascinating. I could tell he didn't take it seriously.

"There's a lot to be said about owls," I told him as I waited for him to unlock the door, but he didn't respond.

We went through the back door into the kitchen, and I followed him into the living room, which was modestly decorated, with a TV and stereo in the corner of the room, pictures of abstract art on the walls and above the fireplace mantel. A red couch, a recliner, a coffee table. Old hardwood floors with Legos, action figures, and various toys. I sat on the sofa while Vin went into another room and returned with a baggie of weed. I watched him roll a joint on the coffee table carefully, sprinkling the weed into the paper and then sealing it. He lit it with his lighter and passed it to me, and we smoked it down. He had two shelves entirely filled with record albums, organized by genre and alphabetized by band name. He was interested in eighties music, bands I had no interest in: Split Enz, Bow Wow Wow, Bowie.

"Why don't you listen to real rock?" I said to him.

"I do," he said. "But I like New Wave bands, too. You like Morrissey?"

"You're kind of a pussy," I said, and he seemed annoyed. I watched him go through his album sleeves and tell me about them. There was a different story attached to each album, to each song. He told me about his first dance with a girl in sixth grade, about a series of firsts: first kiss, first fuck. First drunk, first acid trip, first party in college. Each album held a special memory. His whole life was contained in the sleeves of those albums. I found his obsession amusing and a little endearing.

Around seven in the evening we stepped out the back door onto the porch and sat on his patio. We drank wine as he talked about his own music. He didn't ask many questions about me but seemed more interested in himself, his band, and letting me know he was serious about it. I yawned into my wineglass, stoned but invested enough in him that I wanted to take him upstairs to his bed. We fell silent, and I studied his face, long and stolid, unshaven. His nose was thin and his eyes were gleaming and dark. He stared back at me, and because I was stoned, the look felt long and important. Then, abruptly, he stopped looking at me and stared toward the kitchen.

Luka was there, in the light of the house, watching us through the screen door. I'd assumed he was with his mom, especially since we'd been at Vin's house for what felt like hours, and Vin had made no mention of him. I lit a cigarette and turned in my chair so I could see him better. He was holding a toy in his hand that he kept tapping against his leg as he watched me. For a moment that's all we did: stare at each other, though it was hard to tell for how long because of the weed. His hair was unkempt, but in a way that looked boyish and cute. He lifted his toy to his face, and I realized it was actually a pair of binoculars. He held them there, staring.

"I see you," I said.

He opened the door and stepped outside, approaching us slowly, cautious. His mouth was open as he held the binoculars to his eyes, and I could see his little white teeth, his small chin. His skin was olive-colored, his elbows dry and white. Then he lowered the binoculars and looked at me, and I saw something mysterious in his striking eyes, more than sadness, more than loneliness, probing for affection. In this fragile way he searched my own face, curious, looking as gentle and innocent as any boy I had ever seen. Vin introduced me as Colette, his new friend, and I asked Luka what his favorite thing to eat was, and he said ice cream, so I suggested we all go out for ice cream, my treat. With this, I won a smile from him.

As we all went back inside, the living room was flooded with light, though I was still a little stoned. Vin put on his sunglasses and drove us to the ice cream parlor downtown, observing the speed limit. We pulled up to the drive-thru window, and he ordered our ice cream cones from a boy in black-framed glasses, his hair gelled in a very fifties way. His glasses magnified his eyes as he leaned forward out of the window to take our order. On the drive back Vin kept talking about how the boy held an uncanny resemblance to Buddy Holly, but I was turned around in my seat, watching Luka eat his ice cream with a spoon. "I've never seen anyone eat an ice cream cone like that," I told him, and he responded without looking at me: "I like it this way."

Vin's weed was really good, better than anything I had smoked in a long time, and it took me a while to come down from my high. After Luka went upstairs to his room, we listened to music in the living room, and Vin began to ramble on again about the bands he had played in. I found much of this boring and asked him to be quiet so I could listen to the music. "Goddamn, that's sexy," I said. "Who is this?"

"Sam Cooke."

He kissed my neck a little, and I closed my eyes, listening to Sam Cooke sing about bringing it on home to me and feeling Vin's warm breath, his hands. Soon we were kissing.

He said he wanted me to keep hanging out with him. He would make spaghetti for dinner and open another bottle of wine. "So you'll stay with me," he said.

"Oh really?" I said.

We went into the kitchen, and he backed me against the counter and kissed me, running his hands over my body. He asked me whether I wanted him, and I said I did. "After Luka's in bed we'll go upstairs," he said. He was handsome, but not a great conversationalist. As he made dinner, he talked about how he wasn't registered to vote because politics wasn't his thing. I wondered whether he even knew how he felt on certain issues or if he was a person who simply didn't care. "I don't watch the news or pay much attention to what's going on in the world," he said. "I get bored so easily with anything political. It's all shit. Watching the news is all about fear and violence anyway." He preferred music and movies. He preferred not thinking about the world too much, things like mass shootings, poverty.

"People are dying all around us," I said. Or maybe I said, "People are falling in love all around us." But I knew he wasn't interested.

He said Luka was on the autism spectrum. Luka's mother, Vin's ex-girlfriend, was in jail, he told me, for distribution of meth, adding that he didn't want to talk about it anymore because he became too angry whenever he thought about her. About the only thing I told him was that I knew what it was like to be around kids without a mom, since my mother had been a social worker. While I talked, I watched him set two spots at the table. He called Luka to get his food. A moment later Luka came down and took his plate upstairs to eat in his room.

"What an adorable son you have," I told him.

Later, after Luka had gone to bed and we'd finished the bottle of wine, I followed Vin upstairs to his bedroom. It was surprisingly messy compared to the rest of the house. He clearly hadn't planned on me seeing his bedroom, or maybe he didn't care. There were clothes on the floor and on a dresser, a few of Luka's toy cars in the corner, and the bed was a tumble of covers. In a way I found it humorous. His walls were a faded turquoise, with a few framed pictures of people I assumed were family members on them. A mahogany-framed oval mirror that looked like an antique hung over his dresser. It was charming compared to the rest of the decor.

He came over to me and kissed me a long time, running his hands along my sides, over my breasts. I preferred it this way, to be slowly caressed. I wanted to indulge in him. I put my hand against him and told him I could be loud sometimes, and was that a problem, since Luka was down the hall? "So what," he said, and I pushed him onto the bed, planning to get on top of him, but he took my arms and wrestled me to my back. I watched him unbutton his shirt and pull it off. He clearly wanted to take charge, so I let him, though somewhat reluctantly. In the past I'd found that guys who wanted control were careless and quick. It appeared he wanted to take his time, though. I sat up and raised my arms so that he could pull my shirt off. He was still standing, wanting me to watch him unbutton his jeans and take them off. He did this slowly. He did not take off his boxer shorts but instead leaned forward onto the bed and kissed me without restraint. I could feel the tension in the muscles of his arms and legs. What I can say about that first time with him was that he was not trying too hard, like so many other lovers I had been with.

He wanted me to talk like an Indian, to whisper his name like an Indian.

"Fuck you," I said. He thought I was joking, but I was serious.

I got on top of him and pulled his hair. Then he pulled mine. I called him a little white boy.

"Come on," I kept saying. "Come on, do it!"

He kept making this face, which struck me as funny. Afterward I began laughing, which made him angry, I could tell.

"But you make a weird face," I said, and he laughed a little, so it was all good. Both of us lay there in bed in the dim light of the lamp on the nightstand. He turned to lie on his stomach, and I ran my hands over his back lightly.

"I'm kidding around," I said.

"Whatever, I'm good. Women tell me I'm good."

"Funny guy."

"It's all good," he said.

I didn't care what he said. He could've said anything to me. I felt his skin, sticky and warm from fucking. I put my face to his back and smelled him.

After Vin fell asleep, I texted Edgar: Hey, you around? Are u coming home? Edgar never called Papa or our mom, and I knew it hurt them. Edgar had promised me, too, he'd keep me posted on what was going on. We usually texted once a week, at least, but that hadn't happened in a while, and I was concerned. I kept texting him: Are u ok? Hey, need to talk asap!!! Call me when u can! The more frantic I sounded, I thought, the more he would realize how badly he was needed. Part of Edgar's problem was feeling unloved, being the youngest child. He was so little when Ray-Ray died, and he'd spent his childhood trying to grow up in Ray-Ray's shadow, listening to our mother and Papa talk about Ray-Ray's sense of humor and about everything he did.

I walked quietly down the hall, still naked, to Luka's bedroom and peeked inside. I couldn't hear him breathing over the hum of the ceiling fan, but I was able to make out his figure in the bed. Outside there was thunder, followed by rain thrumming against the window. I pulled Luka's door closed softly, then walked quietly downstairs and turned on the light in the living room, where I stood and stretched. It was raining really hard now, and the wind had come up. A squall battered the back door. How wonderful to walk naked in a stranger's house during a thunderstorm, I thought. Something about it always excited me, being naked in a strange house. There was a picture of Luka and, I assumed, his mother on the fireplace mantel. I picked it up. She was sitting outside somewhere, wearing sunglasses, and he was in her lap. He was wearing a blue Dallas Cowboys T-shirt with the number 8 across the front, and holding a little football. The photo crushed me.

As I put the frame down, I noticed a photo of Vin and an older man I was certain was his father. I picked it up and stared at it, then set it back on the mantel. Outside I heard the rumble of thunder in the distance. The trees were waving in the wind, and it was raining hard now. I opened the screen door and stepped naked into the rain outside. It was dark, and the drops felt cold on my body. I walked to the trees and squatted to pee while thunder rumbled all around.

I don't know what I expected to feel. I suppose I wondered whether Vin would wake, find me gone, and rush outside, but no light ever came on in the house. The moon came out from behind the clouds. I looked up to the blue night sky and saw its glow. Whatever may have happened then, I could feel something stirring around me, perhaps the wind or something else entirely. I won't lie and say I didn't find it exciting, the trembling of wind, the unknown presence of something watching me naked in the night. I sank down to my knees and felt the warm earth and grass. I ran my fingers along hedge branches and bushes. Something was there, I could feel it. I stood up again as if being summoned, stepping toward the house.

I heard the sound of wings. I looked up and saw a large bird perched on the roof of the house, its wings spread, looking down at me. It had me now, whatever it was. It had my attention. Who can say how long I was out there? I heard the wind, the sky, the trees. Welcoming the storm, I let the rain come down on me.

TSALA

Beloved son: when I look at the scope of our history, I can see the longing to hold on to people, to keep them close so they don't leave. We were afraid they would depart and never return. I witnessed the removal of our people from our lands. We each have our own stories, which bring us together.

I loved your mother, Clara, more than any other person I had met. When I was a young man I found her by a stream near the mountains. I brought her gifts: a blanket and sweet corn. I told her about her natural beauty. Her eyes were like none I had ever seen, and eventually we were married, but it was not easy. Our story is similar to the old story of the young man who meets Laoka — a story that holds a special meaning for me. My great-grandfather told the story to my grandfather, who passed it down to my father, who passed it down to me. And now

I will tell it to you, as it possesses a great lesson.

The Story of Laoka

A young man who was very lonely met a beautiful woman by the mountains and told her he was an honest and adept hunter.

"I like hunters," she said. "Show me how well you can shoot a bow."

He looked to the sky and squinted at the sun. He took his bow and an arrow from his bag and looked at a tree across the stream.

"I know when a man is acting a fool," she said.

He stared straight ahead and shot his bow, which hit the tree across the stream. "That is what I was aiming for," he told her.

The young woman was not impressed. She told him he was looking into the sky, not at the tree.

"I can skin a bear with my hands," he said. "I have killed bears and snakes with my knife."

"I don't believe you," she said. She became very suspicious of his stories and told him goodbye. He was sad but determined to win her love.

Walking away, he called out wearily for

132

help. He sat on a rock and said he would give anything to win her. He held his head in his hands.

Would you give anything? He heard a voice speak from the darkness.

A large brown rodent with a dark snout and long tail crawled out of the brush. The rodent stood on its hind legs. This was Laoka, whose belly swelled at the sight of human and animal flesh.

Laoka staggered toward the young man, leaning down to tilt his hairy snout and making gurgling sounds.

The young man had heard stories of Laoka from the elders, stories of how he appeared in different form, as a snake or beast, and how he slaughtered birds and animals and then ate them. How his belly swelled and burst and then swelled again. How wasps flew from his mouth and attacked whatever person or animal he wanted to eat.

"Go or I will kill you," the young man said. "I know who you are."

Laoka was studying him to see what he was going to do. The young man lunged at him, and Laoka moved out of the way.

Laoka hissed, *I can help you.*

Then three sacred stones materialized before the young man: a dark-red stone, the petrified coral, love's wisdom. A yellow stone, the topaz, to think of future generations. And a rose stone that healed a heart overwhelmed by sadness. The young man reached for the stones, but Laoka latched on to his hand with his mouth. The young man felt the teeth in the fleshy part of his hand, and he yelled out in pain.

Laoka let go and said, *You can have these stones if you follow me to the fire.*

The young man wanted to see the fire. Those who entered it disappeared, leaving no remains. It was a sacrifice to enter the fire, to reestablish a good relationship with the land and our nation, the earth, and the sky. It was the most sacred place, and it never appeared in the same location.

So the young man followed Laoka through the woods. The sun went behind a cloud, and the woods dimmed. He could hear his footsteps crackling through leaves and twigs. Soon they came out of the woods and upon a cave, where Laoka stopped and turned.

Before seeing the fire, Laoka hissed, *you must first see selu, the corn.*

The young man agreed and followed Laoka into the cave, where they sat on the ground and Laoka offered him ears of corn.

This selu contains a powerful energy. You should take them and feed them to the woman you are in love with. She will fall in love with you.

"How do I know you're not tricking me?" the young man asked.

I find your young strength admirable. Now go.

The next day the young man arrived at the stream and saw the beautiful woman. She asked, "Where is your bow and arrow, adept hunter?"

"I brought you this corn," he told her.

"Where did you get this?"

"I found it near the river," he lied. "I want you to eat it, please. Taste it and tell me what you're feeling. It's good corn. I ate it myself."

She pulled off some kernels and tossed them to the ground. After a moment a small bird, a sparrow, flew down and hopped over to it and ate it. The sparrow immediately began convulsing and making noises. "This is poison," she said. She stood and went over to the sparrow, which was still shaking. The bird fluttered and shook, trying to fly away.

"You killed that bird, and it would've

135

poisoned me," she told the young man.

He was horrified by what had happened. "No, no," he told her. "I didn't know."

"You told me you ate it, so you lied to me, too."

"I didn't mean to," he said. "I gave it to you because I thought it would make you like me."

But she walked away. He called after her, but she didn't respond.

Now furious, the young man returned to the cave and called for Laoka: "Yo ho, Laoka! Yo ho, yo ho, Laoka! Come out so I can kill you . . ."

He entered the cave, but it was empty. He searched and searched for him, but he wasn't there.

He sat outside and waited. For days he sat there, starving himself, freezing in the cold, but Laoka never returned. The young man knew he was out in the world some-where, but he held his anger inside himself so fiercely that he slowly died out there. While he waited, he heard the hissing of Laoka, but never found him. He heard the shrieks of animals in the woods. He saw black vultures in the moonlit sky.

My son, I had to earn trust of your mother by showing I was trustworthy. I did not lie or betray her. Anger and vengeance were not uncommon in our family. They are dangerous, as you can see from the story of Laoka. We must warn our family about their dangers.

Your mother and I married, and soon you were born. We lived peacefully among our people on our land. But soon, too soon, I began having visions of the coming soldiers.

EDGAR

September 3

My dad used to say the ringing in my ears
was a sign the dead were trying to contact
me. "Your ancestors," he said. "Listen for
them. Pay attention to things around you."
At Jackson's that first night, the constant
ringing made it difficult to sleep. I remembered how Rae used to stay up late with me
and talk whenever I couldn't sleep. She
would turn on the lamp, sit up in bed, and
we would talk about anything. I listened
again to the voice mail my mother had left,
reminding me of Ray-Ray's anniversary.

In the morning I woke to a noise outside,
which I hoped was a cat or raccoon rummaging around and not the red fowl. My
room was still dim despite it being morning. The room had a bluish tint. I heard the
wind blowing, and from the window I could
see the branches moving. I thought of Rae
lying next to me. I thought of my dad's

confusion, walking around the house, forgetting where he put things. I thought of the look on my mother's face while she watched him struggle.

I lay in bed awake for several minutes before I finally got up. In the kitchen, Jackson was clanging dishes around in the sink. He wiped his hands on a dish towel and took a drink of his coffee.

"You should go back to bed," he said. "Sleep while you can. I'm hoping to talk to someone today about getting you involved in the software development and new avatars, now that you're here. If you leave and run into anyone, say your name is Jim, as in Jim Thorpe. You look like him anyway. You don't want people harassing you."

"What the hell?"

"The name Edgar is a loaded name. There was an Edgar in town who went on a killing spree a few years ago, and it's still touchy. Everyone knew the guy as Edgar, plain old Edgar. He took an assault rifle and shot a bunch of people at the park on the south side. Everyone was saying Edgar this, Edgar that. He was the only Edgar in this town. So you should go by Jim for a while."

I rubbed my hands over my face.

"It's a strange place," he said. "People might give you weird looks. Best to just ignore them. You need to trust me."

I got a coffee mug from the cabinet, and Jackson poured me a cup. "I better get to work," he said. "I'm glad you're here, Edgar. I'm going to talk to my work team about bringing you on board for the game development, but for now feel free to walk around town and explore. There's a coffee shop down the street. There's a liquor store. Everything will be fine."

After he left, I drank my coffee, went to lie down on the couch. I put my arm over my face and lay there, thinking about the Darkening Land, where I was, and trying to remember why I decided to come here in the first place, so far away from my family. I sat up and looked around Jackson's rotting house. While Jackson was at work, I made a piece of dry toast and ate it standing up, looking out the window. I sat in the rickety wooden chair and watched TV for a while, read part of a book from his shelf on Eastern religion. I found strange old books, one on the occult, another on General Custer. I flipped through a book on Baron Jeffrey Amherst and Pontiac's War, with a photo of dead men. The book felt dirty in my hands, so I headed out for a walk.

The air was hard to breathe, full of smog. All around, the land was full of dumpy

140

houses, old buildings, small shops. Dead leaves trembled as I walked past them. I stopped at trees and examined the cracked faces in them, wondering whose faces they were. One street I came to was lined with pink weeping trees, which I found somewhat attractive in such a dark place, so I followed that road. I walked past a laundromat. A few steps ahead of me was a woman wearing a long coat and house shoes, annoyed that I was walking behind her. She stopped and waited for me to pass, muttering to herself. Behind the laundromat were three dumpsters with graffiti spray-painted on them: Savages. All the buildings were falling apart, abandoned video rental stores, restaurants, auto parts stores. I saw a man with no legs begging in the street, shouting "Beware Devil's Bridge!" I saw another man pushing a boy in a wheelbarrow along the side of the road. The boy was pointing a toy gun at everything he saw. "POW!" he yelled, pointing the water gun at me as they wheeled past. "POW WOW!"

What did he mean, "Pow wow"? Or had I misheard him, and he'd said "pow" twice? Finally I came to a small cluster of stores on a street of old buildings and stepped into a place called Rusty Spoon Records. Inside, the owner, a bearded man with long silver hair and black teeth, asked me if I was looking for a particular record.

"Browsing," I said.

He told me his name was Venery, and he lived upstairs in the building with his miniature Doberman. He looked like an ex-hippie who'd tripped too many times in the sixties.

"You're a stranger in town," he said. "A stranger in an even stranger town."

I looked at him.

"Where you from?" he asked.

"I came here from Albuquerque."

"No, I mean where you *from,* son?"

"Oklahoma."

"Indian Territory," he said. He looked brain-dead and slack-jawed. I could see bits of egg in his beard. "Woody Guthrie was from Oklahoma, right?"

"Right."

"So was Jim Thorpe."

"Right again."

"You're a dead ringer for Jim Thorpe," he said. "Anyone ever tell you that?"

"Yeah, a few people."

Venery scratched at his cheek. "They say Jim Thorpe died of a heart attack. A victim of racism and intolerance and suffering. Tall, like yourself."

I didn't make eye contact with him, and I

think he could tell I was feeling uncomfortable, so he went over to his space by the register and returned with a good smoke and a large ashtray. "This ashtray was made from the ancient bones of a man from the plains," he said. "I'm not kidding. Look at this thing."

The ashtray was oblong and pale, and we smoked and looked at it, studying its curves and cracks. "I got a forty-thousand-year-old Neanderthal skull," he went on. "I use it as a bong for my good weed upstairs. Is it true the Natives had elongated skulls? What do you know about that? Can you enlighten me, Jim Thorpe?"

His tone was inconsiderate, but then I thought he was partly unhinged. The music playing in the store was loud, something psychedelic from the sixties or seventies. I decided to try to ignore him and began browsing records, flipping through the classic rock section, then on to blues and jazz. Some punk, even old country and western.

He told me he was so obsessed with Procol Harum that he'd named his oldest daughter after the band. "She and her husband live in a farmhouse outside of Kansas. It's a flat and desolate area full of cockeyed mouth breathers. Good God. I haven't seen them since I swallowed a bunch of pills thirteen years ago."

"Pills," I said. "What kind of pills?"

"The good kind."

"Me too."

Venery laughed. "My neighbor Vic got loaded on whiskey and beat his dog to death, then slit his own throat in his ex-wife's kitchen. His daughter overdosed on benzos and died in the tub. Now all they do is talk jive about everyone and never leave the house."

"Why don't they leave?"

"Bad air, Jimster. Wait until you start coughing, you'll see."

He had an eeriness about him, but he seemed harmless. He reminded me of some of the older guys I used to see in Albuquerque. They loved to talk music and drugs. "Sounds like a lot of people who live here tried to kill themselves," I said.

"Go down the street to Hemingway's Pub, and you'll run into Richard Manuel from The Band. Or maybe you'll see Phil Ochs. Both famous musicians, dead of suicide."

He had to think before he decided what to say next.

"You prefer Elliott Smith? I saw him in there drinking raspberry tea and reading something by Virginia Woolf. See the connection, Thorpe? We're all here for the same

144

reason."

"I need to know where I am. This whole place, I mean. It's creeping me out. I can't seem to relax here. You ever see a big red fowl walking around?"

"It's the Darkening Land, Jimbo. Nobody can breathe from the bad air. You'll develop a cough and spots on your lung. You're here like us, pal. Everyone has a fowl. You gotta withstand this evil harridan of a town and kill it yourself."

"Kill what? The fowl?"

"Kill it, JT. The rules are different in this place. Cobain plays the Cobra Room every Friday night. Hendrix does an acoustic set in the upstairs lounge at DFW's. What you need to do is listen to music. It helps." He showed me the album cover of *Their Satanic Majesties Request.* "This is a great fucking record. I also got *Exile on Main Street.* I got Albert Ayler. I got Hendrix live at Monterey."

I glanced at the album cover but told him I couldn't afford to buy anything right now until I got a job. "I'll come back soon," I told him. "I just got to town."

"Did you say your name was Jim Thorpe?"

"Funny," I said.

Venery laughed, coughing dust and smoke.

■ ■ ■ ■

I headed back to Jackson's, down the same street as before. I looked up to the yellow sky full of clouds and tiny birds circling overhead. On the street puddles of rainwater reflected autumn foliage. An older man, spindly and awkward, wearing a long coat and fedora hat, stopped me and asked if I'd been to Devil's Bridge.

"Sorry, no."

"I see," he said, eyeing me closely. "I take it you're not in the military?"

"No."

"Government agent?"

"No."

I saw the face of a deeply sad old man. I saw in his eyes a longing for an answer neither of us could grasp. Maybe he was connected to some universe, some other reality I didn't understand. His eyes watered, and I looked away.

"Heck, that's good," he said. "I carry a blue-steel Colt, sometimes a .38 Special. Back in the seventies I got court-martialed for firing a gun into the ceiling of a base in El Paso. There's a mud pit and firing range out by Devil's Bridge."

"I don't know anything about it," I said.

"Sorry, I need to go."

"I can show you where it is. We can go there. We can go there right now if you want. Are you Native American?"

"Sorry, I'm in a hurry."

I turned and headed back to Jackson's house, past the laundromat and dumpsters. I walked quickly, as quickly as I could, but it felt like I'd been walking around for hours. I turned down Jackson's street and saw his low-slung car parked in the drive.

Inside the rotting house, Jackson was talking on the phone. He looked up at me as I entered. "Hang on, he just came in," he said into the phone. "I'll call you back."

I sat on the couch across from him.

"That was Lyle, asking about the game," he said. "We were talking about avatars."

"What game, the sports game?"

He nodded impatiently. "That's right, the Jim Thorpe game. Lyle wants some specific information from you." He crossed his legs, jostling his foot. "Since the sports game has to do with the American Indian, I guess I need to know what Native Americans eat. Is Indian skillet a real dish? Indian tacos, fry bread? Anything culturally specific to Native American food?"

"I eat what you eat," I told him.

"Beans and cornbread?"

147

"No."

"Possum?"

"No."

"Help us out," he said. "I figured you could help some here. What kinds of food?"

"This is dumb, Jackson. How is this important for a sports game?"

He clicked his tongue, thinking. "Maybe a cultural reference in case a player wants to have lunch with Jim Thorpe. The game's Thorpe hologram should show a man looking forward to a good meal after competition. It's a bonus round: eat with a champ. Eat some possum or rabbit with Jim Thorpe, maybe fry bread too. We'll need accurate cultural references, which is why I need you to tell me everything you can."

"Christ, Jackson, what a terrible idea," I said. "No wonder you guys haven't done much. Nobody will want to pretend to eat as a bonus round."

He crossed his arms, thinking. We both stared into the floor, a long silence between us. When I looked up, he was making a steeple with his fingers and looking at me. "Maybe we'll try something else," he said. "I'll need you to pose for some camera shots."

"You need me to pose for camera shots."

"For the game, yeah. We need to fine-tune

148

our hologram of Jim Thorpe, and there aren't many Native Americans in this town. A year or two ago a Native American preacher and his family rolled into town. They were part of some larger cult, I think. They stayed at a roadside motel out past the interstate and ran church from their room. A few people went, including the mayor and some of the city councilmen and their families. Eventually I think the mayor ran them out of town, though."

"Why is everyone so focused on Jim Thorpe?"

"Thorpe was an Olympic gold medalist," he said, looking at his nails. "A Native American man, a fucking legend, considered to be the greatest athlete in the world, right from our home state of Oklahoma. Think of the decathlon, long jump, high jump, javelin throw. His hologram doesn't do him justice. In fact, it doesn't look like him at all yet, but we're still in development. What better person could there be for others to play against in a simulation? We're building out a full Olympics simulation. Compete against Thorpe in baseball, football, basketball."

He went on, using technical computer jargon I didn't understand. "I'll need to film you, if that's good with you," he said. "I just need to work on something for a few minutes."

I leaned back on the couch and looked up at the ceiling. He worked on his laptop across from me. He typed rapidly, pausing every so often to make little sniffing sounds, which grated on my nerves. All that sniffing. It was as if he was doing it on purpose while he worked. What was the sniffing about, and was it supposed to irritate me? I couldn't handle it.

I wondered where Rae was, and whether she felt sorry that I was gone. I thought, too, about what memory I could share at Ray-Ray's bonfire if I decided to go home. Ray-Ray used to give me piggy-back rides through the house. One time we flew a kite together in the backyard, just the two of us. I was afraid of letting go, thinking the kite would fly away. Ray-Ray held it with me, placing his hands over mine. I remember looking up at the kite and watching how it snapped in the wind, feeling panicked. "It's fine, it's fine," he kept telling me. But I couldn't fly it for very long. Something about it moving around up there so high made me dizzy, almost nauseous.

I wondered if my dad would be able to share a memory at the bonfire this year, too. He was so different from how he used to be. The first time I noticed his Alzheimer's was when I visited home after having been away with Rae for a few months. I couldn't believe how quickly he'd changed. The day I showed up, the first thing he wanted to do was go out to eat at a Mexican restaurant.

"They have good enchiladas," he said. "Good salsa. The hot kind."

I was happy to see him and my mom, but he wasn't well. At the Mexican restaurant he told me he wanted to construct works of art from motorcycle parts that would hang in museums all over the Southwest. In my room that night, I rummaged through old boxes full of photos and drawings. I found a picture I drew in crayon of him when I was little. He had a long beard. He looked like a god. He had giant birdlike wings.

The longer I sat in Jackson's house, with Jackson typing and sniffing across from me, the more anxious I felt. I needed to relax. I remembered I had a joint in my bag, so I stepped out onto the back porch and smoked half of it. I walked around the side of the house and looked at the area outside my window where I had seen the red fowl. There was a cluster of bushes that needed to be trimmed badly. As I drew nearer to that area, I heard something rustle in the bushes, so I turned and hurried back inside.

When I stepped into the front room, Jackson was standing there, waiting for me to join him. I followed him downstairs to the basement, which was too warm and brightly lit. The walls were dark-toned wood. There was a cabinet against a wall, and a stepladder in the center of the room. Some papers and a few cords were scattered on the floor, as well as a basketball, a football, and a video camera on a tripod. Jackson told me to stand by the wall. He tossed me the basketball and then turned on the camera, which beeped and flashed a red light.

"You're filming me for the game?" I asked.

"Right, the game."

"What do you want me to do?"

"Dribble, shoot. Play pretend ball. Raise your arms, pivot, whatever you need to do."

"Shoot? There's no rim in here."

"It doesn't matter," he said. "I just need the movement and your image on video."

I dribbled the basketball while he filmed. I did a head fake and ran in for a layup. I shot free throws. I moved my body across the room, maneuvering right and left, guarding an invisible player. I pivoted with the ball. I blocked out, elbowed, faked left, and drove.

This went on for half an hour. Jackson kept stopping me to get a second take.

Afterward, I watched him edit the clip on his laptop. I coughed, out of shape, weak from smoke in my lungs. Jackson slowed the video down, clipped parts of it. The film was all me, playing in real time, in slow motion and finally in animation. He added music tracks, heavy on drums and screeching electric guitar. I watched myself dribble and shoot, pitiful. There I was, trying too hard. "I'm no Jim Thorpe," I said.

Jackson didn't respond, focused on his editing. When he finished, he powered down the camera. He seemed pleased. "Fuck yes," he said. "It all looks good."

I followed him back upstairs, and he got us beers from the fridge.

"I don't know," I said. "It's all so weird. Today I was downtown, and someone asked me if I was Jim Thorpe. Someone else asked me about Devil's Bridge. It's all so strange."

Jackson felt at his jaw, thinking. "Devil's Bridge," he said. In a way I wanted to grab him and shake him into rational thought. It wasn't paranoia driving me to this line of thinking. It wasn't drugs. I was clearly seeing something very strange happening all around me. I didn't trust it. I was starting not to trust Jackson. He was not the same person he was so long ago.

"Don't be paranoid," he said. "Look, there

153

are nervous citizens here. They see a new neighbor, and they freak out. It's the confined space, the cloudy air, fog all the time. It destroys everyone. There is no happiness anymore. I don't even know where I'll be in the future. The thought of being stuck here doing the same thing forever is miserable."

I coughed a few times, held my chest. "I should just leave," I said.

"You crazy, Chief? You can't."

"Why not?"

"Give it a chance. Before coming here, I tried to develop phone apps with no luck. I applied for a patent that didn't work out. Things take time. Be patient, you haven't even been here a day."

He cracked his knuckles and looked at his phone. "We're just working on software development, that's all," he said. "My colleagues are disappearing. One went missing a month ago. His body was never found. Another added to the missing persons list. Sorry to sound so depressing. This place is a trap. Maybe you can earn your leave, but I don't know how."

"What do you mean, a trap?"

"Where would I even go?" he said. "Some other hellhole? I don't have anyone. I don't have anywhere to go."

"What do you mean, a trap?" I asked

again, but Jackson was too busy texting someone on his phone to answer me. He kept texting and sniffing.

That night, long after Jackson was asleep, I lay in bed watching the ceiling fan whir above me. Outside, the snow-foggy world was in strange form. A rainbow of light reflected on the wall across the room. Something was happening, but I couldn't place what it was. My lungs rattled as I breathed. I coughed and brought up phlegm. Once or twice the walls of the house creaked. The unknown was frightening. I heard soulful groans. I heard the sad howl of a dog's spirit outside my window.

MARIA

September 3

Early in the morning Wyatt and I sat at the table, both of us quiet while he ate breakfast. Ernest had gotten up early, around six thirty, to take a walk. He was now sitting outside on the deck, drinking his coffee and reading the newspaper.

I found myself staring at Wyatt while he ate. His eyes were brown and sleepy, a bit of soot in his lashes. He was dressed for school and ready to go on time, wearing a collared shirt and khaki pants. I had gotten up at seven, not able to fall back asleep, so I made waffles and bacon, which Wyatt devoured. He drank two glasses of orange juice quickly. He was surprisingly calm, adept at making himself appear relaxed and steady.

"I'll drive you to school this week," I told him. "But you'll need to ride the bus home. It will drop you off at the edge of the road,

156

down by the pond. It isn't a far walk."

"Will you be there when I get off?"

"I didn't know if you'd be embarrassed, so I thought you could walk here. My kids used to get embarrassed if Ernest and I waited for them."

"I'm not too embarrassed about things like that," he said. "Hey, does Mr. Echota always drink coffee outside in the morning? It reminds me of my dad."

"Oh, what does your dad do?"

"He's in jail for another DUI. Does Mr. Echota drink much?"

"Not really. Not anymore."

I wanted him to tell me more about his family. I only knew what Bernice had told me, that his mother was out of the state and his father was in jail. But I realized we were running late, so I got my purse and Wyatt put his backpack on. I didn't tell Ernest we were leaving, since we were in such a hurry. It took about fifteen minutes to get to Wyatt's school from our house, but we made it on time, and as he got out of the car, I told him to call if he needed anything. "You don't need to call Bernice," I said. "You can call me directly."

"I don't have your phone number," he said. He stood at the door, looking around, nervous. I borrowed a pencil and wrote down my cell for him on one of his note-books.

"There you go," I said. "Call if you need anything. Don't worry. Just call, okay?"

He shut the door and started to walk away. Watching him, I felt something inside me fall apart.

Onward! I had plenty to do to keep myself busy. I told myself I needed to get the details in order for Ray-Ray's anniversary bonfire, and I also needed to call Edgar. When I arrived home I saw that Ernest was still sitting on the back porch, so I sat at the table and made a grocery list for the bonfire. We needed a dessert. We needed meat and fresh vegetables. Our meal would be plenti-ful, but it would take time to prepare for the family. I started writing out what I wanted to share aloud in remembrance of Ray-Ray. I wrote: *I remember when you were little and liked to pick blackberries with me alongside the road. You always loved picking blackberries with me.* I set the pen down and stared into the table, thinking. But nothing else came.

I got my phone from my purse and called Edgar, praying he would answer. It went to his voice mail. "Edgar," I said. "Please call me when you get a minute, honey. I really need to talk to you."

I sat at the table, thinking about Edgar and wondering whether he was at home or out using someplace, roaming the streets. It terrified me to think he was around dangerous people whose lives hung on the cusp of tragedy. I prayed silently for him to live, to think about us and want to come home. In the kitchen I poured a cup of coffee, then went outside to check on Ernest. He was leaning forward, looking out at the water.

"Everything okay?" I asked.

"I'm looking for signs," he said. "Spirits, messengers, anything." He turned and looked at me, and I could see the seriousness in his face. "That boy," he said.

"Wyatt."

"No, Ray-Ray."

I tried not to let it bother me. I tried to think about what I was going to do about the bonfire, who was going to run things, since Ernest was not mentally able to. I thought he might burn himself trying to start the fire. It was too dangerous in his condition.

"We should be careful talking about spirits in front of him," I said. "Wyatt comes from a broken home. His mother has left, his father is in jail."

"All the talk of music and movies last night."

He remembered their conversation from last night. This was something of a surprise.

"Ray-Ray liked to collect records, too," he said. "Remember he liked jazz? I'm almost positive he alphabetized his records."

Ernest went for another walk while I drove to the grocery store to get food and drinks for the bonfire. I called Sonja while I pushed the grocery cart down the aisle. "Papa's memory is getting better," I told her. "It just happened last night. He remembered his mother and father. He remembered Ray-Ray's records."

"Oh my God," Sonja said.

"I don't know why or what's going on, but something is working."

"Is it the meds?"

"I don't know," I said. "You'll have to come over and see."

When I returned home, Ernest helped me put the groceries up.

"How are you feeling?" I asked him.

"I'm feeling good," he said. He opened the pantry and set cans on a shelf. When we'd finished, he went to the couch to take a nap. I sat in the chair and watched him sleep, then grew sleepy myself and dozed off in the chair.

When I woke, it was time for Wyatt to be heading home. The bus was supposed to drop him off down at the end of the road. I told Ernest we should stand on the porch rather than wait for him at the stop even though he said he wouldn't be embarrassed. We waited for fifteen minutes after the bus was supposed to arrive, but there was no Wyatt. The road was empty.

"Where is he?" I said. "Maybe the bus is late?"

"Call someone," Ernest said.

I went inside to get my phone and called the school. I started thinking the worst: he was attacked, assaulted, got into trouble, had to stay in the principal's office or detention. A nightmare, having to deal with that. But the office receptionist was no help.

"Did anything bad happen at school to him?" I asked. "Did he get picked on?"

While I was on hold, waiting for her to check with the teachers, I told Ernest we needed to start looking for Wyatt. We started down the road, Ernest walking beside me, looking confused. I felt a quick jolt of panic, wondering if Wyatt had run away after getting off the bus. Maybe he didn't like it with us after all. Maybe he wanted to be elsewhere and would send Bernice to pick up his belongings. It didn't seem right, though. In the morning he had been happy. Maybe he'd gotten picked on during the bus ride home. Maybe another kid made fun of him. Had he gotten into a fight? What else could possibly go wrong?

"I knew it," I said aloud, but Ernest didn't respond. "I knew he'd have a bad day."

When the receptionist got back on the line, she said there were no problems with Wyatt at school. The buses had all left. I hung up and thought about calling Bernice, but Ernest and I kept walking quickly. As we got to the end of the road, I saw Wyatt up ahead and felt a strong surge of relief. There he was with a group of other kids from school, huddled in the open field across the road from where the bus dropped them off. There were ten or twelve kids total in the field, in two separate groups, which surprised me until we walked closer.

"They're playing football," Ernest said.

Sure enough, Wyatt had organized an entire game of touch football. We crossed the road to the edge of the field. He was giving directions to both teams, playing referee. We heard him shouting, calling one boy "Captain Oblivious" and another "Blockhead." They were both bigger than Wyatt, but taking his orders like lost children. He removed his cap and threw it to the ground, stomping on it in mock frustration. Then he laughed, telling Captain Oblivious and Blockhead to run back to their respective teams.

"They're having fun," Ernest said. "He's with friends."

The game continued, full tackle without pads, both teams seemingly coached by Wyatt, who ran back and forth along the sidelines to give instructions in huddles or demonstrate head fakes and leg tackles while the boys kneeled and watched. Eventually the game came to an end, and they gathered around him. He showed them speed and agility drills, full circles and half circles, and then ran a receiving route while the quarterback threw a long, perfect spiral to him. He caught it with ease, jogging into the makeshift end zone. The rest of the boys chased after him, cheering.

There were high fives and fist bumps before the players separated. "Catch you guys later," Wyatt told them, walking toward us with his backpack.

"We were worried you weren't coming back," I told him.

"What?" he said. "We were playing football. I've known those guys since sixth grade."

We headed back down the road toward the house. Out of nowhere, Ernest started laughing, patting Wyatt on the shoulder in a proud, fatherly way.

After dinner Wyatt took a shower, got cleaned up, and spent some time in Ray-Ray's room, doing homework. When I knocked on the door to check on him, I found him typing an essay on Ernest's old typewriter, which we kept in the room. It hadn't been used in many years, maybe not since Ray-Ray used it. Wyatt typed with two fingers slowly, and didn't look up when I entered.

"We have a computer in the living room," I told him. "You don't want to use this old thing, do you? It's kind of junky."

"I don't mind," he said, staring down at the keys as he typed.

I watched him a moment. "Well, I can leave you alone if you want. Or maybe you need help?"

He stopped, rolled the paper out, and read it silently. With a pencil he wrote something on it, then inserted it into the typewriter and began typing again.

So I left him alone. Ernest was standing outside the door, waiting for me.

"Well?" he said. "What did he say?"

164

"About what?"

"Is he giving any clues about the Spirit World? I think the Great Spirit may have sent Ray-Ray back to us in another form."

I saw the seriousness in his face and was confounded. We could hear Wyatt typing on the typewriter on the other side of the door. I motioned Ernest to follow me into the front room and told him in a quiet voice that Wyatt was doing homework and didn't want to be bothered. "Let's let him settle in," I said. "Don't be disappointed if he doesn't seem like Ray-Ray."

"He's a spitting image."

"Let's let him work."

We sat in front of the TV for a while, watching a detective show. I didn't care for police dramas, but Ernest loved watching them on TV. Sometimes I watched, but most of the time I did the crossword or crocheted.

"Do you remember our conversation last night?" I asked Ernest as the TV cops drew their guns and chased a suspect down an alley.

"Of course," he said. "My head doesn't feel foggy. I'm feeling good."

"Any other memories come to you?"

He thought a moment. "My moccasins," he said.

"Yes, you mentioned that last night."

"I mean the ones I wore as a kid. I remember those moccasins. My mother made them from buckskin. I remember the beadwork. The red beads."

"A new memory," I told him. "This is a good sign. This is what we've been hoping for. I think you're feeling better."

On TV, the suspect fell hard to the ground, and the cops were on him, restraining him with handcuffs.

"The red beads," Ernest said again, trailing off.

Wyatt came into the room with a few notebooks. He sat down next to me and began flipping through them, pausing to show me his writings — all his poems, stories, and drawings. "I colored this when I was ten," he said, pointing to a drawing of a big red house surrounded by trees. Most of his drawings were of houses, I realized. What did all the houses mean? I assumed he had been deprived of attention, moving from home to home, constantly thinking about what it means to live somewhere.

"I have a whole series of haiku poems in here," he said. "All based on different rooms I stay in whenever I'm in a building or school or house. One of the reasons I'm glad to be here is so that I can write a poem

166

about the rooms in this house."

"I hope it's a nice poem," I said. "I like to write down my thoughts, too. It always makes me feel better."

"Trippy," he said, smiling.

"Trippy?"

"I'm full-body digging talking to you."

I found his speech and mannerisms delightful. So animated and exaggerated, such a funny little guy. He pulled out an essay for school. He needed me to look over it for errors, he said; would I mind?

"Of course I'll look over it," I said.

"What's she checking for, spelling?" Ernest asked.

"I'm looking more for development and ideas, not grammar or spelling," he said.

I put on my reading glasses and moved in closer to the table lamp so I could read easier:

ESSAY FOR ENGLISH CLASS
(IN PROGRESS)

Wyatt Eli Chair

This dazzling "prose fragment" poem from our illustrious textbook is about discernment. The poem tells about the reincarnation of a Cherokee boy (the poem is taken

167

from the author's first book, *The Book of Levitation and a Thousand Deaths*). The "prose fragment" is titled "The Owl and the Eagle" and is his masterpiece. My humble opinion, dearest and vitiated Reader, is that *The Book of Levitation* shows themes of spirituality. (At Sequoyah School some years back, I read and reviewed his other books of prose poems for the school paper. One book I read, *Faces Reflected in a Spoon,* is about spirits and reincarnation.) The eagle in the mirror is a reincarnation. How is this possible? Fondled Reader, allow me to illustrate: with a flickering of strange striated light, the figure floats in a circle before it disappears. Certainly, there is a yellow light, then blue light. Out of nowhere, the appearance of the exiguous Cherokee words: "Tawodi." Its image remains in the mirror. What if the author is a Spirit or a messenger? Historically, Authochthonous Reader, Eagles are considered messengers in Cherokee mythology. Look for spirits here on Earth . . .

"Well," I said, handing the essay to him. "Well. Hmm."

"It needs work," he said. "I can handle it, please correct what you see is wrong. I want it to be good."

"I guess I haven't read a book report in a long time. Who is the boy?"

"The boy in the poem appears in different forms, like as a hawk or an owl. Or an old man or even another boy."

"In the poem?"

"The author is Cherokee, from here in town, my teacher told us."

"I don't know him. Ernest, do you know this author?"

Ernest came over and stood next to Wyatt, looking at the essay in his hands. "Did you say tawodi?" he asked.

"Tawodi means 'hawk' in Cherokee," Wyatt said. "What did you think of me ending it with the ellipses?"

"The what?"

"The three dots at the end."

Ernest felt at his jaw.

"Take a pencil to it," Wyatt told me. "Can you fix it and make it good?"

"It looks good to me," I told him.

Wyatt asked Ernest if they could play chess, so they went into the dining room to play while I stayed looking at Wyatt's essay. I read slowly with a pen, circling exclamation points and parentheses, but I didn't know what to do with them. I crossed out a few sentences. I read it over and over, but it was hard to concentrate because I heard Ernest laughing from the other room, so I got up and walked into the dining room, where I found them playing chess.

I didn't say anything, but I knew Ernest would struggle to remember the rules. Chess had never been an easy game for any of us except for Ray-Ray. He was the only one who really loved it.

"I did what I could with your essay," I told Wyatt and handed it to him. He looked at it, nodded.

"Thank you," he said. "Ernest forgot how to play, so I'm helping him remember. We're talking about spirits, too."

Ernest was staring at Wyatt. "Tell me more about the spirits," he said. "Tell me everything you saw in the Spirit World."

"The Spirit World?" I said.

"Yes," Ernest said, still looking at Wyatt. "Tell me, son. What did you see?"

"Maybe he wants a snack," I said, trying to change the subject. "Wyatt? Are you hungry? Ice cream?"

"The Spirit World," Wyatt said, humoring Ernest, leaning forward and resting his elbows on the table. "Ah, what a place! I met a beautiful woman by a stream. Her name was Clara."

"Did she have raven-black hair?" Ernest asked.

"Yes sir, she had raven-black hair. Her hair was long. She was really pretty."

"What else?"

"She was looking for her husband. She was searching everywhere but couldn't find him there."

This interaction caught me off guard. I was grateful Wyatt was such a sensitive boy, willing to play along with Ernest's strange topics of conversation.

"What else?" Ernest asked.

"I met owls and eagles and other beautiful spirits on my walks," Wyatt said. "I met the Yunwi Tsunsdi, the little spirits. I met Dragging Canoe, too, who told me . . . get this, Pops: 'You will be a visionary with prophetic gifts'!"

SONJA

September 3

I walked down to Barnacle Bill's Marina, which sat on the water a little ways down from my house and where I sometimes went to drink coffee and eat lunch and read. The place was busy during the summer months, when vacationers went there to drink and listen to live bands. This afternoon it was nearly empty, probably because it was fall and the weather was getting cooler out, which meant fewer people were staying at their lake houses. Barnacle Bill's closed for the winter in November, but I liked to go as much as possible in the fall, when it was cool and less crowded.

When I arrived, high water had flooded the deck, where I liked to sit, but the marina was still open. The sun was out, and the sky had cleared. The air was thick with humidity and the movement of birds and insects, pushed by a light breeze that was cool enough to feel welcoming after a storm. A few geese were walking away from the kids playing near the edge of the water, and a dad kept telling his son not to step into the mud. I had my copy of Colette, ready to eat a bowl of soup and drink coffee and read in quiet.

From my small table near the window, I sipped my coffee and watched some kids near the edge of the water. There were five of them, all boys, and one of them was significantly smaller than the others. One boy threw a stick, and the others chased the geese into the water. Then they huddled together, talking. I wondered if they were planning something. I was too far away to see, so I wasn't sure what they were playing, or whether it was a game at all. A moment later two of the boys picked up the smallest boy and carried him toward the water, while he struggled to break free. They dropped him and ran back to the other two boys, hurrying away from the marina. The small boy stood up and ran down the road after them, until I couldn't see any of them anymore.

My phone vibrated then, and I saw that my mom was calling.

"Are you at home?" she asked.

"I'm down at Barnacle Bill's for coffee.

Do you want to come meet me?"

"I can't right now. I wanted to tell you about your dad. Stop by when you can. It's his memory."

"Oh my God," I said.

"No, don't be worried. He's getting better. He's recalling memories better than he has in a long time. We're a little stunned by it."

"His memory is better?"

"Yes, it's amazing, Sonja. Stop by when you get a minute, okay?"

"I will."

"Let's pray it's not temporary. Let's pray he's recovered in some way."

The conversation pleased me. I had been avoiding thinking about Papa's health for months, because every time I did I felt overwhelmed with worry. This improvement meant something supreme was occurring. I told myself that if Papa got better, I could focus on being happy. I thought about the boys who had been playing by the water and their disregard for the feelings of the smallest boy. As I was leaving Vin's house earlier that morning, Vin had said he'd *needed* me to come back over later in the day rather than asking me whether I wanted to. He was very demanding. And when I replied, "Well, if so, I'll *need* you to try to be a better lover," he didn't laugh, pretending it had hurt his feelings, so I told him I was joking instead of apologizing. This was the manner of men, it seemed to me, so often unaware of their own aggression. My whole life, the men I had been involved with would try to make me feel guilty. When I was young and in school, I used to stare out the window, envying the trees. This became a regular pattern of thought for me, at least for a while, that I stared at a tree outside and envied its anonymity, its beauty and silence. One could appreciate a tree for its pure beauty and expect nothing more. A tree could stand over a hundred years and remain authentic.

After our first night together, I found myself less attracted to Vin. This was not uncommon, I suppose. We had spent all morning in his bedroom, naked and rolling our tongues over each other, and I whispered his name and stared at him intensely, trying to strengthen his desire for me. I am a passionate lover, I have been told on several occasions, but I am also able to remove myself from physical sexual acts — and in the middle of having sex with Vin I pretended I was having sex with a married man, which was more exciting than having sex with Vin. I had a fantasy that we were cheating, that it was riskier than it actually was.

At Barnacle Bill's, I read Colette and sipped coffee for over an hour before I left, heading back up the slope toward my house. I stopped at the edge of the lake and looked out over the gray, wind-rippled water, thinking about how I could never feel at home anyplace else. From an early age I knew that I would likely never marry, so different from my friends at school, who all wanted to move away and marry someone and have a family. I never dismissed the idea, but I didn't entertain it either, and while I realized that a desire to live alone was strange, I could never understand why none of my friends felt the same way. The silence of the lake and the solitude was what I enjoyed most. The wind strengthened and felt cool for a moment, like a perfect fall day. I walked back home.

I considered walking down to my parents' house, but my instinct was that I needed to see Vin. Even though I honestly felt less attracted to him, I still wanted him to want me. Maybe it was a strange obsession, but I didn't care. I rode my bicycle in to the YMCA down on Main Street, where I knew Vin and Luka often went in the afternoons.

There weren't many cars in the YMCA lot, and I pulled my bicycle up to the front. I waited outside for a few minutes, thinking about what I would say if they saw me. I would tell him I was checking out prices for a membership. I was considering joining. By mere coincidence, that's what I'd say to Vin.

For a moment I watched some kids dance in the spray of a fire hydrant down the street. I headed inside, where I saw three guys at the front desk. They were young, probably college age, and only one looked like he lifted weights. The other two were thin and gangly. They looked more like the type of kids who spent summers home from college sleeping until noon and playing video games all day. I asked them where the youth program was meeting, and one of them told me they were upstairs in the game room and should be down any minute. I thanked him and walked down the hall to the vending machines and tables, where I sat and watched a group of elderly women do water aerobics in the indoor pool. I played on my phone a while, until I heard a group of kids and saw them coming down the stairs. They were out of control, hurrying and laughing. I'd walked back down the hall about halfway when I saw Luka running out the door. From the front desk I could see him outside, walking away with Vin. I decided not to follow them and stood still as they got into the car. One of the gangly guys at the desk kept asking me if I needed help, but I didn't say anything. I waited until Vin drove off before I went out the doors and back to my bicycle.

That evening Vin called as I got out of the shower. I hurried to my bed to answer my phone.

"Do you want to go out to dinner?" he asked.

"I'd rather just fuck you somewhere," I said.

"Whoa," he said. "Hell yeah. I got a sitter for Luka, so let's do it. But I need to eat first. I'm fucking starving over here."

"Me too," I said.

About an hour later he picked me up at my house but waited in the car for me to come out. He wanted to go somewhere nice but couldn't decide. I suggested we drive to Tulsa and go to the restaurant in the Cherokee Casino because I knew the manager there, and we could sneak into the buffet by entering through the kitchen. Vin said the idea of a buffet sounded good, but I wondered whether he just liked the fact that dinner would be free.

The restaurant was crowded, so it wasn't hard for my friend Lucille to let us in. Lucille never let me pay even when I offered. Leave it for the tip, she would tell me, which I told Vin about at our table. Lucille was a friend I'd been at school with years ago, whose mother held a high position in the tribal council. The casino was a gold mine for the tribe when it opened, and it only got better as it increased in size and development, soon adding a hotel and pool next door and bringing in concerts and boxing matches and other entertainment. I hadn't seen Lucille for a while, so we talked for a few minutes about her family, and I introduced her to Vin.

As we ate, we settled into a silence that, strangely, felt awkward despite the night we'd spent together. The silence irritated me, I realized as we ate, and I watched him devour his food without saying much. I was unsure what he was thinking about us, or if he was thinking about us at all. I asked him if he ever took Luka out to the casino's pizza buffet, where kids eat free on Fridays, and he said it was one of Luka's favorite restaurants, except that the noise of the arcade games and music was too much stimulation for him. It was too much stimulation for all of us, I said.

"I saw my dad today at his house," he told me.

"He's still sick, huh?"

"He's lost a lot of weight. The in-home nurse was helping him. It's horrible to see."

"You have a really cute kid," I told him, changing the subject. "Luka's a real doll. You spend a lot of time with him? I could watch him sometime if you need someone."

"I guess," he said, eating.

"He's a great kid. He seems interested in lots of things. Artistic, huh? Imaginative?"

"I guess," he said. "I'd probably coach Little League sports if the opportunity ever arose, but that's probably not happening with Luka."

Clearly Luka was not at all what Vin had hoped he would be. Because of his autism, he was more interested in sitting outside looking through binoculars at squirrels and birds than throwing a baseball. But I liked Luka. In a way, he felt like he could be a son to me, or a little brother. I was so wounded after Ray-Ray died that I was never a very good big sister to Edgar. I wanted to know more about Luka — what his favorite color was, what he liked to eat and drink. I wanted to know his teacher's name, his friends' names, his favorite subject in school, his hobbies. He was a wonderful boy, I could tell, and I knew he liked to ride his scooter in his driveway, play with a remote-control car, and also pretend to be a bird, which was odd for a boy his age. I could teach him Cherokee words — *tsisqua* ("bird"), *osiyo* ("hello"), *Agiyosi, inalisday vhvga* ("I'm hungry, let's eat") — and help him do his homework, teach him about girls and school and life. I'd helped Edgar with his homework when we were young because Mom and Papa worked so much. We didn't have much time for ourselves back then. I could tell Luka I knew what it meant to struggle for time with loved ones. I could tell him I'd always wanted a son.

"I guess I'm wondering if the middle school years will be too hard socially," Vin said. "He already has to deal with other kids playing too rough with him, or making fun of him. I want him to like sports or guitar or drums or something like that. But he wants to be in the goddamn chess club."

Luka was in a local chess club that met once a week at the community center downtown, Vin said, and one of the kids there had mocked Luka's behavior. When I asked what this behavior was, he told me that Luka sometimes rocked back and forth during the game, a way to channel his thinking

181

and anxiety, which was not unusual. But it was eccentric behavior for boys not familiar with autism. Vin had witnessed the boy making fun of Luka's rocking and talked to his mother about it.

"What did she say?" I asked.

He took a bite of his corn on the cob and told me he didn't want to be around her in that moment, so he stormed out before she had a chance to respond. "She needs to learn to control her goddamn kid and learn some parenting skills," he said. "Her kid needs to learn how to show some respect."

At this, I could tell he was getting worked up, bothered by the memory. "Does Luka like any other board games besides chess?"

"He'll play anything as long as it makes everyone happy." He took a drink of his beer. "He doesn't like conflict. Anything too competitive is hard. He isn't aggressive enough, and I don't want him to grow up weak."

"Don't be such an asshole," I told him.

"I don't want him to be bullied. I wish he liked sports."

"You want him to be aggressive?"

"I don't want him to be a pushover."

"He's so adorable," I told him. "He reminds me of my brother when he was alive. He looks like him, even."

182

I wanted to tell Vin about Ray-Ray then, but it wasn't the right place. I wasn't ready yet for that conversation. Still, I grew irritated. "You don't want to hear about my life," I said.

"I want to gamble for a while," he said, not paying attention to me. "We saved money from a free dinner, right? Let's go play while we're here."

I didn't say anything. I followed him to the slot machines and sat down at a Triple Seven machine and played. I lost twenty dollars quickly, more than I cared to lose. I watched Vin play for a while. At one point he looked around for the cocktail waitress and said he wanted a beer. He handed me a twenty and asked if I'd go to the bar and get him one and buy myself a drink as well. It was this kind of behavior that he was completely clueless about, making assumptions that any woman would immediately do as he told; he was buying my drink, after all, so I'd fetch him a goddamn beer? Or maybe I was wrong, maybe he knew exactly what he was doing. Maybe he had gotten away with it for too long. The quick surge of anger I felt toward him surprised me.

"Oh sure, let me just run off and fetch you a beer," I said. "Okay?"

He kept slapping the button on the machine, his stupid mouth open. He glanced at me. "Don't be like that," he said.

"Like what?"

"I'm doing pretty good here. Up forty bucks." He kept slapping the button and staring into the machine.

On the way out, after Vin had lost over a hundred dollars and was shaking his head in disbelief that he had allowed himself to drain his cash, I suggested we stop somewhere for a drink. "We should go back to my place while Luka's still with the sitter," he said, and put his hand on the small of my back as we crossed the parking lot.

"With the sitter there?" I said.

"She won't mind," he said. "It's cool, trust me. She'll keep him downstairs. She's cool."

"I can't," I said. "Not tonight, okay? I should check on my parents. My dad's Alzheimer's can be difficult for my mom."

"Right," he said, but I knew he was pissed off.

He drove me to my house without saying anything. His silence made me uncomfortable. When he pulled into my driveway, I leaned over and put my hand on his leg and rubbed it lightly. I kissed him, running my tongue over his lip, touching his cheek with my hand. He pulled back and gave me a distant look, as if he were unsure what to make of this.

"I'll talk to you later?" I said.

"Yeah, talk to you later."

When I got out of the car, he sped away.

I didn't want to think about Vin for the rest of the night. I felt wired and anxious, mainly because I was so annoyed by his behavior. I reminded myself that he wasn't really a very nice person and probably ignored his son too much. I tried not to think about him for a while, but a strong fear came over me. I have always had anxiety, but this was stronger. I worried he would come back to my house and become violent. He would get drunk and return to confront me. I felt a strong spiritual connection to this warning, but I brushed it off and decided to distract myself with chores.

I worked in my backyard in the darkness, raking leaves. I watered the grass, watching the sprinkler spray thin arcs of water around the lawn, and as I watched I saw a hawk swoop down and land across the yard at the base of a tree. The hawk spread its wings and took a few steps. It noticed me, or so it seemed, and it watched me. It wasn't even midnight, but I still felt troubled.

I decided to clean the basement, where I never spent time. I turned on the light and carefully walked down the stairs. The room was drafty, and mostly empty. My old bed from when I was younger was there, along with piles of old possessions I hadn't seen in years. I started stacking boxes near a wall — all the framed pictures, old newspaper clippings, toys. There were boxes of Christmas decorations, tinsel and ornaments, colored bulbs, and old-fashioned magazines. There was a shelf holding some books, two empty cans of paint, and some old paintbrushes. There was a half-eaten cube of mouse poison and an old mousetrap from when I had mice last winter. I swept and dusted until the entire basement was neat and tidy, and afterward I removed all my clothes and got into bed with my Colette book and was quite happy.

TSALA

For most of my life I was not an angry man. I never expected to feel such fury, but the earth sent us warnings: there was a drought. The summer solstice had burned up the soil, and one could taste dust in the air. The wind rose up and howled. Beloved, it was crucial we paid attention to these warnings. We knew the time was near.

Our prophets, too, had warned of the soldiers coming to remove us from our land. This was a terrifying time. We were frightened but ready to defend our home. Our people would refuse to leave, even though we had been tricked by the government with their fraudulent treaty. We did not trust them. It was a time, too, for hope. Some of the missionaries introduced us to the Christianity religion and read from the book of Matthew as it had been translated by one of the men from New Echota. We discussed peace and sacrifice. We also talked about the treaty and our humility. During this time, I saw visions of the dying before I understood what it means to die.

Visions of the Coming Soldiers

The night before the soldiers arrived, I looked up to the yonder sky, where I saw visions of the dying. I saw people walking alongside oxcarts, carrying their children and their food while soldiers sat in wagons with their guns. I saw the fighting of warriors and soldiers across the land as my people hid in the bloodstained grass. I saw people dying of starvation and disease. I saw the slaughter of the fattest cattle and the passing of the war pipe while our people mourned for the dead. I saw horses dying and snakes lying in the red dust at night. I saw a deaf boy running through a field while soldiers called for him to stop; when he didn't, they shot him dead. I saw the burning of ranches and stage stations, and afterward the feasting and dancing. I saw a wind sweeping down into a dead body and giving birth to an eagle, who flew away into a red dawn. I saw bursts of fire in the sky and bodies trailing away like smoke. I saw deer and smaller animals running toward the mountains.

Later in the night I woke to the drumming of spirits, or so I thought. I walked outside to look to the trees. The drumming stopped, but I saw nothing. I looked to the sky: there I saw the great blacksnake, the screech owl, the horned owl, and a group of people walking, all moving toward a giant tree in the sky. The tree was on fire, and burning so fiercely I could feel the stinging in my eyes as I watched. Then smoke began to cover the people, and the ashes fell from the sky like falling stars. I had to cover my eyes and go back inside, where I lay awake until dawn. My wife said this was a strong vision of what was coming our way. All the pain and suffering. All the walking, all the deaths.

I, too, dreamed of soldiers arriving in Kusawatiyi, and I knew then that we needed to go to the mountains, where they wouldn't find us.

The Yunwi Tsunsdi
The Yunwi Tsunsdi were believed to be Little People living in the mountains, which worried many of us. You could hear drumming coming from the caves there. Some believed it came from these spirits, as they were quite fond of music and dancing. They had lived there even when our ancestors were alive. In the time of the

smallpox epidemic, a hunter in the middle of a snowy winter afternoon found small footprints leading to the mountains, which he believed were the footprints of children. Concerned that these children were freezing to death, he followed the footprints to a cave. A few days passed. People began searching for him, thinking he had been eaten by a bear, but when he returned a few weeks later, he told them that he had become ill with smallpox, and that the Yunwi Tsunsdi people had taken care of him until he was feeling well enough to leave.

They were no taller than his waist, he said. They comforted him. Their hands and eyes were fire. They were nocturnal, night travelers like owls, and did not wish to be seen. Their teeth were crooked, their eyes bulging. Our people say that if you hear music and drumming coming from the mountains at night, it is likely the Yunwi Tsunsdi. No one knows why they are so secretive, but you can hear them in the mountains. We would soon come to know the mountains very well. The mountains were as mysterious as the Yunwi Tsunsdi.

But here is an important story of the Little People: in the beginning, people started to believe that the sun was growing angry as it grew hotter outside, and they feared the world would burn during a drought. The land went one hundred days with no rain. The grass and crops were dying, the rivers were drying up; even people were dying during the hottest days. What do we do? people thought, and decided they would go to the Little People in the mountains and seek counsel. When they arrived, the Little People told them that the sun was jealous of the moon because people loved to look at the moon, and they squinted at the sun. The sun did not understand its power over the earth, only that it provided light, which was a good thing. It could not understand why people were so afraid to look at it, shielding their eyes and spending time in shady areas.

For days a dog howled from the mountain. It was believed that the dog was howling as a signal that rainfall was coming. The dog's owner could not get the dog to stop howling. He tried feeding the dog, comforting it, but the dog kept howling and howling, pacing back and forth, pacing and howling. The Little People made medicine that changed two men into hawks. Both men flew high into the sky, directly toward the sun, but they became blind and burned and fell to their deaths.

Soon afterward, the Little People said that the sun felt so sad that it went into hiding, and a great rainfall came, and people rejoiced. The sun loved the earth too much to burn it up.

It rained for six days and brought a great flood. Rivers overflowed and destroyed houses, and some people died. The man and his dog disappeared after the flood. Their bodies were never found. It is said that late in the night one can still hear the sad howl of the dog's spirit.

Beloved: as we packed our clothes and supplies to prepare for the journey, we could hear a sad howl coming from the mountains.

The night before the soldiers arrived, while you were sleeping, I reached down and touched your hair, your back, your forehead. You stirred in your sleep. Across the room, your mother was stripping corn. Your beautiful mother, her hair hanging down her body, facing away from me. I moved silently so I could see her face. Back then we grew corn and squash, sunflowers and pumpkins, and we dressed deerskins together. We walked at night together to be alone. Then I began to silently weep. I lay down beside you and wept, for you, for your mother, and for our people, who would soon have to hide in the mountains. I wept for the people who would be beaten. I wept for the people in wagons and the ones who would walk west. I wept for all who would soon be suffering and dying.

My son, that night when the soldiers arrived, you dreamed of their arrival. You woke crying. Your mother consoled you until you were able to describe what you saw in your dream: the people dying all around us, in wagons and in fields and snow. You saw the frostbite on children's hands. You saw people falling to the ground. I told my people that we would need to protect the land from the threat of the coming winter. I had a very unsettled feeling about it all. While you fell back asleep, I lay awake, worried that your prophecy was worse than you dreamed. I was correct. The soldiers arrived a few hours later.

EDGAR

September 4

In Jackson's rotting house, I watched him whittle a devil's flute from a piece of wood. He carved out the holes so that when he played it, I heard the songs of past centuries I'd never heard before. He explained that a friend of his had taught the songs to him while they were working on the projections of Indians for the games he was developing.

"I don't understand the attraction to these games," I said.

"They're games, nothing more. People like to play sports games." He held the knife out and glared at the blade. "The possibilities are endless with gaming."

He whittled and made sniffing sounds.

"I'm going downtown," I said.

"Where to?"

"Rusty Spoon Records, to look through music. There's a guy I like named Venery who works there."

"Oh, Lyle knows him. He's bought weed from him. Trying to get him to sell some ammunition, too. Apparently the guy's got all kinds of ammo for hunting. Ask him about it and let me know."

I left and walked downtown. On the way I passed trees with low-hanging branches, old cars with busted-out windshields. I walked along the sidewalk at a steady pace. A few kids were riding skateboards up ahead. One of them saw me and pointed. I watched them as I walked. The others got off their skateboards and congregated. They huddled together and talked for a minute, and then they all looked at me. I watched them until they turned and ran off.

When I got to Rusty Spoon Records, Venery was thumbing through a stack of records. He looked up at me, his long silver hair hanging down in his face. He could've passed for someone living deep in the woods of the Oklahoma northeast, somewhere outside Quah, and the longer I was in the store, the more I wondered whether he in fact had lived there.

"Jim Thorpe," he said, laughing.

"Jerry Garcia?"

He wheezed laughter, causing him to cough a couple of times. "I met him many years ago," he told me. "I was at a party in

San Francisco in the seventies, back when I toured with a psychedelic band called Venery and the Voyeurs. We smoked hash, and he gave me an earring I wore for twenty years."

I looked at him. He wasn't wearing an earring.

"Lawd knows my ear got infected, and it was never the same," he said. He told me his band used to play in the Paseo district in Oklahoma City and then down in Deep Ellum and at terminals at the Dallas/Fort Worth airport. He drove west to California to stay with a cousin outside of Venice Beach. He was there about six months before he ran out of money and had to move back. "We could never get anything to work out," he said. "My buddy and I did this thing in LA where we pretended like we didn't know each other. We would go into bars and clubs. He would sit at the bar, and later I would come in and sit alone at a table. At some point he would pretend he recognized me and start telling people around him that I was the brother of Jerry Garcia. We could eat peyote or score free weed or booze. I met some real weirdos out there. One told me there were narwhals hiding behind dumpsters in Paseo. I existed in the fantasy of pretending I was someone else."

"That seems to be what's happening around here."

"You may be right. Are you flummoxed?"

"I can't figure anything out."

"You look anxious," he said. "I could tell the moment you walked in here. Everyone can tell, so choose carefully where you walk. Some roads lead to pain, others to your past. Anyone come up to you and ask you a bunch of random questions or make equivocal statements on purpose? Folks with twitchy mouths or protuberant eyes? Don't dicker. Best thing for you to do, Chief, is just keep walking. Don't talk to anyone unless you know them."

"Why me?" I asked.

"There aren't many Indians around here, JT."

"It's fucked," I said. "Have you heard anything about this Jim Thorpe game?"

"Games? All I do is run the store and read hagiographies upstairs until I levitate. I don't know much anymore. I don't trust no one."

Venery's cell phone was ringing. He went over to the register and answered it. I wanted to browse through records and focus on something I enjoyed, since music always

197

put me at peace. The more I thumbed through records, though, the more I realized I couldn't find the motivation to continue browsing. I looked over at Venery. I couldn't hear what he was saying, but he kept glancing over at me, so I waved goodbye and left.

I found myself thinking about fantasy, about what Venery had said about pretending to be other people. Part of why I liked leaving Oklahoma was that I could go places nobody knew me. I could walk around with Rae and be a new face. I never planned to stay in one place for very long.

Back at the rotting house, Jackson was preoccupied with an approaching storm. He sat on the edge of the couch, watching a meteorologist on TV. "I'm really high right now," he said. "This is all freaking me out."

"You smoked?"

"Yeah, while you were out. I was feeling anxious or something. Don't look at me."

On TV, the meteorologist looked pale and ghostly and exhausted. The radar showed red and yellow flashes of blocks ticking slowly eastward, indicating a severe thunderstorm. "This is the one they've been talking about for the past week," he said, staring at the screen.

"Maybe tornado season is over," I said.

"There is no tornado season in this goddamn hell," he said. "It's all the time. Tornadoes form even in the winter. Last year an F-four blew across the southern part of the land, ripping the roofs off houses and knocking down power lines. There are no seasons, haven't you noticed?"

"The weather seemed fine just now."

"Storms can stir up quickly. They've been talking about a flood for the past fifteen minutes. Here it is, heading right toward us. See those streaks of red? The flashing colors?"

We both stared at the TV screen as the meteorologist tapped his earpiece and we heard the static of a storm chaser's voice saying something about winds blowing up to sixty miles per hour. The meteorologist kept tapping his earpiece.

"And the rain could flood us again," Jackson said. "This house was underwater once. This house has mold. They all do. I hate floods. My lungs are probably black. A big rain would really put a damper on our game production." He glanced at me. "Isn't there a rain dance or something you could do to make it stop?"

I went into my room without answering him. I stayed in there for a while, looking out the window at the graying sky. Rae and I were once trapped in her apartment in

199

Oklahoma during a terrible thunderstorm. Hail the size of softballs battered cars in the parking lot, shattering windshields and damaging the roofs of houses. Amazingly, there was no tornado then. The electricity was out, and Rae and I drank vodka with cranberry juice and lit candles and placed them all around the room the rest of the night. It was a miracle we didn't burn the place down.

I thought of that night, the way the sky had turned the same yellow as the sky here. And soon the sky turned gray again, and it was raining hard outside. The wind came up, blowing the trees outside. I heard Jackson talking on the phone to someone about the wind speeds. The television was blasting loudly. The only way to pass the time during these storms was to focus on something else.

I was lying on the bed, staring at the ceiling, when Jackson came in and said the storm had shifted. "It turned north, so we're in the clear. I was a little scared, Chief. You never know."

"You never know," I said.

"Storms do something to me. I can't explain it."

"Frighten you?"

"But the fear does something else, excites

me, I guess. I don't know how to explain it."

"You're high."

He laughed a little, then sat on the edge of the bed near my waist, and we were both quiet. I had my hands behind my head, staring up at the ceiling. Jackson pulled off his T-shirt. I didn't think anything about it. He turned to me and waited for me to look at him. When I did, he put his hand on my leg. I hadn't seen him without a shirt on. His skin was pale, his body gangly and thin, not much different than mine. I wondered if he was waiting for me to say something. Then he leaned in to me, running his hand from my upper thigh toward my crotch. I stopped him with my hand and sat up.

"Sorry," he said, pulling his hand back and looking away, embarrassed. I was a little shaken by what he was doing, not having understood.

"Oh man, I'm sorry," he said again. "I thought maybe you wanted to."

I shook my head.

He got up and left the room, closing the door behind him. I stayed in bed for a few minutes, wondering why, how I had given him the wrong impression or said something to lead him on.

Soon I got up and stepped into the front

room. Jackson wasn't there, but the door to the basement was open, so I went downstairs. It felt too warm and smelled of cigarette smoke. Jackson was sitting at a desk down there, working on his laptop. There were some military and sports magazines scattered on the floor. Other than a cabinet against the dark-wood-paneled wall, the walls were bare except for two screens: one against a wall and the other on the floor. Jackson looked up at me, then back at his laptop. Our shadows spread across the floor from the light.

"I don't know what to say," he said, typing without looking at me.

"What?"

"It was uncomfortable, I get it."

"Yeah, I didn't mean to give you the wrong impression."

"I shouldn't have done that, Edgar. I'm embarrassed."

"It's not a big deal, though."

He stopped typing and looked at me. I could see he felt bad about trying to manipulate me. "Seriously, I'm embarrassed."

"It's all cool," I said. "Really, no big deal."

He nodded. "Can I at least film you for the game, since you're down here?"

"That's fine."

"For the game," he said. He got up and

went over to a cabinet, took out a plastic assault rifle, and handed it to me.

"It's not real," he said. "Just pretend like you're firing it at the camera. I'll get some shots with the camera."

I looked at the assault rifle. He had me stand against the paneled wall and point it at the camera while he recorded me. I saw the red blinking light on his camera. He had me stand in various poses, holding the rifle in one hand or at times with both hands. Then he handed me a fake hatchet, an old Halloween prop, and told me to pretend I was attacking the camera. I lunged forward with it. Jackson got down on one knee, working the camera. The red light kept blinking.

Finally we stopped, and he told me he was happy with the way I looked. "It'll be great for the game," he said.

"I guess I don't see how this is all part of the game," I said. "I mean, what it has to do with playing sports."

"It's tricky," he said. "I'm working on bonus features, those kinds of things. It'll be great, Chief."

"I'm stepping outside for a smoke," I said.

"I'll be down here working."

I went upstairs and stepped out into the backyard and smoked a cigarette. I tried to think about how I felt about Jackson. It was confusing. While I smoked, I noticed a creek nearby, with muddy water that rippled and bubbled. I walked to it and found myself staring at something in the water. It resembled a thin snake but was moving very slowly. The water, though shallow, was so dirty that I couldn't see how long the thing stretched, but it looked too long for a snake. I saw no head, only a silvery body moving underneath the water. I remembered my dad telling me a haunting Cherokee myth wherein a boy reached down to a snake and was pulled underwater. I had a snake phobia. I didn't like rivers or lakes, even though I grew up close to them.

A man sitting on the porch next door called me over. "Hey, who are you?" he called out, and then stood up and walked over to me. When he got closer, I could see he was old, and his face was sagging and covered in blemishes. "Who are you?" he asked again.

"Edgar."

"Have I seen you before?"

I shrugged. "I don't know. I'm staying with Jackson Andrews."

"The game maker?" He had a low, gravelly voice and sounded out of breath when he spoke. "You take a bunch of pills?"

"What?"

"Pills," he said. "You take a bunch of them? Like all the people walking around, stoned on death. How we got here."

"I took pills in Albuquerque."

"Well, I don't know about you, but I'm looking for a way out. We all are. You're stuck here with the rest of us."

"What do you mean?"

He coughed dust, shook his head.

"My stomach is in knots here," I said, unsure what I meant.

He looked toward Jackson's house, then back at me. "I need to go," he said, and he started to walk away.

"Wait, what does it all mean?" I said, but he wouldn't stop walking. "Wait," I called out to him.

Back inside the house, I went straight to my room, closing the door. I lay down on the bed and thought about what he meant, being stuck there, unable to leave. I could leave anytime I wanted, it seemed to me. I imagined myself walking around town, people staring at me. I had a sudden coughing fit in bed. My eyes started watering. After a few minutes I relaxed and was about to drowse into sleep when my ears started ringing. I turned over on my side in bed. My eyes were tired. I heard the toilet flush in the hall bathroom, and then fell asleep quickly.

Now this happened. At some point I woke in the middle of the night, confused. It took me a moment to remember where I was, my surroundings. A steady rain was thrumming on the roof. I could see a glass of water on the nightstand beside me, as well as my bag and my shoes on the floor. When I sat up, I saw the figure of an old man standing in the doorway, an apparition. I didn't recognize him. His hair was long and silver and hung languidly. I was too afraid to say anything.

For a moment I had a sense of our mutual awareness of each other, of a state of confusion, although it felt way more definitive than that. When he turned and walked away, I got up and followed him. He walked into the bathroom, where he looked at his reflection in the mirror. He raised his hands to touch it, tilted his head, studying himself. I could see his reflection in the mirror, but it was much blurrier than he appeared. I reached to turn on the light, and he disappeared. When I turned it back off again, he was still gone. I turned the light on and off again. He didn't reappear. "Where are you?" I whispered. I called for him, but he never responded. I turned and walked through the quiet house looking for him, my feet creaking on the old floors in the dark. I peeked into Jackson's bedroom and saw him asleep with his back to me, snoring over the hum of a ceiling fan.

I stepped quietly back to the bathroom, but I couldn't find the old man. Again I turned the light on and off, whispered for him. I returned to my bedroom and went to the window. Outside, at the back of the yard, a hawk was resting on a fence post, sitting very still. The moon shone blue in the dark sky. At one point something flashed by in the darkness, but I wasn't able to tell what it was. I sat on the bed and saw that it was almost four in the morning. What was I supposed to think about the man I saw? I wasn't able to go back to sleep, too unsettled by what I had witnessed, too afraid of whatever it meant.

I saw many people that night: apparitions of women and men with blankets over their shoulders, walking down the hallway. I saw children being carried. I saw people crawling and reaching out to me for help. They kept coming and coming, walking down the hallway past my bedroom. In the dark I couldn't see their faces, but their bodies were struggling against a wind, pushing forward. My ancestors, I thought. My ancestors walking the Trail.

My ears were ringing when I got back under the covers. What did this mean? The ringing was as severe as it had ever been, growing louder. I pressed my hands against my ears and stared into the dark hall. I felt compelled to watch these people as they walked. They pushed forward and kept walking, falling.

MARIA

Ernest used to tell me I had always been good at maintaining composure even in times of extreme stress. After Ray-Ray died, I made it my sole purpose to do whatever I could to keep my children alive. I looked after them closely, watched them play outside even when they weren't aware, listened at their bedroom doors if they talked on the phone or had friends over. My blood pressure rose; I developed panic attacks, something that I had never experienced before. I always made sure that if Sonja and Edgar left with friends, they called and checked in with me every hour. I kept photo albums near my chair and looked at pictures of all my children, including Ray-Ray. My sister Irene said it would always help me feel better, and I was surprised to discover she was correct.

After I took Wyatt to school, I returned

209

home and sat in the living room and flipped through pictures of Edgar in the photo albums. The ones I enjoyed most were the ones when he was little, all the birthday parties and Christmases. They brought me joy no matter how many times I looked at them. When Ernest came into the room, he smiled at me. Something happened to the configuration of the room, and we felt what I thought was the slight trembling of an earthquake.

"Did you feel that?" he said.

"Was it an earthquake? It was an earthquake, wasn't it?"

"Maybe so. It wasn't too bad."

I noticed that his eyes were dark and full of wonder. His eyes could speak to me better than his mouth sometimes, and I knew he was about to say something about Ray-Ray's spirit.

"I know what you're thinking," I said.

He sat in the recliner across the room and put on his sneakers. He bent forward to lace them. He sat back and looked at me.

"I have a good feeling Edgar will come home," he said. "I feel better than I've felt in months. In years."

"I doubt it," I said.

"What do you mean?" he said. "I have a hunch things will look up. And last night

210

the boy wanted to sleep in bed with us."

"Who, Wyatt?"

He nodded.

"Did I sleep through it? I don't ever remember waking up last night."

"You were asleep. He came to my side of the bed, like Ray-Ray did."

"No, you dreamed of Ray-Ray. I do it all the time."

"He walked into our room in the middle of the night," he said. "He tapped my arm. I woke and saw him standing there. There he was, standing there like Ray-Ray."

I looked deep into his face and tried to see what was happening to him. I remained quiet, looking at him.

"It was Wyatt, but it was also Ray-Ray standing there," he said.

I felt my face flush. "What did he say?" I said quietly.

"I followed him in here," he said. He looked around the room, gesturing with his hands. "Colored lights were hanging all over. There were balloons. I sat on the floor, and he brought me one. He brought me a rock that lit up in my hands. He told me to look into it."

I shook my head. Now the Alzheimer's was making him sound crazy again. I didn't want to hear anything else.

"I held the rock in my hands," he said. "I looked into that light. It was a yellow light. I held that rock like a bird in my hands. Then I gave it back, and he told me to go to bed, to rest, because I needed to get well."

Sunlight brightened the room as it streamed in at an angle from the window overlooking the back deck. I could see in that stream of light the particles of dust floating in air, and they held my gaze until Ernest walked out of the room. I had an overwhelming urge to do something, but I didn't know what.

I thought again of Edgar. In the coffee-table drawer we kept a list of phone numbers, and I looked through them for Desiree's number. I couldn't find her name or number anywhere. I did manage to find Edgar's friend Eddie's number. Eddie was also living in New Mexico. I reached for my cell phone and called him. When he answered, I immediately asked if Edgar was okay.

"Who is this?" he said.

"Eddie, this is Maria, Edgar's mom. Is he doing okay? Have you seen him?"

"Oh," he said. "Oh, well, I saw him a few days ago. He seemed fine to me. What's up?"

"Did he say anything about coming home?"

"I'm not sure. I think he said he was taking a train. He seemed fine, no worries."

I felt an enormous relief — that he wasn't hurt, and that he was planning on coming home. "That's good to hear, Eddie. If you see him, can you tell him to call me? He hasn't returned my calls, and I'm a little afraid. But I'm glad you say he's doing okay."

"Yeah, I think him and Rae broke up, I guess. Don't worry. If I see him, I'll tell him you called me."

"Thank you, Eddie."

After we hung up, I took a deep breath and sat back in the chair, wondering if Eddie was being truthful or covering for Edgar.

It was very possible I was starting to believe Ernest when he said Ray-Ray's spirit was inside Wyatt. It wasn't so crazy to think such a thing. What mother wouldn't long for her dead child's spirit to be near? For years I had looked for Ray-Ray, for signs and evidence of his watching us. I once found a feather outside that held turquoise, red, pink, and yellow colors. It was unlike any feather I had ever seen, certainly not from any bird around here. Sonja said it was a gift for us from Ray-Ray, and though at the time we laughed it off, I secretly wanted it

213

to be true, and in some ways, I actually believed it.

When Wyatt arrived home from school that day, I found myself staring at him. Something was different, either in me or in him, I wasn't sure which. But I felt a much stronger connection to him. It was my evening to volunteer at the youth shelter, to read to the residents staying there, and when I mentioned it to Wyatt, he told me he knew some of them.

"Those kids are from my school," he said. "I know some from the chess club. Drama Club. We're sort of like a family, even though I've never had to stay there."

A family. What an odd term for describing the others, I thought. Some of the kids came to the shelter with bruises or welts on their legs. Some came with lice, skin infections, even serious illnesses like hepatitis C. Wyatt asked if he could come along, and whether it would be possible for him to bring his notebook so he could read a story to them. Of course I let him.

When we arrived, sure enough, many of the kids already knew him, all the lost boys and girls, even the older ones in high school. They welcomed him with high fives, fist bumps, some questions about whether he was still acting president of the Youth

Foundation for Nonviolence in Elementary Schools, which was news to me, something he hadn't mentioned.

"Principal Holt said I was taking on too many extracurricular activities once I started cracking jokes about the *Dewey* Decimal System," he told them. "I mean, seriously guys, do we really need to know the Dewey Decimal System? *Dooo we? Dooo we?*"

Laughter all around, more fist bumps. "They're a good group of kids," Sarah, the youth services coordinator, told me. For a while Wyatt played Ping-Pong against an older teenager named Antonio, a former gang member. Antonio spent six months in a secure lockup placement down in Altus before getting released and placed back into the state's custody. "Angry" was how everyone described Antonio, but that had been proven false, Sarah told me; he'd been at the shelter for three months without one incident or angry outburst, even when he was told to do standard chores like cleaning the kitchen or picking up around the facility. Wyatt lost the game, joking that he let Antonio win. He said something in Antonio's ear that made Antonio laugh so hard he doubled over.

"Dude is cray-*zeeee,*" Antonio said, still laughing, as everyone began to gather in the commons room. The kids gathered on the floor in front of Wyatt, all of them; even the older kids with the basketballs and Ping-Pong paddles sat down to listen to his story. Sarah and I watched, a little surprised at how natural it all seemed, Wyatt's sway over the other kids, his easy mentorship, all of it at such a young age.

"The story is called 'Doe Stah Dah Nuh Dey,' " he told them, but he didn't bother translating it to English for them or, for that matter, me either. I was unfamiliar with this phrase, even though I knew some of the Cherokee language. One of the younger kids asked whether it was like the other story he used to tell them in Drama Club, "The Boy Who Never Grew Up," a story based on *Peter Pan* that Wyatt had written a year or so earlier. At this point Wyatt launched into a long explanation about stories based on stories, and how sometimes the same characters appear in various forms.

"Look, look," Wyatt said, "the stories all have something in common, right? They're like medicine, but without the bad taste, right? It's good for you. No painful needle in the arm or hip." Finally, he assured them that this was a new story.

There was once, in a small town called

Quah, a quiet boy who lived near a dark river. One day the boy ran away from home after disobeying his father. The boy went to the river to swim, not knowing it was the home of a giant snake, e nah dah, who was known to leap out of the water and drag people to an underground world full of darkness. The snake opened its mouth wide and grabbed the boy as he was swimming, pulling him down into the land . . .

Wyatt held his hands up like claws and made a face, which reminded me, oddly, of Ray-Ray. Such a strange expression, it occurred to me. Now I could understand what Ernest was seeing in him, or at least how he resembled Ray-Ray in this particular way. His face, the way his lips curved downward, the way he talked and smiled. I could see it.

. . . and the boy looked around to see he was in another world, the Darkening Land. All around him were other people who had been pulled under by the snake. He saw dead buzzards and dead fish along the side of the road. He saw a cloud of vultures in the sky. Nobody would look at him or talk to him. In the distance, he heard gunshots.

"Someone help me!" he called, but nobody answered.

So the boy ran. He didn't know where he was going, but he ran until he came across a group of people. He saw a few men holding rifles, following a group of people who were walking and falling. The men with their rifles kicked and yelled, making the people walk and walk, even when they fell.

The boy hid behind a rotting building and watched, feeling helpless. He saw birds gathering, making noises. He saw rain lifting from earth to sky.

The residents were all entranced. Wyatt was so charismatic. That he resembled Ray-Ray so strikingly in this light was bewildering. I was reminded of when Ray-Ray used to do his impersonations, gesturing broadly with his hands, so entertaining. Wyatt talked with the same mannerisms, had the same ornery smile, even as he recounted a story of such despair and pain.

Suddenly a giant eagle, bigger than the boy, landed in front of him. The eagle spread its wings, then turned into a man with long silver hair. The man approached the boy and told him not to fear what he saw. "Their suffering is for you," he told him. "Now go home."

"How do I go home?" the boy asked.

"I'll take you," the man said. Then he turned back into an eagle and told the boy to climb on his back. Carefully, the boy climbed on, and they flew westward into the pale sky.

Wyatt closed his notebook and looked out at the kids.

"Wait," one of the boys said. "That's it? What happens?"

"I have one more story for you," Wyatt told him.

I saw Wyatt now as a reflection in the sky, dreamy and mystical, surrounded by kind spirits. He was an eagle soaring in the clouds one minute and back in the shelter the next, a boy entertaining deprived kids. I had a vision of him in a hospital with the sick and disabled, the addicts, the mentally ill — the dead with self-inflicted gunshot wounds, scars on their wrists and necks. I saw him comforting our people who had died of sickness and fatigue along the Trail, the young and the elders. And now these kids were all there listening to him, our strange and wonderful Wyatt, the boy who could seemingly do anything.

219

There was a man named Tsala, a Nunnehi.

"What's a Nunnehi?" a girl asked.

"A spirit. An immortal who lives every-where," Wyatt said.

One day, he searched for a beautiful woman to become his wife. He searched every opening in the woods. He walked and walked but never found her. That night he had a dream. A giant hawk appeared before him. The hawk spread its wings and told him, in a voice he recognized as his own: "Go forth to a mountain far away, and there you will find the woman who will become your wife."

"Who are you?" Tsala asked, but the hawk flew away into the night.

Wyatt outstretched his arms like wings to illustrate the bird flying away. Again I pictured Ray-Ray, could almost remember him in this exact room, making the same gesture with his hands. A déjà vu. And yet I knew that Ray-Ray had never come to the shelter with me when he was alive. I tried to remember a time when he had fluttered his hands like birds, but I couldn't recall. He was in an elementary-school play once — maybe that was it. The vision dissolved as quickly as it had come.

220

Late the next morning he awoke to find himself surrounded by a group of children. They were all looking down at him, their eyes wide in wonder. One of them said, "Are you Tsala? The man who will save us?"

"I'm looking for my wife," Tsala said. "But first I will help you find your way home."

He began to lead the children back toward their village, determined to return them safely. They walked past the mountain where the Yunwi Tsundsi lived, then followed a trail through the woods. They walked under dark clouds, thunder sounding in the distance. Soon a light rain began to fall. By the time they reached the village, the thunder grew louder, and the rain was coming down harder.

"I have to go," Tsala told them.

"Beware of the soldiers," the children warned him.

"Wait," a boy said. "Who are the Yunwi Tsunsdi?"

"The Little People," Wyatt said. "From old Cherokee stories. But that's all for today. Now go and think about what I told you."

I was a little stunned by listening to him, almost entranced myself, even as Wyatt got

221

up and returned to playing Ping-Pong. The rest of the time at the shelter, Wyatt seemed like a normal kid again, talking about movies and music with the others.

"Wyatt has something special," a supervisor named Hank told me. He put an inhaler in his mouth and sucked in. "I put out fires all day, every day," he said. "Some of these juveniles are runaways and criminals. Some get kicked out of long-term placement for getting high or stealing from staff. Others get picked up by the police and brought in. It's a rare day when there isn't a fire to be put out."

I had seen kids come in and out of the shelter for twenty years. The court placed them in the custody of social services, and they sat in the shelter and waited to be placed in group homes. Then they might run away from the group homes and return to the streets, and the whole cycle would start over again. When I worked at the shelter, it was my job to meet with the kids when they were first brought in. After they changed out of their street clothes and showered and put all their money and jewelry in baggies, after they carried their bedsheets and pillows down the hall past the medical supply room to their rooms, I would sit with them as they told me everything that happened on the streets. They opened up to me — it was a gift. I rarely had to do much, maybe smile and tell them I would try to help them. Part of my job was listening to them, these kids who had seen enough in six months to provide a lifetime of nightmares.

One of the older boys came over to Hank and said he needed his medicine. Hank called for a staff member to come over.

"Paolo needs his asthma meds," he said, then showed the boy his inhaler. "I have mine right here, so I feel for you, son. Hang in there, it'll get better." After Paolo walked off, Hank told me that Paolo was sixteen and had lived in seven different foster homes since he was twelve.

"I remember working with a lot of kids exactly like him," I said.

"Paolo's dad is one of those low-grade knuckleheads who wears flannel shirts and drives a 1993 Firebird and chews Red Man. Paolo's a good kid, though."

"Maybe I helped a few over the years. I hope so, anyway." We watched Wyatt give high fives to some of the smaller kids. Then he came over, and I asked him what the title of his story meant.

"I thought you knew Cherokee," he said.

"Only a little. But I didn't catch the title

223

when you said it."

"Doe stah dah nuh dey," he said. "It means 'My brother.' "

On the drive home, the town felt quiet and isolated. The road took us past empty and decayed buildings, carrying us east toward the bridge leading to our house. A few welding trucks were parked in the otherwise barren lot of an old roadside motel. "Way out in the distance," I told Wyatt, "way out there among the trees and hills, Woody Guthrie once walked on a dusty road, mumbling lyrics to a folk song with his guitar strapped to his back."

"We sang 'This Land Is Your Land' every day for three years at Sequoyah," he said.

We rode in silence for a while.

"I think you're a good mom," he said.

I put on my sunglasses and cried then, quietly, but I don't think he knew. When we arrived back home, he went into his room to do homework while I went into the kitchen and took out a pan to make supper. I stepped out onto the back deck, expecting to find Ernest, but he wasn't there. I called for him, but he didn't answer. Now I felt terrified — what had I done? Left an Alzheimer's patient alone to wander off? I checked the house, hurrying from room to room and calling his name, but he was nowhere. Wyatt came out of his room and asked me what was the matter.

"Ernest isn't here," I said.

His eyes widened, and he looked distraught. "Did you check outside? Maybe he's out there. I'll help you look."

While Wyatt rushed out, I got my cell from my purse and called Sonja, but she didn't answer, so I left a message: "Sonja, it's Mom. I think Papa has wandered off. If you get this soon call me." Then I rushed out the door and called out for him again.

The moment I stepped outside, I felt a surge of pain in my chest, which I recognized as fear. I felt dizzy, short of breath, as I hurried around the side of the house.

And there he was, by the garden.

"Ernest," I said, holding my chest. I was still short of breath. "I thought you'd wandered off."

I approached him and took his hand. "My God," I said.

He was looking at me in a way he hadn't looked at me in a long time. He took my other hand in his. "Maria," he said. "I can remember things I've had trouble remembering, like the combination to the safe in our closet. Thirty-six, eleven, twenty-two." He took his keys out of his pocket and started going through them one at a time, telling me what each was for.

I couldn't believe what I was seeing. "You remember each key," I said.

"Just like that. Dr. Patel said he wears a Titleist cap when he plays golf. Last week at the Cherokee National Holiday, I watched a girl from Sallisaw win Miss Teen Cherokee. Her name is Aiyana, and she wore the same dress her grandmother once wore. Her favorite subjects in school are science and history, remember?"

"What's happening?" I said.

He started laughing, and I put my head against his chest and let him hold me.

Maybe this was a season for miracles to occur, I thought. Maybe the earth was healing itself of trembling and drought, maybe the bees weren't dying, and the swarms of locusts jumbling tunelessly around were feeding all the rodents and reptiles and crawling creatures. As the sun came out from behind a cloud and Ernest asked if we could call Dr. Patel, I kept thinking we were due for a season of healing ourselves. "I want to tell him I'm feeling damn great," he said.

"Yes, yes," I said.

"Although I think the doctor's offices are closed for the day."

226

I didn't care. I pulled out my phone and called Dr. Patel's number anyway. "This message is for Dr. Patel. This is Maria Echota. My husband is Ernest Echota, and something remarkable is happening with his memory. We think his Alzheimer's is gone. He can suddenly remember things — can you believe it? I think — I think he's been healed!" I hung up the phone, my hands trembling.

Wyatt came around the corner of the house, looking flushed and breathing heavy. "She found you," he said. "Wow, you look like a new man."

"I feel better than ever," Ernest said a little later, back inside the house. "And look at this boy who's blessed us with his presence."

Wyatt came into the dining room, dressed in a collared shirt and khaki pants, his hair combed and wet from a shower. "I always feel better after a good day of work and a shower," he said. "Smooth water, the smell of shampoo."

I started sweeping the back deck while Ernest raked the leaves outside in preparation for the bonfire in two days. I decided to postpone dinner so I could enjoy the beautiful evening outside with him. I couldn't believe his energy. He bagged what he raked, tied the trash bag, and carried it to the trash can by the side of the house. When he came back to the deck, we talked about our kids. We talked about Ray-Ray, too, Ernest laughing as he told the story about the time Ray-Ray dressed up as a ghost for Halloween when he was little. "Remember we just threw an old white bedsheet over him and cut two holes for eyes?"

I laughed hard at that memory. We were both laughing. Then Ernest wanted to go out for ice cream and celebrate how well he was feeling.

"I feel drunk," he told me. "It's like I've been drinking all day. I want dinner and ice cream. I want a good glass of wine."

"You haven't touched a drink in months and months," I said.

"Not since April of last year," he said. "It was the day I met Wes Studi downtown. He was in town for a funeral, I remember. He liked my hat."

"Yes, I remember," I said.

He was already putting on his shoes to go. So I quickly changed clothes and drove the three of us to a nice restaurant downtown for dinner. Ernest ordered a glass of rosé, which made me uneasy, but he held a finger up and said he didn't want to hear it.

"Let me enjoy this while it lasts," he said. "I haven't felt like this in a long time. My energy is up. My back doesn't hurt. I didn't get winded walking from the car to the restaurant."

"You're healed," Wyatt said.

"Your back is feeling better, too?" I asked.

He stood up then, with people around us, stretched his arms forward and did a knee bend. He jogged in place. I was getting embarrassed and told him to sit down.

"Maybe our prayers are finally answered," he said, settling back into his seat and taking a drink from his glass.

We enjoyed a long, unhurried dinner, then went for a walk downtown. We stopped in Morgan's Bakery to buy Wyatt a cream puff, which made him happy. I was elated.

"If only Edgar was here," Ernest said on the walk back to the car.

I immediately called Edgar and left a message. "Honey, please call us. We want you to come home for Ray-Ray's bonfire, sweetheart. I'm not mad and Papa isn't mad. We want you here. Please call me back."

"Fear the beard," Ernest said, back at the house. "Remember when the Thunder lost James Harden?"

"I'd like to grow a beard someday," Wyatt said.

"You're fifteen, so you can start trying."

"Says who?"

"Says my smart wife." Ernest winked at me. "She knows the good bearded ones in sports: Johnny Damon, James Harden. Right? You think I'm kidding, son, just ask her."

"Ernest used to watch sports all the time," I told Wyatt. "For years it's all he watched, and I just started watching, too."

"Kareem had a beard," Ernest said.

I tried to remember the last time Ernest had even remembered an athlete's name. It was as if the boy had showered him with some strange invisible angelic dust that reset his memory, if only temporarily. Ernest talked about a baseball game in Arlington, Texas, when the Rangers beat the Red Sox after clobbering Wakefield's knuckleball. "Wakefield," he kept saying. "That knuckleball either hissed or missed. Go watch the big league sometime. Of course in terms of Oklahoma sports, Jim Thorpe was the best athlete we've ever seen, just ask anyone."

Wyatt wanted to hear more. Ernest was invigorating to listen to, and it occurred to me that Wyatt brought out an energy in Ernest that had been stagnant for months, even years. Listening to him talk now was like the Ernest thirty years earlier, before all his ailments, all his arthritis pain and high blood pressure, pre-Alzheimer's, when he was more social. To be young again, to share stories, to laugh — how wonderful. To sit in lawn chairs in the backyard and look up at the fireworks in the sky. To drink lemonade on a humid summer evening. It would all be possible again, I realized.

"Maria," he said, unable to conceal his excitement, "remember that old Chevy I had back in the seventies? The one with the bucket seats?"

"Of course," I said.

"You'd love them," he told Wyatt. "I remember recovering them, removing the seat-back rubber bumpers and hog rings to get to the burlap. I stripped the backrest, popped off the headrest. Remember, Maria? My pal Otto helped me. We used a special set of wires to hog-ring the upholstery to the foam."

"What kind of Chevy?" Wyatt asked.

"Nova."

Wyatt nodded approvingly. "A good solid car."

"I had sideburns back then," Ernest said. "Otto worked at the body shop downtown. We would listen to rockabilly on the radio.

231

Elvis and Eddie Cochran. Oklahoma's own Wanda Jackson. Otto worked with a guy named Phil who picked a guitar as fast as Chet Atkins or Jerry Reed. You heard of them guys, son?"

"True pickers."

"Goddamn legends. I got records in the basement."

"Trippy." Wyatt nodded.

They headed downstairs, Ernest leading the way. He was energetic. His posture and overall body structure even looked different. How had his posture improved so quickly? While they were downstairs I called Irene, and told her what was happening to Ernest.

"Are you kidding?" she said. "He's *cured*? Is that even possible?"

"It sounds crazy, but it's true. He's cured."

"I wonder if his medication is finally working?"

"He's happier. He feels alive. He's standing up straight."

"Strange his memory improved so suddenly."

"His memory is sharp," I said. "Earlier he even told me about the upholstery in our Oldsmobile forty years ago. *Forty* years ago. I can barely remember what color that car was, much less remember the upholstery."

232

"Maybe you should call and talk to his doctor? If he can suddenly recall specific details from so long ago, that seems so odd to me. But how wonderful he's talking like his old self again."

"It really is wonderful," I said, a little uncertainly, looking out the window at the dim shapes of trees and their complicated, twisting branches.

SONJA

September 4

September 4

I woke in the middle of the night from a horrible dream. I was in Quah, being chased down the street where Ray-Ray had died. Vin and Calvin Hoff were running after me, gaining on me, until Calvin was close enough to grab me and press his hands against my throat. I looked into his face and saw his sagging jowls, his furious eyes. He tried to choke me. Suffocate me. He pressed his body against mine, but all I could feel was his hands on my throat. Vin yelled at me to keep my mouth shut, not to move. I struggled, unable to break away, and when I woke I felt a heaviness in my chest like never before.

I didn't sleep well after that, only a few hours. Finally I got out of bed and sat in the kitchen with my morning coffee. I left Edgar a voice message for what felt like the hundredth time, then went outside to work in the flower bed. The sun was out, and it was warm and humid. Bugs and mosquitoes were swarming, so I didn't work too long. Inside, I took a long shower and got dressed. When I checked my phone, I noticed that Vin had left a message.

"Come over tonight," he said. "I want you. I wanted you last night, babe. Call me when you get a minute."

I didn't call him back. Whatever desire I had felt for him, I'd lost, but I still held my anger toward him. Since last night at the casino and that awkward goodbye, my feelings for him had fluctuated between anger and apathy. It saddened me a little, because I'd developed such a connection to Luka, sweet Luka, who reminded me so much of Ray-Ray. But I knew that I had let things go too far with Vin. I wondered if he would say something to his father about me. Every time I thought of that dream I'd had, I felt weirded out. Was the dream a warning to stay away from the Hoff family? Were the spirits telling me I was wrong?

In the kitchen I rifled through the cabinets for a Valium, but I couldn't find one. It took me a while to let my frustration settle. I thought my parents might have a Xanax or something to calm my nerves, so I walked down the road to their house. "Hi, Mom," I

235

called out as I opened their front door. "I'm here to meet the foster kid." I felt a little bad for lying.

"Wyatt's at school," my mom said from the living room. I told her I needed to use the bathroom and rummaged through the medicine cabinet, but I couldn't find anything. My mom asked me to take a walk with Papa, which I thought might take my mind off Vin, so we walked down the road to a spot in the trees where Papa used to like to paint, a place we had both come to often throughout the years when we wanted solitude and quiet. Papa talked about wanting to paint an orchard full of apple, pear, and plum trees. He liked to paint in concentrated colors, yellows and reds and greens. I remember watching him, as a girl. I would study his hands, his grief-stricken eyes, noticing how he worked with such precision and heightened sensitivity. I saw artful shadows and reflections in his work, beauty in an unstable world. I recalled the sheer brightness of a lazy afternoon when I played in the area so long ago, the tall grass and thickets of maple and oak around me.

"I loved to paint when I was a kid," he said. "We lived out near Briggs in a small house, all eleven of us. Did I ever tell you about the creaking floorboards in that house? My sisters and I used to step on them over and over just to annoy my mother."

"I love hearing about your childhood," I told him. I kept it to myself, but I was absolutely amazed by his memory.

"I feel better than I have in a long time."

"What's happened?" I asked.

"This boy Wyatt, he reminds me of Ray-Ray," he said, looking away from me, as if he was thinking aloud. "Maybe our prayers are being answered."

"Our ancestors watch over us," I said.

"Yes, they do," he said. "I've been telling Wyatt some of the old stories about our family."

"I remember some of those."

"You and Edgar used to love for me to tell the story of Tsala when you were young. About how soldiers shot him dead because he refused to leave the land. It's an important one." For a moment he looked down at his hands and said nothing. "I haven't seen Edgar since the intervention."

"I think he'll come home," I told him. "I think he'll look for work here. Last time I talked to him, Desiree had broken up with him and he didn't have any sort of plan. I kept bugging him about it, but he didn't tell me anything about what he wanted to do.

He didn't know. He should just come home and let us help him."

"He knows we want him to come home."

"I've told him that over and over."

He looked at me with uncertainty. "Desiree was good for him. She called a few days ago, worried about him."

"What did she say?"

"Nothing. She wouldn't say anything except they split up and she wanted to let us know. I told your mother maybe we should drive out to Albuquerque again."

I looked at him and saw that he was serious. "For another intervention?"

"Whatever we need to do," he said. "Bring him back to live with us so he can save money. Anything to help get him out of this situation."

When we returned to the house, we sat on our back deck for a while. I was feeling overwhelmed to see Papa this way again — so supportive and protective of his kids during a crisis, exactly as he'd been after Ray-Ray died. Soon my mother came outside and suggested we all go down to the lake.

"You'll have to meet Wyatt when he gets home," she told me. "He is so charming and smart. I have to tell you, he reminds us of Ray-Ray."

"That's what Papa said. The guy I went

out with the other day has a son named Luka who resembles Ray-Ray in a way. The way he looks, his facial expressions. It's so strange."

"Wyatt's more than just a resemblance," Papa said, and I saw my mom tap Papa on the arm for some reason. They were holding back something from me. Sometimes they acted secretive like this, and I decided not to press it. Honestly, I didn't care much about the foster kid — I was more concerned with my own problems, with Vin and with Edgar not contacting us.

We saw a hawk swoop down at the edge of the road, ahead. Papa pointed. It perched and turned to us before flying into the woods. "I see that hawk from time to time," Papa said. "I've always wondered if it's Ray-Ray watching us. Or maybe an ancestor."

"I like that it could be Ray-Ray's spirit," I told him. "He would play tricks on us, for sure. Right? I can totally see that."

As we walked, we heard a girl's voice from down the road, and a moment later she came into view. She was running toward us, calling out, "Wolfie! Wolfie!" When she reached us a minute later, she was out of breath. "Have you seen my dog?" she asked, breathing hard. "His name is Wolfie."

"What kind of dog is he?" I asked.

"He's a shepherd mix," she said, still trying to catch her breath. I guessed she was
eight or nine years old. "He ran away. He
has light-brown fur and a collar with his
name on it."

My mom took her by the hand and promised we would help her search. We all hurried down the path toward the water, calling Wolfie's name and whistling. "Where is
he?" the girl kept asking us.

After a few minutes, my mom knelt down
to the girl. "What's your name? Is your
mom or dad around? We should find them,
too."

"My name is Sarah," the girl said. "I live
with my daddy in that house over there."
She pointed to a gray house across the lake.
"He's looking for Wolfie, too."

My mother asked, "Why are you by yourself? What happened?"

"I ran off to try to find Wolfie," she said.
"My daddy's looking on the other side."

Papa and I knelt down to her, too. "But
he's probably looking for you," I told her.
"We should go find him."

"It's going to be okay," Papa told her.
"Everything will be fine."

The girl was near hysterics by now, and
my mom held her for a minute. Papa put
two pinkies in his mouth and tried to

whistle. "I used to whistle this way," he said, disappointed, then looked down to see Sarah's face wet with tears. I could see his compassion for the girl. He understood that she was so afraid of her dog never returning she could barely breathe. It was a feeling we all understood. In such a moment, there is never enough comfort to soothe that fear.

My mother announced that she would take Sarah to find her dad, and we promised to keep looking for Wolfie. Papa and I walked back toward the house, calling Wolfie's name. The woods could be thick in parts, and also dark. When we were almost to the house, my phone rang. I saw that it was Vin, but I didn't answer it.

In the kitchen I made Papa a glass of water with ice and took it to him in the living room. The window overlooked the yard, where we could see some birds pecking around. They flew away, scattering. When I was young, Edgar and Ray-Ray spent Saturday mornings in this room, watching old black-and-white movies with Papa: Laurel and Hardy, the Marx Brothers, Mickey Rooney — but I didn't like slapstick, couldn't understand the juvenile humor.

In the kitchen I made myself a salad. I found some blueberries and apple slices in the fridge, along with salad dressing. There was a half-full bottle of white wine, so I poured myself a glass and sat at the kitchen table. While I ate, I played the balloon game on my phone a while. Afterward I stepped outside on the back porch and smoked a cigarette. A little ways down the trail I saw my mother talking to the little girl and a man I assumed was her dad. He was dark-haired and rugged-looking, wearing a vest and boots. It was difficult to see exactly what he looked like from where I was stand-ing, but he reminded me of someone I had seen in a movie somewhere, or on TV, maybe his overall posture and what he was wearing. I could make out his face a little, but not entirely. From afar he looked to be built, in good shape. He leaned down in a fatherly way to comfort Sarah as she em-braced him, all the while talking to my mother. And then she turned and headed back, and I watched the guy walk the other way with Sarah.

"Well?" I said when she reached the porch.

"That was Sarah's dad, but we couldn't find the dog," she said. "Poor thing, she was so upset. Her dad's name is Eric."

"Well, that's good," I said. "Is he mar-ried?"

"Married? He didn't say."

"Did he say how long he's lived over

there? I haven't seen him before."

"He didn't say," she said. "Hey, Wyatt should be home from school soon. Do you want to meet him?"

"I should go back home. There's a phone call I need to make."

"Call Edgar, maybe he'll talk to you."

"I've called him so many times, I'd be surprised if he talked to me," I said. "But who knows? He's so unpredictable."

I walked back home. My quiet house breathed sadness. Every room I entered held a dim silence, and I started listening to the rooms breathe their presence into me. I could hear their whispers, or maybe they were the whispers of ancestors' spirits. I thought about what Papa was saying about our ancestor Tsala walking the land around us. I knew I should listen for him, for courage. I imagined Papa speaking to the wind and sky as our ancestors watched us. Listening to the quiet house, I was again plunged into fear. I worried too much, the sort of unsettled, troubling concern one feels before a line of tornadic storms approaching. I knew my anxiety was stirring again, and I felt tense at the thought of Vin coming over.

I sat in the armchair in my living room

and watched TV for a while, some movie about a pilot who went blind and refused help from his wife. He threw things around the house, shattering glass, knocking over lamps and tables. I looked outside and saw a cardinal on the windowsill. It spread its wings and flew away.

I turned off the TV and tried to relax, but I couldn't. I called Edgar, but he didn't answer. This time I didn't leave a voice mail. I took a hot bath, which helped me feel better temporarily. Soon enough a weariness came over me, and I had the sense that something disorderly was flowing throughout the house. I felt restrained in the drowsy warmth of my bathwater, as if something was pressing down on me.

That night Vin called, as I knew he would. He was a little drunk. Again, I let it go to voice mail, and then listened to the message. "I'm coming over after a while," he said. That was it, nothing more. I played a dumb balloon game on my phone, then turned off the lamp beside my bed and smoked a cigarette in the dark. Colette had become the smoke in my house, drifting around from room to room. I felt her presence in the darkness. I felt her presence everywhere lately: in my bedroom, in the hallway, when I was in the bath at night. Or was it the presence of someone else entirely?

How aware my senses were in the middle of the night, in the darkness, as if I could access some place I wasn't able to during daylight hours. I felt the room's pulsating heart, its breathing. I heard, too, a rhythmic sound, like soldiers marching in the distance. I had a vision of an intruder watching me through the window, then breaking down the door and dragging me out of the house. I felt like a young girl again, terrified after hearing a noise, and then waking Papa to tell him.

I drifted in and out of sleep, I think, hovering in that space between dreams and visions. At one point I heard the Cherokee phrase whispered in my ear: "Aniyosgi anahili, aniyosgi anahili." *Soldiers are marching, soldiers are marching.* I heard it over and over, nudging at me like a bad dream.

At three in the morning, a knock on the door startled me. I sat up in bed. The knock came again, and I peeked out my window blinds, somewhat relieved to see Vin's car. I turned on the light in the living room, and when I opened the door, he was already letting himself in, smelling of cigarettes and whiskey.

"You're drunk?" I said.

He could barely keep from falling over.

245

He moved in close and kissed me. I let him, but just for a minute. Then I pulled back and asked where he had been — and where was Luka? He frowned, moved in close to me, and kissed me again, sliding his hands down my arms. He started kissing my neck, and after a moment I pulled away.

"What do you want?" He laughed. "Tell me what you want."

I felt him gripping my hair, as he did during sex, but this was more forceful and way more irritating.

"Stop," I said, pushing away from him. He grabbed my arm and squeezed, unexpectedly.

Something flashed in my mind then, and when I looked up to meet his eyes, he was dressed in uniform, a face of the past, threatening me. Something about his face, his expression, as if he were someone I didn't recognize. "You're hurting me," I said. "Seriously, Vin, stop."

"Come on," he said, squeezing my wrist. "I drove all the way over here from downtown just to see you. Come on."

I jerked my arm away more forcefully this time, pushing him away. "Stop it, Vin," I told him. "That hurts." Now I was angry.

"You're a crazy Indian woman," he said, releasing my wrist. "Just an old slut."

246

Without thinking, I swung at him, but he grabbed my arm again and twisted it, dragging me down to the floor. I screamed, but he didn't let go. Then he slapped me, hard, and I collapsed, covering my face.

I had never been struck in the face like that by a man I thought I knew. My cheek was burning from the blow, and the stinging only seemed to grow worse as I sat there holding my hand to my face.

I screamed "I'm calling the police!" at him and ran into the hall bathroom, locking the door behind me. My heart was racing. I quickly realized I didn't have my phone, though, and paced in the bathroom until I caught my breath. It didn't sound like he was outside the door, luckily. I wanted to scream again, start smashing things in there. I must've bitten my lip because I tasted blood. In the mirror I saw that my cheek and lips were red. I ran cold water over my face and over a washcloth by the sink, then held it to my skin.

I sat on the edge of the tub with my head in my hands, unable to bring myself to tears despite what had happened. A feeling comes in an instant, a restlessness, an irritability, that alerts you to leave before something terrible happens. I felt it pressing against me, suffocating me, warning me to separate

myself from him. What was I supposed to do? There was no window to crawl out of. I was alone in a locked bathroom with no phone, trapped.

I stayed in the bathroom for at least twenty minutes, maybe longer. It felt like forever. Thankfully he never tried to open the door. At one point I wasn't sure whether he'd left; it was so quiet, and I couldn't hear him walking around. Even so, I needed to feel safe, I needed something for protection. I opened drawers under the sink, where I found a pair of scissors. I found rubbing alcohol, which I could throw in his face if I needed to. None of this made me any more prepared to face him. I stood at the door for a moment, listening, but there was still nothing but silence. Finally, gripping the scissors firmly, I unlocked the door and stepped out.

I walked slowly, quietly, into the living room. Vin was slumped on the couch, asleep. I hurried to retrieve my phone from the floor, against the wall, and returned to him. His mouth was open, and he muttered something when I said his name.

"Vin," I repeated. "I'm calling the police, and you have to go now. Do you hear me? Hey, Vin."

He was too drunk to even respond, and

obviously in no condition to drive himself home. I wanted to slap him while he slept. I could've slapped him, right then, and he wouldn't have been able to do anything about it. I thought of calling the police, but the thought of Luka entered my mind. What would happen to Luka if his dad was in jail? I couldn't do that to him. I couldn't even think straight. Vin was completely passed out, and I told myself I was probably safe at this point.

I thought I could call someone to come get him, but it was four in the morning; who would I call? In the kitchen I poured myself a glass of wine, trying to think what I could do with him by the time he woke in the morning. As the minutes passed, I kept thinking about how I would not forgive him. I watched him sleep, thinking about how pathetic and weak he was. He slept deeply with his mouth open, snoring. I couldn't stand watching him. I couldn't stand to be in the same house with him.

In the hall I turned on the light and opened the door leading downstairs to the basement. I walked quietly back into the living room and shook him awake. "Vin," I said over and over, "let's go to bed. Come on, Vin, let's go to bed," until he stirred and opened his eyes. I kept pulling on his arm, and finally he got up and mumbled something, and I led him by the hand to the hallway and helped him down the stairs. At one point I thought he said something about Luka, but I ignored him. I just wanted to make sure he got down there. Once we were in the basement, I told him to lie down. "Go to sleep, go to sleep," I said.

He lay down on his side, on my old bed, and fell back asleep. I was so nervous about it that I had to sit down on the basement steps and rest a moment. He stirred and mumbled something, which startled me. I could still smell the liquor on him. I stepped over to him, reached into his front pants pocket, and carefully took his phone. He still had his wallet and car keys. Then I went back upstairs, closing the door behind me and bolting it so that he couldn't get out. I felt safe with him down there, locked inside.

In the kitchen, I set his phone on the table and stepped outside to the back porch, where I lit a cigarette. Then I walked down the trail near the lake, as I had done so many nights before, with the moonlight reflecting on the water and the soft dirt beneath my feet. I was calm, even being out alone so late at night. A little ways along the bank, I sat down and hummed a song, a lullaby my mom used to sing. *The wolves go away, the wolves go away, and sweet baby will stay.* I hummed other songs from my childhood, songs I didn't understand or barely remembered the words to. Then I spoke a prayer to the Great Spirit to bless me with protection and to give me peace. After about twenty minutes I walked back to the house.

I didn't go down to the basement — Vin needed to sleep it off — but I felt the need to go back inside and check all the rooms. I peeked inside my bedroom, then I closed all the blinds in the house. I checked the hall closet, the bathroom, under the bed, and in the shower. After all that, I sat quiet on the kitchen floor so that I could hear Vin in the basement underneath me if he woke up. It was five in the morning, and the sun would be coming up soon. I wasn't even tired. I picked up his phone and scrolled through his messages, emails, and photos.

Fuck him, I thought. On his phone there were several photos of other women. I deleted them, along with all his other photos, except for the ones of Luka. I deleted his phone numbers and contacts, and then I posted on his social media accounts: "I hit a woman tonight. I hit a woman. I hit an Indian."

251

Tsala

Beloved, the earth will always speak to us when we need to hear her the most. Even in my time we were worried about rising oceans and burning land. I always looked for warnings. Our family believed strongly in Tecumseh's warning of the soldiers coming to remove us from our land: there was a drought. There were high winds and a bitter cold winter.

You are aware that this was a terrifying time for us. We were frightened but ready to defend our home. Our people would refuse to leave even though we were tricked by the government with their fraudulent treaty. We did not trust them.

It was raining the night we rounded up a few families and quietly snuck away to hide in a cave in the mountains. I told the other people in the Cherokee language: *What we do will affect our people for years to come.* I thought of all my visions, our visions, the

252

prophecy of the coming migration, and hoped they would be proven false. That night, in the cave, one of the wives was so afraid for her new baby that she ran out into the rain with a tomahawk, yelling, "Kill! Kill!" She felt the presence of a spirit's strength so powerfully that she threw the tomahawk into the night sky, in the rain, and it never came down again, was never found anywhere. That night it hailed large ice pellets.

We were there ten nights before they arrived to destroy our homes. We watched from afar as the ones who swarmed on our land like a pack of wolves began firing their weapons. Now there was a great threat upon us. The soldiers were ordered to be civil, but they destroyed our cabins and barns. They slaughtered our chickens and hogs and cattle. They prodded our wives and elders with bayonets as they forced them out of their homes and to stockades. By the end, many of our people had nothing but their clothes — everything else was gone. We felt a great misery spread throughout our land. Soldiers dug into graves to steal the gold from our dead, never bothered by the stench of corpses that filled the air. Though we were safe in seclusion, two other men and I couldn't stand that we were not helping our people, so we set out, armed with our weapons. And you, my brave son, you came with us.

At once the soldiers saw us approaching, and soon they surrounded us. We attacked and fought, but there were too many of them. One of them hit you with a shovel, and I lunged at him with my knife, cutting his arm. The other soldiers pulled me off and held me down. They tied us with rope. I told them to kill me first, but they did not agree. I closed my eyes and lowered my head as they pointed their rifles at us. I begged you not to open your eyes, even when they told you to.

EDGAR

I kept waking up, coughing. In sleep I dreamed that a woman brought me a seed basket full of rainbow-colored corn, turkey gizzard beans, and trumpet vine seeds. She was very beautiful, slender with long raven-black hair.

"My gift for you," she told me. "I'm planting pink cherry blossoms to swell in the gray world. The Seven Dancers, the Pleiades star system, is our home. Look for my cherry blossoms along the road and follow that road out. Remember the Tsalagi is about harmony." I saw smoke drooling from her mouth as she walked away.

After that I drifted in and out of sleep until the room brightened and I knew it was morning. I woke feeling I needed to leave Jackson's house. I lay in bed for a while, then got up and saw that Jackson was gone. I made an omelet and coffee and turned on the TV in the living room. The Darkening Land was on fire, according to the live newscast. Flames were roaring everywhere. Chopper 8 showed the view from above a bridge, heavy plumes of smoke and flames. The reporter said fire crews stated that someone had started the fire near Devil's Bridge. The reporter interviewed a witness, a young man holding a red helmet, who said he was looking for people in the restricted area of radioactive mud pits near the bridge. "I've seen people all around here in the past," he said.

"What's the helmet for?" the reporter asked.

"It's for a game. That's all I'm saying."

On TV I saw plumes of black smoke floating over the bridge. I saw dancing flames. I finished my breakfast and watched. "This is a former military base for nuclear testing," the city manager told the reporter. "We've detected underground nuclear explosions for the past fifty years and I can tell you with the utmost certainty that the explosions have left radiation in the area. That's why it's restricted. Someone started a fire in an act of arson."

I stepped outside on the back porch for a smoke. A light drizzle fell. Across the yard, a blurry image hovered around the bushes like a dark fog, and through the drizzle I saw a solitary bird on the horizon. The bird circled in the sky before disappearing into the low clouds. It was quiet outside, too quiet, and soon enough I heard a church bell ringing in the distance. Back inside, I put on a Bauhaus record. It was after five in the afternoon. I lay on the floor and listened, staring at the ceiling. When the music finished, I turned the record over and played the other side. I kept doing this, listening to one side and then flipping the record and listening to the other.

When Jackson came in, it was dark outside and the music was still playing. He set his briefcase down and stood over me. "There's a gathering tonight," he said. "Some folks involved in the games. It's not far, maybe a mile or so down the road. My friend Lyle who's working on the Thorpe game with me wants to meet you. Maybe take some video, have you stomp in a headdress or shake your head like an animal."

"Shake my head like an animal?"

"People will be fascinated, Chief. Who knows — maybe someone will have some good gak you can get geared up on. Good gak, Chief. Sometimes Charlie has Mexican speedballs."

He took a shower while I turned the

album over and started it again. In the kitchen I heated up leftover pizza in the microwave. When he was ready to go, he came into the kitchen and ate leftovers while I looked in my bag for a toothbrush. I couldn't find one and then wondered when I'd last brushed my teeth. My teeth were bad from meth use. I changed my T-shirt before we left.

Jackson wanted to get there quickly, so he drove us, taking a road I hadn't seen. We crossed over the railroad tracks, and a flock of blackbirds fired into the dark sky. I thought about the fowl, which I hadn't seen in a while. I knew it was still lurking around, waiting to swoop down and attack me, dig its talons in my shoulder or hair. We drove down a desolate road until we came to a warehouse.

The warehouse was crowded inside. A band of old men with gray beards and straw hats played some type of sad country music, droning slide guitar and low singing. The people around me were wearing loose-fitting flannel shirts and boots, the only alcohol a domestic beer served in red plastic cups. I saw people engaged in serious conversations, looking at their phones. I saw the intensity and pain on their faces, no laughter at all. This is supposed to be a party, I thought. There were NO SHOOTING signs all around.

Jackson left to get us beers. While he was gone, I overheard two guys talking near me. "I played for twenty-seven hours straight, stopping only to piss once," one guy said to the other. "The game is really addictive. The whole town is buzzing about it."

The other guy rocked on his heels. "I played three days without sleep. Fought about two dozen Indians. My wife prefers TV, but I need something more interactive."

Suddenly one of the guys made eye contact with me, and I realized I had been staring. He squinted at me, and I looked away. No matter where I looked, I felt threatened by everyone I saw. Before she left me, Rae had encouraged me to go to counseling and figure out why I never wanted to be social, why I preferred isolation, and why I always wanted to stay home. She said I was constantly running away, never facing my problems or emotions. I wasn't confrontational enough, that was the problem. I'd struggled to look her in the eye as she told me this. Maybe she was right.

Jackson returned with Lyle, who was thin and pale. Jackson handed me a beer, and Lyle introduced himself. "I'm mighty glad to meet someone who can help us with this

Thorpe game," he said. "We understand there's a way Jim Thorpe dominated sports with his body. He used his weight, had a low center of gravity, so he had certain poses that gave him a whole lot of power."

Jackson coughed hard into his fist. "Well, that's all purely speculation, Lyle."

Lyle had narrow eyes and sculpted hair. He was short, with a slender chin and a bony nose. It made him look a little like a badger.

"We met a Depp-like Indian who told us his grandpa works for the government here," he told me.

"To be fair," Jackson said, "the Depp-like dude was not really an Indian, I don't think."

"Shit. The grandpa just fathered a child at eighty. He runs three miles every damn day and still works for the government. That man is a god."

Jackson nodded impatiently. "Let's not get excited here, Lyle."

They both looked at me, waiting for me to respond, but I didn't say anything.

"We really need to talk gaming," Lyle said.

He motioned for us to follow him and led us to a foldout table by the far wall of the warehouse, away from the music and crowd. Lyle put a cigarette in his mouth but couldn't get the lighter to work.

"Lyle has some questions for you," Jackson said. "We're beta-testing the game I told you about. There's a mud pit we're using. Lyle can explain it better than I can."

"A mud pit," I said.

Lyle kept flicking the lighter until he finally got his cigarette lit. He exhaled a stream of smoke from the side of his mouth and leaned forward. "It's an area near Devil's Bridge," he said. "Do you know where that is?"

"I've only been here a couple of days. How would I know where that is?"

"It's on the outskirts of town. There's a mud pit we want you to see."

"You want me to see a mud pit?"

Lyle nodded, eyeing Jackson.

"We actually need you to get muddy," Jackson said. "We'll take video. We just need you in the pit."

I took a drink from my cup and frowned at them. I couldn't figure out if they were serious or if this was some strange joke at my expense.

"For a football simulation," Lyle added. "We need better footage, like playing in mud and bad weather. You get the idea. It's a mighty good game, friend." He stopped talking to watch a woman walk by. She wore a black leather jacket and blue jeans. Her hair was long and dark and hung down her back. I wasn't able to see her face, but Lyle was staring at her.

"We could all go tomorrow," Jackson said.

I finished off my beer and set the cup down. "This is for the Thorpe game?" I said.

"Yeah, for the Thorpe game," Jackson said. "It's killer."

Lyle laughed. They both laughed.

I told them I needed to find the toilet for a piss and walked away. Fuck it, I thought. Fuck Jackson for bringing me there. I felt paranoid and antisocial and knew I had to get out of that place. I was able to move quietly and unnoticed along the wall to the front door, where I stepped outside into the cool air of the moonlit blue night.

I walked away from the warehouse, following a road heading south to a small field. I thought I recognized the street on the other side of the field from one of my walks. Squeezing my way past a large bush and a wooden fence, I walked down a small slope of grass to the dark field, where I heard things around me creaking in the night. It was still warm enough for bugs, night insects and creepy sounds. I felt the urge to get high then. It came out of nowhere, and suddenly I saw it: the fowl, running toward me with its wings outstretched. I ran. The red fowl chased me as I scrambled through the darkened field toward the main street, breathing heavily without looking back, feeling the soft dirt underneath my feet as I made it to the edge of the street. I saw glimpses of red traffic lights up ahead. I turned around, then, and saw the fowl was gone.

When I finally made it all the way back to Jackson's, I was still trembling from anxiety, and I desperately wanted to get high but I had no more weed. I drank a couple of beers from the fridge and sat in the chair for a while, trying to relax. The urge to leave the Darkening Land made it difficult to calm down. I missed Rae, too. She hadn't called once, which made me feel awful. She wouldn't want to be with me anymore, not with my lying to her about my drug use, but I still hadn't accepted this.

There were too many unanswered questions. I sat on the couch for a while and started to doze. Maybe I fell asleep for a while, but soon enough I heard Jackson come in. He was a little drunk, I could tell, and asked me why I left so suddenly.

"I fell asleep, I guess," I said.

"But why'd you take off?" he asked again. "Lyle was annoyed. We looked everywhere for you."

"Too many people there for me. You know me. The place was crowded."

He staggered into the kitchen and opened the fridge. He took something out, unwrapped it, and heated it up in the microwave. He sat in the kitchen and ate.

"I should go to bed," I said.

"Wait a minute," he said, turning to me. His words were slurred a little. "Let me show you something new I've been working on for the Jim Thorpe image on the projector downstairs. The hologram."

I agreed, though somewhat reluctantly, and followed him downstairs to the basement. He turned on the light, and the air felt warm and heavy. There was a stepladder. He pointed above it, and I saw a gray device that resembled a projector installed in the ceiling. "This is it," he said. He stepped on the ladder and reached up to the device. He was a little wobbly, drunk, and I worried he might fall.

"Maybe we should do this tomorrow," I said.

"It connects to the Wi-Fi," he said, ignoring me, "but it's a little spotty most of the time. The light from here projects to the screen on the floor and then bounces to the Mylar screen on the wall over there. All of it creates a hologram that looks very fucking real." He turned and barely kept his balance, drunk. "You'll see in a minute."

I watched him work. His face twisted as he tried to focus. He powered up the device, and blue lights blinked around it. "Here, yeah, you'll see an image of Jim Thorpe in a minute," he said.

The projector began clicking, and a moment later a robotic voice spoke: "I am the Indy Ann," the computerized voice said. "Shoot the Indy Anns."

The light on the device blinked, and I saw a blue light project from it. In front of us, a cloud was forming into something human-shaped. The image that slowly appeared in front of us was not Jim Thorpe, but a hologram of an Indian man in full head-dress, with feathers, standing before us. I stood up. He was maybe six feet tall, with his arms at his sides. His body was in focus, but his face remained a little bit blurry. There was a cool tint to his body, as if he were standing under a blue lightbulb.

I lost all awareness of my surroundings, if only for a moment, lost my interest in the image and the technology and in Jackson, consumed as I was by the reflection of blue light, but the moment reasserted itself and almost immediately I felt the absurdity in the situation.

"That's not Jim Thorpe."

"Fuggin' glitch," he said. "Must be a damn glitch in the software. I need to get in there and screw with it."

"Glitch? It's a man in a headdress."

I watched the image of the man flicker while Jackson, still up on the ladder, looked inside the machine. He picked up a tiny microphone and spoke into it: "Testing, testing," he said.

Slowly, the apparition began approaching us. He didn't so much walk as he glided slowly toward me. I couldn't believe what I was seeing. When he reached me, I could hear a ticking sound coming from his head. The expression on his face was horrific, a cry for help.

"Testing," Jackson said into the tiny mic again.

The apparition said, "I am the savage. Shoot the savage." Then it froze, staring out into the distance. I realized it had paused, fallen into sleep mode, unresponsive and still.

"Shit, shit, shit," Jackson said. He had the projector's lid open and was leaned way over, trying to rewire or repair whatever was wrong with it. "Give me a minute," he said. "Is it still the same image?"

"What the fuck is going on?" I said.

"Trying to get the Jim Thorpe image to appear. This was a model, a stock image. Shouldn't be there. Please ignore."

I watched him bite his lip, concentrating. The image of the unblinking Native man kept flickering in front of me, eyes wide open. Finally Jackson clicked it off, and the image disappeared.

"Thing's gone apeshit," Jackson said, wobbling as he climbed down the ladder. He slumped down in the chair. "Voice activation is damn hard. There are speech patterns. Fuggin' glitch."

"This isn't for the sports game," I said. "It wasn't Jim Thorpe. What's going on?"

"Shit."

"Tell me the truth, Jackson."

He stared into the floor, drunk.

"Seems like this is a different game about Indians," I said. "Is this what you were filming me for?"

Jackson didn't say anything. He wouldn't look at me.

"What's going on?" I said.

"I didn't want you to know."

"Why not?"

"It's nothing, just a harmless game. I don't even want to talk about it. Let's head back upstairs, I need to get to bed."

Jackson stumbled a little and steadied himself as he trudged slowly up the stairs, not seeming to care that I wasn't following him. I stood for a moment, reeling from what I had just seen. Then, not really knowing what I was looking for, I started going through Jackson's belongings to see what I could find. I opened the cabinets. There were papers, receipts, notes with scribblings. I shuffled through them. I wasn't sure what I was looking for. Next to the ladder I found a game manual:

SAVAGE

— Ready for Beta-Test IMMEDIATELY! —

PLAYER GOALS: Determine whether the savage Indians are real or holograms by interaction. Capture and torture. Shoot to kill.

SPECIFICS: Single- or multiplayer. First-person shooter. Ages 10 and up. Players may purchase game weapons from local dealers in DL (DT's Gun Supply; Conway's House of Guns and Ammo; Gunz R Us; etc.). Please register code tracking # for game.

LOCATION: Darkening Land city limits is approximately 1,970 feet (600 m) below sea level (located at 35.20388S, 97.17735E)

GAME OBJECTIVE: Players take on the role of police officers, special agents, soldiers, or assassins who are fighting a local threat of a savage (SAV) invasion. Weapons can be mounted on steady surfaces for shooting, but fewer points are collected. Players shoot Savages.

RED HELMET BONUS: Players earn red helmets for information gained from SAV, so in order to reach the Reward Tier, player must earn ten (10) red helmets. Red helmets can be traded in for experience points.

TORTURE BONUS: Players can place SAV in the Torturous Radioactive Mud Pit (TRMP), located approximately 69 km south of Devil's Bridge, where they can question SAV and gain information and points before destroying SAV by slow radioactive torture in the mud pit. The radioactive mud creates a slow memory loss (based on historical records of deaths near Devil's Bridge); therefore, the more torture a player uses, the less information is gained. TRMP is the worst of possible tortures for SAV and is used as a strategic gameplay for long-term players because it earns them red helmets.

REWARD TIER: Experience points are saved in system to encourage long-term gameplay and can be redeemed for a Missile Launcher Fighter (MLF) or Petroleum Fuel Freeway Fighter (PFFF) in case of rare SAV escapes from TRMP. *Note: PFFF redeemers be aware that PFFF/MLF trades are not accepted because MLFs are in much higher demand and take more experience points to redeem. **Once a player collects three (3) different MLFs, player then has opportunity to enter the Jewel Zone (JZ) and purchase Native jewelry stolen from SAVs suffering in TRMP.

COMMUNITY RULES: Never share personal information with other players or SAVs, even when SAVs are in TRMP, unless you are redeeming red helmets for PFFFs or MLFs through Andrews, Jackson Media Inc. Cheating, Impersonators, and Trollers: See TRMP. We at Andrews, Jackson Media want you to be careful and have fun.

I tore the guide to shreds, then climbed the ladder and looked up at the projector. I touched it, felt for buttons until I heard it power up. The lens lit, and I climbed back down, waiting for the image of the Indian to appear. The screen was hazy at first, but after a minute the hologram showed a child, a boy with dark bushy hair, sitting cross-legged, resting his elbows on his knees and his chin in his hands. I moved closer. The image remained still until I knelt down in front of him. He looked at me, and I recognized the face.

"Ray-Ray," I said quietly.

He blinked slowly, giving me a curious look. His eyes were dark and piercing. His eyes held a complicated gaze, as though I was staring into his spirit. The structure of his face, his hair and body — it appeared just as it did in photographs of Ray-Ray at home. My own memories had grown hazy by this point, I realized. Quickly I stood and moved away, nervous. What was I afraid of? Maybe it was the haunting silence of the late night, or the thought that something could look so much like my brother and yet be a blatant fabrication. The urge to recoil gave me a dizzy feeling that almost made me ill.

"Talk to me," I whispered. "Say something."

I coughed into my hands, waiting, but he kept staring at me. I moved closer to him. I held up my hand, and he looked at it. I waved, and he waved back.

"Hello," I whispered.

I saw his mouth move, but no sound came.

"Ray-Ray," I whispered again, and he kept forming his mouth as if trying to speak. I couldn't hear anything. I reached to touch his arm, but when my hand touched the image, it burned badly, and I quickly withdrew it. I held my hand, grunting in pain. Ray-Ray was an image, nothing more. A hologram. A hallucination, a mirage.

Finally, he spoke: "Brother," he said softly.

My heart was racing. What did it mean? Did he recognize me? Was his spirit somehow present in the projection, or was it programmed?

His eyes looked upward, and he evidently fell into sleep mode. He sat frozen, not moving. I climbed the ladder and pushed every button I could reach, anything to get a reaction. Then I saw the image of Ray-Ray looking up at me as he slowly dissolved into nothingness.

MARIA

A cool morning in fall and perfect weather
for an outing, our first in a long while. It
was a teacher conference day, and there was
no school. Wyatt told us he had never seen
exotic fish or sharks, so we decided to take
him to Jenks, near Tulsa, to the big aquarium. While I drove, Ernest engaged in a long
conversation with Wyatt about old-time
music and various dances: the Charleston,
the fox-trot, the waltz. Wyatt pulled out one
of his meticulously organized notebooks and
read from an alphabetized list of his favorite
old standards: "All of Me," "Have You Met
Miss Jones," "In a Sentimental Mood," and
so on, along with a list of musicians by
genre. They talked jazz — Coltrane,
Gillespie, Wyatt naming off little-known
anecdotes he had read in various online
sources. Ernest listened, delighted. "The
boy is a walking encyclopedia," Ernest said

273

to me. "He has class. Not many kids have such good taste these days."

I looked at Wyatt in the rearview mirror and saw him staring out the window at the rolling prairie outside. Ernest was as happy as I had seen him in a long time.

At the Jenks Aquarium, Wyatt scanned the map, wanting to see all the exhibits, every one of them: Sea Turtle Island, the South Pacific Reef, the Ecozone. We entered the Extreme Fishes exhibit, a large, dimly lit room encircled by enormous tanks filled with exotic fish. The room had a magical quietness about it the moment we walked in, as if we were underwater, deep in the ocean. I saw a rainbow of light as the fish darted back and forth behind the glass. Ernest went over to the tank and touched the glass. A blue fish drifted over and stared at him. They were looking at each other, Ernest and the fish. He tapped a finger on the glass, but the fish wasn't frightened.

"This fish is giving me the stink eye," he said, winking at Wyatt.

"Must be a female," I said.

"She's jealous of a fish," Ernest told Wyatt.

For a moment I felt envious. Oh, to be so happy. How did this work again? I was in control of my own emotions, my own needs, and everything felt stable again. I recognized what made me happy or sad. Seeing Ernest like this made me feel elated.

Another family had entered the room, and I noticed that Wyatt had made friends with a baby in a stroller. The baby's siblings, an older brother and sister, were with their father, looking excitedly into the glass at a yellow fish. The baby was wearing a pink outfit and a bow in her hair. Wyatt was making her laugh. I heard him make little baby sounds. The mother smiled politely, then strolled away to join the rest of her family. I walked over to Wyatt.

"What about the fish?" I asked him.

"They're fantastic. But babies? Babies are my jam."

He joined Ernest at the glass, and we continued to walk down alongside it, looking at the vast underwater world. My phone rang, and I stepped away to answer. It was Bernice from Indian Child Welfare.

"How's everything going with Wyatt?" she asked. "Is he behaving himself?"

"He's an angel," I said. "Can we keep him?"

"Well, the hearing is tomorrow. It looks like he'll end up going to stay with grandparents."

"That didn't take long," I said.

"Sometimes it doesn't. The school said

he's doing well, as I expected. He really is a doll, but his grandparents are here in town, and they want to take him. The hearing is at ten in the morning."

I watched Wyatt lean in to Ernest. From behind, they looked like grandfather and grandson. "I don't want him to go," I breathed into the phone. "We want him to stay with us. Is that even possible?"

"Oh, Maria," Bernice said. "Are you serious? Is everything okay?"

They were leaning into the glass with both hands, staring at the fish, and standing there watching them, my heart broke thinking this could be their last day together.

"Maria?" Bernice kept saying.

The drive home was silent, and I didn't want to bring up the hearing to Ernest and Wyatt. As I drove, I tried to imagine Wyatt's reaction to the news that he would be leaving us. Would he be sad, or would he be relieved? How would Ernest take it? I didn't want to think about it. When we arrived home, Sonja was in the kitchen, stirring blackberries in a saucepan. She turned and looked at Wyatt and said hello, smiling.

Wyatt removed an invisible hat and bowed, which made Ernest laugh loudly.

"He can do impersonations," Ernest told Sonja. "Do you want to hear him do a

Frenchman?"

Sonja looked confused.

"Maybe later," I told them. "Why don't you two go in the other room and let me talk to Sonja."

Wyatt bowed again and turned, heading into the living room, Ernest following him.

"He's cute," Sonja said.

"Very cute."

"I've been texting Edgar," she said, her voice low and serious.

"Is he coming?"

"I don't know. He won't reply."

"Not at all?"

She set the mixing spoon down and leaned against the counter. She took a deep breath. "I don't know. Something tells me he'll show, though. I have other things to think about."

"Like what?" I asked.

"Nothing, it doesn't matter."

We were silent a moment, and I waited for her to open up, but she didn't. She turned and went back to stirring the blackberries, so I went into my bedroom and gathered the laundry. I took it into the basement and started a load of laundry. When I returned to the kitchen, Sonja had left.

After lunch, Ernest and I watched a crime

drama we had recorded on the VCR. Sonja had said many times that we were the only people on the planet who still watched videotapes on a VCR, but it was easy enough for us to operate, and we liked watching TV.

"Tomorrow is Wyatt's hearing," I told Ernest.

Ernest was eating peanuts from a small bowl on the TV tray. "Already?"

"He's gone," the TV said. "He's dead."

Ernest looked at me, waiting for a response.

"We're a temporary placement, remember?" I said. On TV, two police officers sat in a squad car, talking. One of the police officers was shaking his head, disappointed.

"The timing of it all," I said. "Think of the timing. Tomorrow is the hearing. It's also the sixth, the day of our bonfire."

"The timing," Ernest said, setting his fork down on his plate. He leaned back in his chair and watched TV. We sat in silence for a few minutes, then I pointed the remote at the TV and turned it off. We were both still staring at the screen even though the TV was off.

"I want to put on my sneakers and go for a run," Ernest said.

"A run? What are you talking about, a run?"

"What do you think? A run. A jog. To go out into the night and jog down to the lake and back, like I used to. I haven't done that in a long time."

"Nobody's going for a run right now," I said.

He looked at his hands and made a fist, cracked his knuckles. He rubbed at his knees. A moment later Wyatt entered the room quietly. It almost startled me.

"Do you want to watch home videotapes?" he asked. "Old home movies?"

Ernest and I both looked at him. I knew I should tell him about the hearing, but I couldn't bring myself to say it just yet. "Well," I said. "We don't watch them often, but we could if you want to."

"Play the one with Edgar following Ray-Ray in the parade," Ernest said. "It's the one with the bicycle."

I didn't want to watch home movies. Ernest could tell but he wouldn't let it go.

"It's just a videotape," he said.

I dug through a cabinet where we kept all our old videotapes. I found one labeled KIDS PLAYING/BIRTHDAYS but didn't know the year or what was on it. I put it in the VCR and pushed play, then left Wyatt and Ernest on the couch. I stepped into the kitchen and poured a glass of water. For a moment I stood at the window. I could see my reflection in the door of the microwave, my face unrecognizable, blurred. My hair was pinned up, but it looked strange in the reflection, as if some stranger was staring back at me. Some faceless presence watching me.

I knew what they were watching, but I couldn't bring myself to watch it. The tape was old, full of static. A tape of Ray-Ray at his birthday party. Edgar kicking a soccer ball in the backyard. Sonja riding her bicycle, ringing the bicycle bell. A vacation camping trip to the Southwest.

"I don't recognize my voice," I heard Ernest say from the living room. "Is that my voice?" I heard Wyatt laughing.

I sat at the dining room table for a while, thinking about Edgar. I imagined him packing a bag to come home, boarding a bus for Oklahoma. Tomorrow morning, maybe, he would call and ask me to pick him up at the bus station. Or he would show up at the house, without a knock on the front door, just letting himself in the way he used to, with a smile on his face, and asking me to make him something to eat. Yes, I wanted to cook for him again, bring him a plate of spaghetti or a bowl of soup and sit across from him and watch him eat. He would tell me about his friends, everything he did during his day at work. Maybe I would ask him about a girl he liked, or if he was going to tuck his shirt in. He was always easy to embarrass. I pictured him laughing into his glass as he took a drink the way he used to.

When I heard the tape end, I returned to the living room. Ernest and Wyatt seemed somehow more approachable, at least in this instance, maybe because they seemed so happy. I didn't want to disrupt their contentment, but I had to bring up the hearing, and this was as good a time as any. So I told him. "Wyatt," I said, "earlier today Bernice mentioned you would likely go stay with your grandparents."

I didn't understand the impact of what I said at first. His entire demeanor fell as he looked down, nodding. It was the saddest I had seen him.

"Do you want to go live with them?" I asked.

"I guess so," he said.

"We wish you could stay here."

He looked at me, and I felt as though his eyes reflected the pain of my words.

"I have a story to tell you," I said to him. "Once there was a girl named Maria who met a Cherokee boy. The boy was very poor, and he was also embarrassed of his speech because he stuttered, but the girl still thought he was quite handsome. Her mother and stepfather were afraid he wouldn't provide a good life for her, so he set out to prove them wrong."

"Ernest had a speech impediment?" he asked.

"I stuttered like a goddamn fool," Ernest said.

I said, "And my life was hard when I was little. I had a stepfather who wasn't very nice. My father had passed and my mother remarried an older man when I was a teenager. My sisters and I didn't like him. He wasn't nice to us, and he certainly wasn't nice to my mother. But what I want to tell you is that I met Ernest when I thought things would never get better. I met Ernest and saw that boys could be nice, and the more I got to know him, the more I saw how caring he was."

"Things can always get better," Ernest said.

Wyatt smiled and thanked me for the story. "I better go to my room and pack up the records," he said.

While he was in his room, I tried to talk to Ernest about the hearing, but he fell silent. His manner had changed, too. "Ernest," I said, "you have to remember, this was a temporary foster placement."

His hands were trembling. Something was wrong with him, which frightened me. I could see it in his face. The day had turned. He went into the kitchen, and I heard the water come on. A moment later the back door opened, and he walked out alone to the deck. I knew he didn't want to talk about it. This wonderful boy, so much like Ray-Ray, had come into our lives. And tomorrow he would be leaving as unexpectedly as Ray-Ray had left us. No more impersonations. No more jokes or singing or talk of happy music from the Golden Age. Funny how quickly things change, I thought, then felt guilty for trying to let go so easily. He was still a boy. He was still a boy without a home. Maybe I should try to fight for him to stay with us, I thought.

Before dinner, Wyatt came into the living room with one final request: to give the shelter kids one last, special storytelling time. "I may never see some of them again," he told me. "We'll lie down in the grass behind the shelter and stare at the stars tonight. We'll gaze up at the sky like it's our last night alive. Sound good? One last story time?"

I could see how important it was to him,

so I called Bernice, who called the shelter, and they all decided that as long as I accompanied them as chaperone, it would be fine. Wyatt was pleased to hear it. When I asked Ernest if he would like to go along, he shook his head.

"It's Wyatt's last night with us," I said. "It might mean a lot to him for you to go."

But he wouldn't budge. He was stubborn like that. I could tell him to be more considerate of others' feelings, but that would lead to worse things, like him losing his temper and walking out of the house, which had happened before. So I let him sit there by himself on the deck.

"Fine," I said. "You can stay, but we're going to the shelter for Wyatt's story time. It's important to him, and I want his last night with us to be special. If we stop for ice cream, I'll bring you back a scoop of chocolate in a cone."

"Rocky Road," he said.

"Rocky Road."

Wyatt was fine with Ernest staying there. In the car, on the drive to the shelter, I told him he was a wonderful storyteller and that all the shelter kids would miss him.

"It's about fulfilling my purpose," he said.

"And what purpose is that?" I asked.

"The purpose to be a storyteller. To help

people."

"You've got it all figured out, kiddo. How did you figure out so much so young?"

"I learned to trust my instinct," he said calmly.

When we arrived at the shelter, by the time I checked in with the staff and signed everyone out on the chart, Wyatt had gathered an entire troop of residents to join him outside on this warm night, under the trees in the backyard of the shelter. They lay on their backs with their hands behind their heads, sprawled across the dark grass, yawning under the blue glow of the moonlight. There were few clouds in the sky. Once everyone fell quiet, we could all hear crickets and cicadas all around us.

I watched from nearby, texting Bernice: They're like a pack of little wolves. It's a quiet, starry night, perfect for storytelling.

"What are our chances of survival?" a boy named Lewis asked.

"I'd say it's ninety-eight, ninety-nine percent," Wyatt said.

"Not a hundred?"

"It's never a hundred for anyone. But think about it. We're on the outskirts of town, away from businesses, right next to the woods. There's critters out here. The area's open and clear, with a big sky full of

285

stars. Look at that open sky up there, all that space and expansive darkness."

"Those sound like decent odds," another one spoke up. "Will it be on the ten o'clock news?"

"Who knows? Just close your eyes."

The night lingered on. The wind picked up, rustling the trees all around us. After a moment all the kids stood and gathered around the monkey bars, sat on the swing set and the merry-go-round. Wyatt began his story:

There was an orphan boy from far away, and he was very afraid. They brought him and put him in our room, where he slept for a long time. He was younger than the rest of us, and much sadder. When he awoke, night had fallen and we were in darkness. The room was cold. The only light we had was a small lamp. Every night it was turned on when they brought us dinner. The light flickered and threw our shadows against the wall, which looked like images of the crucifixion. Most nights the older boys whispered prayers in a language we didn't know. Upon waking, almost immediately the young boy began to cry.

The older boys grew angry. "Stop it," one

of them said. "They'll kill you!"

"They'll cut out your tongue," another told him. "Do you want to die?"

But he wouldn't be quiet. He kept moaning and crying until they came downstairs and opened the door and looked at him. They looked around the room at the rest of us, rubbing their fat bellies like devils.

They were all silent, waiting for Wyatt to continue.

"It's weird," a girl said.

I watched him speaking, a half-grin on his face. I watched his mannerisms, the way he gestured as he talked. I saw Wyatt looking at me, then, and I knew this look was it. This look, so familiar.

He put a finger to his lips for everyone to be quiet. He cocked his head to one side, as if he were trying to listen to something from far away, but everyone looked confused. Then he jogged over to me and asked, "Can I please take the others into the woods for a minute? I need to check on something. We'll be right back, I promise. Just wait here."

I hesitated, but something in his voice made me agree. "Be careful and come right back," I called out as he motioned for the other kids to follow him. "All of you."

What was happening now? The boy had

something planned. I took out my phone from my purse and saw a text from my sister, Irene: Ray-Ray's spirit is strong today, sister. Earlier I saw a vision of the mountains and remembered how much he loved the stories of the Tunwi Tsunsdi.

I texted back: You sense his spirit today?

I sense it right now, she wrote. It's as if he's near me.

Before I realized it, I looked up from my phone to see smoke rising in the distance — a fire had started somewhere in the woods. Smoke was streaming from the trees, visible even in the darkness, and I began to panic. I rushed toward the woods, yelling Wyatt's name. They must have walked directly into the fire, which scared me so badly I felt my chest ache. Frantic, I called out to them but heard no response — they had disappeared into the woods. And now guilt came over me suddenly: What had I done, letting them walk into the woods alone? I pulled out my phone to dial 911, my heart racing. Flames jumped, burning fiercely now, the smoke billowing larger. Ashes were falling from the sky. I heard voices crying out in the distance.

Suddenly they emerged, each of them, like ghosts in the night, running out of the trees together, holding something white above their heads. A white owl with glowing eyes in the night. I couldn't make sense of what I was seeing — was the owl attacking them? But then I heard their laughter. They were having fun. And what of this owl? It perched high in all the kids' hands, this owl rescued from the flames, which was exactly what the kids were calling out for me to hear: *We rescued the owl! The baby owl! See it? It's alive!*

They ran in a cluster, with Wyatt leading the group, in the dark night, under the moonlight. I heard the fire engine sirens in the distance now, the smoke billowing heavier from the woods. The kids stumbled to a halt, turning back to look at the flames, yelling and talking over one another excitedly. A small girl was holding the owl now, and I saw the owl begin to rustle, eyes glowing. Then the owl outstretched its wings and flew away, soaring away from the woods, the kids cheering.

"Rescuers!" they chanted to each other. "Long live the owl! We saved the owl!"

They were elated as they walked back to the shelter, checking their hands for scratches from the talons. I followed behind them, trying to catch my breath, my heart still racing. Firefighters were swarming to the woods, the flames slowly subsiding.

Smoke was everywhere. We made our way back inside the shelter, where the kids were still reeling from all the excitement. They talked excitedly about the owl and the fire, all of them still breathing heavily.

We gathered in the commons room, and the staff was able to settle everyone down. A counselor served cookies and lemonade. Soon the fire chief told us that the fire had been started by someone burning trash and had gotten out of control from the wind. Firefighters were able to put it out quickly before it spread. A few of the kids were bleeding a little on their hands and needed Neosporin and bandages, but they all claimed they didn't feel any pain. One boy, Nicholas, had a deep scratch on his right thumb, which he said didn't even sting.

"It's all adrenaline," one of the shelter volunteers said. "The rush, the endorphins."

"Speak English," one of the boys said.

"Calm down."

Another boy: "Don't you understand something majestic has happened here? We saved a baby owl. We found its nest in the woods, and the baby owl wasn't moving! It was too scared, and we rescued it."

"Everyone take it easy. Everything is fine."

"Nobody is hurt! The owl would've died if we hadn't rescued it. The fire was pushing it out. It was magic. It was all thanks to our leader, Wyatt."

Wyatt didn't look nearly as excited as the others. I sensed something was wrong, so I took a seat next to him on the couch and put my arm around him. "Are you okay?" I asked. "What a night. What made you want to rescue the owl?"

But he didn't respond. His silence was an answer I came to understand. He was leaving the next day after the hearing, and everything would be different.

SONJA

September 5

I shut myself in my bedroom all morning. This was not so much out of fear as out of a desire to remove myself from the noises, at least for a while. I took off my clothes and lay in bed, trying to read Colette. I was too nervous to sleep. When I was thirsty, I stepped into the kitchen for water. I sliced a lemon with a knife, then put the wedges into the glass of water. I chopped carrots and broccoli and put them on a plate. Vin must've heard my footsteps, because he started yelling again while I was in the kitchen. I took the knife with me back to the bedroom. I checked my phone for any messages.

Outside it started to lightly rain. I turned my phone off. I tried not to think about anything, but I found myself thinking about the bonfire, and whether Edgar would come home. I imagined us sitting around the fire with Edgar. I looked forward to telling him how much I missed his sense of humor, hearing him laugh, even how he would knock on the door at three in the morning, wanting to talk about nothing in particular. In bed, my body felt cool under the sheets. I imagined walking downstairs to see Vin and giving in to the pleasures of cruelty, watching him weep and huddle in the corner. It was merely a thought, nothing more, and I allowed myself to enjoy it.

A heavy silence fell throughout the house. Would he start shouting again? Breaking and throwing things? I looked out my front window at his car. Farther away, I could see the yellow sky and rain clouds, past Indian Hill Road and beyond the bridge, where chimney smoke from houses drifted in the wind like ghosts. I could see the bait and tackle shop in the distance, and how abandoned and empty it looked. The day was very calm, like looking at the face of a sleeping lover.

Vin's phone was ringing again, but I ignored it. I heard a dragging noise from the basement, as if he were moving a mattress around down there. I powered up my phone and walked throughout the house, turning all the lights on. There was nothing to be afraid of, I told myself. I was defending myself from him. But still I was starting to panic. I felt a slow, creeping fear connected directly to Vin, though it also flowed deeper. Papa had always told me to confront fear, so I did just that. What kind of person was I, to keep him downstairs? He had hit me, but that didn't give me a reason to keep him hostage, did it? I began to think about what I had done. Questions came to mind about what was legal and what was beyond self-defense, especially after so much time had passed. I started to feel paranoid. Maybe I would go to jail for this. Was it morally wrong to protect myself from harm? Was I still protecting myself? For a while my thoughts raced back and forth between what was moral and immoral, which made me feel pressured about what I should do next. No matter what I thought, nothing made me feel any better about the situation.

Slowly I retreated back to my bedroom and searched for a Valium, a Xanax, an edible, anything. I started reading again, looking up at the hallway every now and then. Someday I wanted to be the type of woman who could read in solitude while my lover worked outside, coming into the house to ask for my help. The type of woman whose lover waited patiently while she raised a finger and finished reading. My ideal lover was a person of patience and fortitude, which Vin was not.

Soon his phone was ringing again. The battery had not run down completely. He must've heard it ringing down there, because he started yelling again: "Hey, let me out of here, you crazy bitch!" I took his phone from the kitchen into my bedroom and closed the door. When I answered, I heard Luka's voice, sweet little Luka, crying on the phone. "Are you coming home, Dad? Where are you? Are you coming to get me?" He was crying really hard, and I couldn't bear listening to it. His crying absolutely broke my heart.

"Luka," I said. "Luka, settle down. This is Colette, your dad's friend."

"I'm at my aunt's house," he said, and I felt overwhelmed with sadness. He kept asking where his dad was, near hysterics, and I had to work to get him to hear me. "Luka," I was saying over and over. "Luka, your dad will be there soon. Your dad's coming to get you, Luka, okay?" By then I was near tears myself, very upset. I felt confused, trying to sound like a mother calming her son. A mother, this is what I told myself to sound like. Show empathy, understanding. Comfort him the way a mother would.

When I hung up the phone, I felt my heart racing. I thought of poor Luka, sweet Luka. Why should he suffer for his father's weaknesses? Overcome with guilt, I told myself I should let Vin go to him. Luka needed a dad right now. Depriving him of that only made me feel worse. So I grabbed a can of Mace, which I kept by my bed in case I ever needed it.

I stood in the hallway for a moment. I thought about my intentions with Vin. I wanted him to see me as a strong woman, not someone he could take advantage of. Not someone he could slap in the face. He needed to understand this, and I would make sure of that. I was an older woman, more experienced, one who held grudges. I was an angry woman who never learned to forgive. I sought revenge when I needed to. I'd learned to take up for myself.

When I knocked on the door, Vin didn't respond. I called his name. I unlocked the door, opened it slowly, and saw him sitting cross-legged on the floor at the bottom of the stairs. A few empty water bottles were scattered on the floor. The blanket was balled up in the corner. When he realized the door was open, he struggled to sit up. I didn't enter the room, but stood there waiting for him to speak. He managed to stand up. "Are you a fucking lunatic?" he said. "Why did you lock the door?"

Something flashed in my mind as I glared at him. He was of some other presence. Maybe he could've killed me. Maybe I could've killed him. But I saw where that anger would lead me: a place in which Luka had no dad, a new pain that would not resolve an old pain.

"Do you remember hitting me last night?" I asked him.

He looked down at his hand, and I wondered if he felt remorseful. He was shaking his head in disbelief. I hadn't thought he could ever be capable of being so cruel, but now I knew, and I needed to let him know. I felt as though I were staring into the face of a different man, someone I had never seen before. He seemed fatigued, unkempt, pitiful, like someone who had been through hell, through turmoil, and realizing this, if only briefly, gave me a sense of satisfaction.

"I'm bleeding," he said, compliant and not defensive. "My hand is bleeding."

"Fuck you."

He wiggled his fingers, and I saw a little bit of blood on his knuckles.

"Do you remember that your cop dad shot a teenage boy?" I said. "It was fifteen years ago. Do you remember that?"

He looked up at me, trying not to blink. He was like a weak soldier, and I was like a spirit before him, full of rage for what he had done.

"What does that have to do with anything?"

"That boy was my brother, Ray-Ray. The boy your dad shot and killed. That was my brother who got shot."

"My dad shot your brother," he said, as if he was thinking aloud.

"Your stupid racist dad shot and killed my brother." I could hear my voice go weak.

"I'm bleeding," he said again. He kept wiggling his fingers.

"Christ, Vin, you make me sick. You deserve to bleed. You deserve to suffer for the murder your dad committed."

He looked serious, but I couldn't tell what he was thinking. "Look, I'm sorry," he said. "I didn't know he did that. There must be some kind of explanation. My dad's not a killer. He was a police officer, there were some messy cases over the years. Lots of people died."

"Please."

"I don't know everything he did at his job. I was a little kid back then."

"Fuck you."

He panicked. "Hey, I really didn't know.

298

Why are you bringing this up? Have you just been waiting to confront me about this?"

"My God, Vin, he got away with murder!" I told him. "Your dad should've been tried. He saw an Indian kid and just shot at him. Ray-Ray never even owned a BB gun, much less a real gun. Some other dude was the shooter, not Ray-Ray. There was no trial. It feels like a cruel joke on my family."

He ran his hands over his face, then clenched his jaw. His hands were fists. I saw a vein bulging in his neck. "Settle down, Sonja," he said. "My dad's got lung cancer. He's on chemo. He's weak and dying."

"It feels like a cruel joke," I said again. "The pain we went through. Every single person in my family is still fucked up. My dad's tried his best to keep us together, but he has Alzheimer's and can't even recognize us sometimes. My brother is an addict, and my mother has been depressed for years because of this. Where could we find justice? Can you tell me that?"

He shook his head.

I didn't say anything more, nothing. I set his phone on the floor and left, leaving the door open, then headed outside and began walking down the road toward my parents' house. A moment later I turned and saw him walking to his car. He started the engine and pulled away.

In the end, whatever I thought didn't matter. Calvin Hoff was old, and someday soon he would be eaten by cancer and die. That was the only justice I could hope for.

For the rest of the afternoon I thought of Luka. If I could've snatched him up from Vin, I would have. He would've been safer with me anyway. He would love living with me. I would push him on a swing and see the rush of wind in his hair and eyes as he looked at me. I would take him shopping for clothes and to get haircuts at the barbershop downtown. I would take him swimming, like I used to take Ray-Ray.

Thinking of Ray-Ray reminded me that I needed to visit his grave before the bonfire, so late in the day I rode my bicycle to the cemetery. It was a long ride, and my legs were tired from riding uphill. I felt a sense of density when I got there, as though the air had left my body. As I walked my bike toward Ray-Ray's grave, I saw a young girl reaching down to pick up rocks beside the road. She was alone, talking to herself, I think, though I couldn't hear exactly what she was saying. She wore a white dress and a long necklace. Her hair was long and dark and hung loose to her waist. I walked toward her to see her better. She was classically lovely, with sharp cheekbones and contemplative lips. When she looked up, she stood and smiled.

"I'm picking up rocks," she said, and laughed.

"Who are you with?" I asked. "Is your mother around?"

She held the rocks out in her hand, ignoring me. "They're jewels," she said. "Look at them, they're all around us. Do you see how pretty they are?"

"Pretty," I said, glancing at them. "But are you with your mother or dad?"

"I'm here to see my sister who died on the Trail."

"Your sister on the Trail?" I said. "Do you mean your ancestor?"

"No, it's my sister. My name's Clara."

"Where's your mom?"

"She's over there," she said, pointing, but when I turned I couldn't see anyone.

"Look at these," she said, holding out the rocks again. She ran a finger over them in her palm. They were sparkling in the sunset. I knelt down to get a better look, but she turned and ran away from me. I considered following her, but then I noticed a woman at the end of the road. She was an older woman, wearing a red coat.

"Is she with you?" I called out. "I was worried she was alone."

"Thank you," the woman called back.

Clara ran to her, grasped her by the hand, and the two walked away together.

I walked on to Ray-Ray's grave, and on the path I saw a man up ahead wearing a wolf mask with feather trimmings. Beside him was a woman and child. "We finished the Snake-Mask Dance," the man called out to me. His wife and daughter were waving. The little girl pointed to the sky and shouted at me to look up. Papa had told me the tale about the seven dancing boys who turned into stars, and when I looked up to the graying sky, I saw them dancing, even in the daylight.

"The seven dancing boys," I called out, but when I looked back at the people, they were gone. I continued walking down the path, looking around. They had disappeared so quickly. I remembered Papa once saying all cemeteries are connected, and a wave of sadness passed through me as I thought about how many bodies were underground. Death was all around me.

Mosquitoes and insects buzzed in the air, which was humid and warm. The cemetery was colorless and grim, as all cemeteries felt, with the smell of rotting wood and damp grass. When I reached Ray-Ray's grave, I saw his name engraved on the gray stone. The stone still looked new, after all these years. The engraving was so prominent. I reached down and touched it, ran my fingers over the letters of his name.

As I looked down, underneath the earth I saw him, my brother Ray-Ray, lying on his back. I saw his mangled body, his corpse. His face was disfigured, unrecognizable and without eyes. I was stricken by the horror of the image, my dead brother looking so different. It filled me with anguish, seeing such an unhinged and cryptic apparition. But how different, too, I must've appeared to him — or had he watched me grow? Had he in fact been watching all along, with our ancestors, disguised as an animal or bird?

Only then did I begin to see his beauty blossoming. Death opened like a cave into his body, a passage to somewhere; and I entered it, collapsing into him, entering my little brother, and the two of us watched a bird circle in a cloudless pale-blue sky.

TSALA

Resurrection

Beloved: Regarding my death, I do not understand the reason why I awoke when I did. The soldier had taken my life and your life from us, from our family. We were no longer of this world.

I saw only dark red, the color of blood. In death, as we slept beneath the earth with the worms and the cold mud and rocks, hearing the soulful howl of the coyotes and the drumming of our people, as we slept beneath the feet of those who stomped the ground and shook the heavens, I felt your mother's aching.

I felt her suffering as if it were my own, a suffering so great I felt my spirit move restlessly in an unfathomable darkness. How long was I dead? Surely not long!

I crawled out of the earth like a beast in the night, with necklaces made of bear claws and gold, with wet mud and worms matted to my hair, which hung to my chest. I crawled out of the grave and felt as strong and mighty as a horse, even though I knew I had died. I remembered the story of the tribe of root eaters and acorn eaters whose wives were buried in the same grave as their husbands, and I feared I would look down into the grave and see my wife. In the old story of the root and acorn eaters, a lighted pine knot was placed in a wife's hand, a rope was tied around her body with a bundle of pine knots, and she was lowered into her husband's grave, where she would die after the last pine knot was burned. I feared I would find my wife's body in the grave, burned and dead, and the fear consumed me like a great fire.

When I looked down, I was happy to see that the grave was empty.

And here I stood, not of flesh but of spirit, not of bone or skin as I had known. In this world around me I saw a great fire, right there in the same world where I had lived. A great fire spreading across the sky, heavy in flames, flashing and blinding, and I saw animals running to the trees and birds flying in the sky. Soon the birds changed into children and then disappeared into the flames. I saw columns of smoke leading to the heavens. I saw snakes with their heads chopped off; their mouths were still biting. Their bodies slithered into the ground and turned into dust. The dust rose into more columns of smoke. I saw figures in that dust, figures whose faces I did not recognize but whose bodies were strong, who rose up and drifted away as dust. They rose up and drifted as dust, falling into the great fire, and this sight was beyond anything I had ever dreamed. I saw the winged bodies of others forced into a vortex of wind and smoke, disappearing into the great fire. Yet I was not afraid.

I could see for miles. I saw boys from my childhood dragging their dead mother around so that corn would grow. They were wailing in fear. I called out to them, but they couldn't hear me. Most of our people were at stockades, waiting to be moved west. Our people were being forced out of our land, this I knew, but I could not understand why. My thoughts were cloudy and confused as they can be in sleep. I tried to remember my name, but I fell into a strange loss of thought. For what reason did I awake? Why did I see these visions in the night? I saw oxcarts and soldiers with rifles. I heard the crying of children and saw our feeble elders being lifted into government wagons. I saw a flash of light across the sky. A pale mist swirled before me like a small tornado, holding the image of someone I recognized: you, beloved, a strange vision unlike anything I had ever seen before. I wasn't able to speak or call your name, and in an instant you dissolved. Across the land I heard the wailing of someone in pain.

"We are Ani-yun' wiya!" I shouted.

But when I spoke, I heard no language, no sounds of words. Instead I heard from my mouth a tiresome moan. The soldiers must not have heard me, as I was very far away. I shouted again: "Ani-yun' wiya!" and this time again, a weary moan. Nobody seemed to hear me. I became frightened of myself, and for a moment I wondered if I had changed form or identity. As I examined myself, I saw I wore a buckskin, and I could not feel my skin. Clearly, I was a spirit now. I felt the earth beneath my feet, but when I stomped, I heard nothing. I tried to adjust to the elements, breathing deep. I did not hunger or thirst. I cried out in Cherokee like a wounded dog.

I saw myself as a strong, fierce presence. The air sharpened the sting in my eyes, and I knelt down and felt the ground for dirt, which I rubbed together in my hands to create heat. I placed my palms on both eyes, and when I opened them this time, I saw the spirits of those who had died before me, warriors, hundreds of them. I saw their sleek figures and raven-black hair and a thick, swirling dust building behind them. They wielded black and red clubs, the colors of courage and blood. They were watching me from a distance — for what reason I do not know. And I could hear them calling out:

Ayanuli hanigi! Ayanuli hanigi!
Walk fast! Walk fast!

In the distance I saw fires aroused from smoldering coals. I was left alone in the night, alone, near a stream reflecting the quivering moonlight. I approached the water and leaned over to look at my reflection. The image peering back at me in the water was not the face I had during my life, but some hazy figure whose eyes I could not see.

I stood and looked to the sky, where I saw two twinkling lights in the darkness. The stars told me our people were being held at a campsite nearby, and I needed to help them. I heard the howling of a wolf across the stream and saw that the wolf appeared to be in pain, lying on its side. Wading through the stream in shallow water, I felt no bottom to the stream. I crossed the water to the wolf, which howled again in pain, and I could see that the skin on the wolf's neck had been ripped out, exposing blood and bone. I knelt down and placed my hand on the wound, which made the wolf stop howling. Then the wolf stared at me. His eyes held my gaze. He spoke to me through his eyes.

There is a great sadness coming to the people and this land, he said. *Your people are being forced to leave, to move west, and many will suffer and die.*

I did not speak to the wolf, but he knew I did not trust him.

He continued to stare at me: *If you want a sign that I speak the truth, you must first throw me into the water.*

So I lifted the wolf and placed him in the shallow water, and I saw that the wound had healed. Then I stood back, and the wolf came out of the water and shook its body dry.

For this I will protect your family. For this, because you are a spirit, you should know that you can transform yourself into a creature for eternity.

The wolf turned and walked away, and I shouted to him: "Wolf, how do I change my form?"

He turned his head and looked back at me: *Believe you have wings, and you fly. Believe you are an animal, and you roar.*

Believe you are dead in the mud, and you sleep with the worms in the mud. No matter what you decide, provide counsel to your people as they are removed.

Then I followed the trail leading to the campsite on the westward trail. I never tired. I walked and walked. Along the way, I stopped and knelt down to wash my hair in a stream. My reflection was too dark to see, even in moonlight. The water rippled. I cupped my hands with water and drank as I had done in my life. Despite the winter, the water running down my chest and back didn't feel cold.

In the ground I saw horse tracks. I saw footsteps, handprints, all leading toward the mountains, and I knew the soldiers were looking for those hiding in the caves there. I leaned down and smoothed the dirt, erasing the tracks with my hands. I kept smoothing it, and strangely, my back was not in pain as it had once been during my lifetime. Time was unknown to me, and I kept crawling and smoothing dirt for what must've been hours without pain or fatigue. After a while I stood and saw that the sun was on the horizon.

Ahead, I saw the long trail of wagons and horses and our people walking. I saw all the guards, the ones who slept with their ugly mouths open and their white bellies uncovered, their jugs empty, their bodies drunk and freckled and light-haired and stinking with sweat and evil. The migration had begun.

I saw, too, the manifestations of others like me: the roaring bear in the woods; the soulful, howling coyote; the eagle circling in the endless sky; and I knew I was not alone. A satisfaction came over me when I saw these things, and for a moment I felt my anger lift away in the silence of the night. I was calmed by the sounds and visions of the night as I moved forward. I thought of what I taught you, beloved: harmony and peace. Anger is like flooding water, slowly building to destruction.

I looked to the yonder sky, as Dragging Canoe had taught me when I was a child, and I saw visions of the Trail. This was revealed to me, my son: I saw that disease, not exertion, was the enemy to many. Dysentery and vomiting, head colds. There were very few white doctors on the march. The medicine men attended to children and babies who had intestinal cramps. I saw unclean campsites, bowls wiped with rags, sickness spreading rapidly. I saw people sick with tuberculosis and pneumonia. They grew weaker with each hour they walked until they had to ride in the wagons. The hot sun tortured them, especially those not in the wagons. I saw the soldiers make men dig a trench for the garbage so that rats and coyotes and other animals wouldn't congregate near them overnight. Traveling on, they continued the brutal walk, moccasins were worn out and some people went barefoot. I saw mothers struggling to feed their babies when their breasts went dry.

After seeing these visions, in sadness and anger, I flew west along the trail with my people.

And now, beloved son, you emerge like a harsh wind in circular gusts, no longer a messenger but a spirit. You emerge with arms spread, rising into the sky, swooping like an eagle. Listen! This is the end:

As I made my way toward the stockades where our people were being held, I saw the soldiers loading the wagons. They were the ones who had killed us. The ones who had executed you, taken you from me. I was overcome with anger. I moved quietly as I approached them, but I knew they could hear me, knew my sound was threatening, or at least fearful, because one of the guards responded to me.

Listen to that, he said to another.

312

I don't see anything.
But did you hear it?

The second guard never responded. He walked away from the wagon and left the first guard alone. I moved in closer. The guard took a drink from a jug and wiped his face with a rag. For a moment he glanced around to see whether anyone was watching him. Though I wanted to attack him, I knew it was not the right time; still, I moved in his direction out of the darkness until he turned and saw me.

I told him: "Adahnawa asgwali! There is a war going on!"

He seemed confused, then took a step to the side and gripped his rag.

"Your plan is to hurt us," I said, moving forward.

The soldier shook his head, unsure of what was happening. I felt compelled to attack and tear into his body with my hands and kill him instantly. I felt a burst of rage at the sight of him looking back at me.

Beloved: I did nothing.

The soldier looked at me through narrow eyes, and I whispered, "Look around you, soldier!"

He stepped back and spoke the name of his god. When I moved in closer, he turned and ran.

The night filled with the smell of meat cooking, and I thought of the many times I had snared and skinned rabbits for stew, though I did not hunger, even with the strong smell. I remembered chopping wood near this place in the middle of winter. Thinking of my family only angered me more. I stomped the ground. I moved from one wagon to the next, looking for the man who had run from me. There were men's voices, and next I heard a crowd of people, my people, walking up ahead. I saw wagons and soldiers with their guns. I saw women and men, the old and young, all walking. They kept their heads high, this was evident. The night was so dark I don't know how they could see anything in front of them, but the moon glowed in the sky. I looked up to it, knowing my people were looking to it as well. The moon shone like a white flower. The moon, an offering of hope from the Great Spirit, because what else was there to see in such massive darkness?

The nights were freezing. They came to a stream that needed to be passed. The soldiers made one of the men enter to see how deep it was, and as he crossed, he yelled out from the cold as the water reached his chest. He rushed to the other side and fell, hugging himself. Men and women began entering the freezing water, carrying their children over their heads.

The breeze was cool as the night went on, and I followed in anger and sadness. Wagons were pulled by oxen or mules or horses. I walked with the people. I walked beside them until the children began to cry from fatigue. I walked beside them until an elder man fell. Then another fell, followed by many others. Many people were falling behind, trying to help others, but the soldiers yelled at them to keep walking. People were crawling, crying out. You do not want to hear the voices of the ones who were crying out. Their voices linger.

Soon the sun rose, and they were still walking. Aniyosgi ana'i. And I walked along with them, following the children, helping them as I could. It was as if each hour grew cooler than the last, and soon I was no longer aware of how long they had been walking. I looked to the hills and saw, in the morning daylight, that there were over six hundred wagons.

I heard the laughter of soldiers. Laughter! They were careless toward our people. How badly they treated them. I watched it day after day. I heard their laughter over the cries of pain and wondered how their souls could be so corrupt and without empathy.

Where was their sense of humanity?

I thought of the triumphs and struggles our people had experienced in my lifetime, and in my ancestors' lifetimes, all the pain we had endured throughout cold winters. My mind filled with angry thoughts once more, but I could not be consumed by this torment any longer. My rage would not affect them. I knew my people would continue to treat one another with dignity and kindness. These soldiers' evil actions would haunt them for the rest of their lives.

Beloved child: My people would survive and prosper, and I would be there alongside them, through the temperamental winter, to help them walk when they felt they couldn't.

EDGAR

I tortured myself over thoughts of the game *Savage,* wondering whether I would be captured or shot and killed. I wondered how many others had died in this place. Jackson and Lyle wanted me dead, I was convinced. I started to panic, then. I wore myself out imagining I was dodging bullets, running down alleyways, crouched between buildings. Bombs, explosions, pistols fired. I pictured myself near Devil's Bridge, being exposed to radiation and covered in mud while men in gas masks questioned me about whatever they wanted to know.

For a while I felt the urge to vomit and sat over a wastebasket with a finger down my throat, gagging myself. But I wasn't able to vomit, only dry heave, which made my eyes water. I tried to relax in my bed. I told myself to stay calm, stay civil. It had rained all night, a steady rain for a while. Outside

317

the window I could see branches of the oak tree waving in the wind. The thunder woke me up a few times with flashes of lightning, and I was coughing, which made me worry about my health, so I didn't sleep well. I thought about that projection of Ray-Ray. I looked out the window and saw puddles around the tree and in the road. I saw trees with low-hanging branches in the distance, white clapboard houses beyond a rickety fence. Everything appeared dreary, as usual, the world gray-blue in a darkening land. It rained hard for a while and then tapered off.

Time started to feel heavy. Lying there, I started to think about my mother and all the weight of her responsibilities, having to care for my dad. My thoughts turned to images. A memory of when I was six or seven years old, and she pretended to cry when I said I was going to run away but didn't make it farther than the fence out back. I don't remember why I made the threat or where I said I was going, only that I was running away from home, from her. I stood there for what felt like a long time, listening to her sniffles, her fake cries. I felt terrible about it. All these years later I still felt bad about it, threatening to run away, even though I knew she was only pretending to

318

cry. I stayed in the backyard and played with our dog Jack, rolling around in the grass with him. We played tug-of-war with a twig until it snapped. I let him chase me around the yard, and eventually I forgot about running away. My mother must've watched the whole thing from the back door, because when I came near the back porch, she was pretending to cry again. "I don't want you to run away," she said, putting her face in her hands.

Jackson stepped into the room and said my days were numbered. I sat up in bed, and he walked out. I got up and followed him into the kitchen.

"What does that mean?" I said. "My days are numbered."

His back was to me. He was stirring his coffee cup with a spoon. "I've been trying to create these augmented realities," he said. "This whole place is an alternate reality. Just look how many pillheads live here. People coughing, sick from decayed lungs, craving an alternate state of mind. We all overdo it."

"What are you talking about?"

He turned to me and took a sip of his coffee. "We've been using you to develop our gaming here. Now your days are numbered. It's an expression."

"I know the expression."

"We've got images of you all around town, Chief. People filmed you last night at the warehouse. It's a live shooting game."

"Fuck you."

His eyes widened, but he didn't say anything. It felt good to lash out at him. I could feel myself wanting to go on and on. I couldn't take him any longer.

"Another thing," I said. "I saw Ray-Ray's image last night in the projector downstairs. What the fuck are you doing?"

He waited for some time, thinking. "You saw whose image?"

"Cut the bullshit."

"Oh," he said. He looked at me and blinked slowly. "The machine projects images I feed it. I feed it images I get online all the time. I use Facebook photos or whatever, and I included photos of you and Ray-Ray and your sister."

"You're pathetic, Jackson. You deserve to be alone. I'm getting out of here."

"I wouldn't try to leave if I were you, Chief. You're the star of another game I've been working on. It's called *Savage.*"

"Yeah, I saw the manual, scumbag. Another dumb failure."

"That's what you think," he said. "We're beta-testing it now. People use real guns to

320

shoot Indians. That's why people act so weird around you. That's why I took video of you."

"What a cruel piece of shit you are. I can't believe I felt sorry for you."

"Maybe you should just leave," he said. "When people in town see you, they might assume you're a hologram and shoot. But you could take your chances, right? I think I'll just kick you out."

"Fuck off. I'd rather die out there than stay here with you."

He set down his coffee mug and stared directly at me. It was a look that took time, an attempt at intimidation, but it wasn't working. Jackson was deceptively strong, but not very tough. For as long as I knew him, he had never been tough but had always pretended to be. In school he was always getting into fights and never winning. I started to walk away, but he pushed me. I turned and struck him in the chest with the palm of my hand, and he grabbed my arm. We started to grapple right there in the kitchen. We wrestled like teenagers. Neither of us threw a punch, but we were telling each other off, wrestling. Finally I hit him on the side of his head, and he crouched down, crying out. I could see he was in pain. He held his head with one hand and started swinging blind with the other, but I moved back and went into my room and shut the door.

He didn't come after me or try to open the door. I tried to catch my breath. My mouth went dry, making it hard to swallow. A moment later I heard him leave, so I opened the door and went to the living room window. I saw him drive away. Then I went back to my room and packed my bag. How quickly everything had changed. I decided I hated Jackson Andrews, hated the Darkening Land and everything about it. I headed straight for the bathroom and opened his cabinets, looking for anything else, I didn't know what, anything he had hidden. There were bottles of pills, laxatives, mouthwash. There were Q-tips and creams, gels.

I left the bathroom, kicked open the door to his bedroom, and went through his dresser drawers, his closet, looked under his bed. I searched the whole house, going through everything I could find. Then I went downstairs and climbed the ladder to his projector. I ripped the lid off and threw it to the ground. Coughing, I kicked it against the wall, then stomped on it, but none of this made me feel any better.

■ ■ ■

Twenty minutes later I took my bag and left the rotting house for good, thinking Jackson might as well stay there forever, trapped in the darkness and unwilling to change. I walked away still angry, fueled by an intense desire to confront anyone who glanced at me or mentioned my being Native. I quickened my step as I walked away. I wanted to find my way to the train station. Surely I could get a ride. I thought of the apparition of the woman with the basket I had seen in the middle of the night. She had talked about a trail lined with cherry-blossom trees.

Bulbous clouds assumed strange shapes. The mist hanging above the grass was dense. I remembered a time growing up when my family took a walk around our house. We took lots of walks together, and it was a way for me to gather my thoughts, a type of meditation. On this particular walk, my dad told Sonja and me that our ancestors had hunted only for food, not sport, and that once an animal had been killed, we should ask for forgiveness and explain that we needed the animal for food. Animals were not to be exploited, my dad explained.

Neither were people. This had to do with our fundamental concern for harmony, and should always be followed. As I walked in the Darkening Land, I thought about my anger and how important it was to try to keep peace within myself. I thought about Ray-Ray's death and how I avoided talking about him with Rae and my family. How all anyone ever wanted to do was talk about him when he was alive, and that for some reason I despised him a little for getting the attention. I was no longer angry about that attention, I realized, and telling myself this made me feel better about myself. Spending time away from my family had helped me, I felt.

The road I walked seemed to open up into a new world, with a brilliant sunlight that appeared from behind a cloud. For the first time since I came there, the sky was very blue, the humidity stifling and causing me to sweat. I heard gunshots from somewhere, which frightened me. I followed the road as it wound around and downhill. I walked until I saw the road dead-ended ahead, past a park with a swing set, merry-go-round, and monkey bars, on which I saw children playing. Looking farther ahead, past where the road ended, I saw tall trees towering over the horizon. I walked toward the playground, past plum trees and peach trees and pink cherry trees. It was a land of enchantment. A boy on a bicycle rode past me, ringing his bicycle bell as he passed, and I watched him ride down the hill toward the playground. He climbed off his bicycle and ran to the others. There was a small pond and an old house at the end of the road beside the playground.

Once I got closer, I saw an older man working in his yard. He wore overalls and had long white hair. He was down on his knees, digging through a trash bag. When I passed him, he stood and looked at me.

"Siyo," he said.

I gave a slight wave and kept walking.

"Wait a minute," he said. "Come over here."

I turned and looked at him. He waved me over. He was holding up sheets of notebook paper. "These are all my writings," he said.

I approached him, and he handed them to me. "I think these are for you," he said.

There were scribblings in blue and black ink. "It's Cherokee," I said. "I recognize the symbols, but I can't read them."

"I'm Tsala," he said. His eyes held an intensity, full of years of pain and abandonment. I was struck by how intense and mysterious he appeared. "Maybe you should read my writings?"

"What for?"

"For help. There's the road with the pink cherry blossoms down yonder." He pointed toward the woods, and I saw swelled pink cherry blossoms in the distance. I felt overjoyed by this. In the blue-gray world, it was the brightest color I had seen.

"I need to leave this place," I said. "Where does the road lead?"

He paused a moment, then asked if I would join him for coffee. He was too old and frail to be dangerous, so I agreed, and we walked along a little trail to the back of his house. He invited me into his kitchen. The walls were covered with wallpaper with flowery designs, and darker ovals and rectangles where pictures used to hang. I saw dishes piled in the sink, spilled coffee, vials and prescription bottles on the counter. There was a small kitchen table with two chairs. He sat in one and pointed for me to sit in the other across from him.

He offered me coffee and poured a cup for himself as well. I drank it black from a red coffee mug. It wasn't too bad. I imagined him living alone, going to bed at night with no one to talk to or lie down with. I thought of him getting no help cooking or cleaning or washing his clothes. Tsala, poor old man, enduring the pain and loneliness of his old age. Still, I sensed a calm spirit about him.

He chewed on sugar cane and spoke in a low, serious voice. "A long time ago I built this house for people to stay in. I hauled lumber and erected strong beams. I built a solid roof and laid good floors. I built it for all the travelers to stay here. I devoted my life to this house. After my wife followed the road lined with cherry blossoms, I've kept my writings with me all the time, so people can read our stories while they stay here. You can stay here, but you should leave. Your heart is in the right place, beloved."

He brought his pipe, and we shared a smoke while I told him about my family. Oddly, the smoke wasn't making me cough, and when I told him this, he merely smiled. I told him about Ray-Ray dying. I told him about Rae leaving me. And I told him about my dad's forgetfulness in the early stages of Alzheimer's. All this flowed out of me with the smoke, and Tsala listened quietly and with full attention. As he listened, I noticed one of his eyes was blue and the other gray.

"Keep talking," he said, bringing the pipe to his lips.

"I feel guilty for not going home," I told

him. "My family is having a bonfire. I haven't seen them since they tried to help me with my drug problem."

He leaned in close and looked at me. "Drug problem?"

"Drug problem." It felt awkward to say, but maybe I had not been able to admit there was a problem. My denial overwhelmed me with guilt. "My family came to Albuquerque to confront me about it, but I wouldn't listen."

He stared at me intensely. He was a good listener, I realized, and soon I found there were tears in my eyes.

"I feel terrible about it," I said.

He got up and left the room for a few minutes. When he returned, he set a handful of stones on the table in front of me. He took a pencil and drew a triangle and placed stones within it. "These are the stones that represent the wisdom fire within you," he said. "Look for the fire."

I leaned in and studied the triangle and a stone within it. "This stone is a rose quartz," Tsala said. "It's for overcoming grief. I want you to take it and keep it with you. Go ahead, take it."

I reached in and took the stone. I looked at it in my hand. It was rose-colored and smooth.

"Remember your ancestors," he told me. "Remember they were removed from their homes, and then they had no homes. They walked the Trail, walked and crawled and died. They suffered. But you already know this. Come with me, I want to show you something."

I followed him outside, and that was when I saw the red fowl strutting around the yard. "The fowl," I called out, and stopped walking. I realized I hadn't seen the fowl in some time — I had almost forgotten about it. The fowl saw us, and Tsala moved toward it. He reached down to pick it up. I saw the fowl trying to peck him, its wings fluttering like crazy. Tsala held it with both hands, wrestled it until it stopped moving and went limp. The fowl was dead. Then he took it over by his garden, where an ax was on the ground. He dropped the bird and lifted the ax, bringing it down hard, cutting the fowl's head off. I could barely watch.

When I approached him, he showed me the bloody carcass. "For you," he said. "This fowl is now dead. Do you understand?"

"What now?" I asked.

"We bury it."

He set the carcass down and went inside his garage to get a shovel. I found myself staring at the dead fowl. I saw the severed head with its dark eye, staring at me. I saw the carcass lying dead in blood and soil. No matter how hard I tried, I could not stop looking. A moment later Tsala returned with a shovel and dug a small hole in the ground right where we stood. He used the shovel to toss the carcass and head into the ground. I crossed my arms and watched the whole thing. Each shovelful of dirt made a hard sound as it hit the carcass, and after a moment Tsala had buried it completely.

I was exhausted, but felt like a great burden had lifted from me. I looked at the cherry trees around me and felt somehow connected to each one. I wondered how many people Tsala had helped before me — maybe as many people as there were trees. Tsala then led me to the trail with the cherry blossoms. We heard voices approaching and, turning around, saw a group of men walking down the road toward Tsala's house. They were wearing masks and headsets, talking loudly. In their hands they carried sticks, long clubs that looked like broom handles. They saw us and stopped walking.

Tsala shouted at them to leave. "Go!" he yelled. "Go away from here, cowards! Leave us alone!"

He made a shooting gesture with his

hands for them to hurry away, and, miraculously, they did. I had been bracing myself for a fight, and I stood there stunned for a moment, shocked that they had obeyed Tsala.

"Go follow the trail lined with cherry blossoms," he told me. "It is not a trail of tears, son. It is a trail leading westward, without sadness or sickness or death. It is a trail to your home."

He shook my hand, and I told him goodbye. As I started to walk, I turned back to him and asked, "What are your writings? I never asked."

He called out, "I'm writing the Cherokee stories, beloved. The stories about vengeance and forgiveness."

I watched his body crumple, and he turned into a phoenix. He spread his wings and flew into the gray sky.

Then I left the darkening land. I followed the trail lined with cherry blossoms, looking ahead to the distance, listening to the sounds of owls and frogs around me. I walked down this trail and wasn't afraid. I knew I was walking west because I could see in the distance the setting sun. The sky was pink and yellow, and cherry blossoms spilled onto the trail ahead. Feathers were soon falling all around me, flooding the trail, as white as a fresh winter snow. The winding trail was beautiful. I saw my ancestors ahead, but they were not crawling and wailing, they were standing. Their bodies filled the distance. I walked to them and did not grow tired. The trail before me was blazing with light.

MARIA

September 6

I woke early, at dawn, while Ernest snored beside me. I made coffee in the kitchen and sat at the table, thinking about the day ahead. Barely awake, I stared into the texture of the wall, creating tiny shapes, little bodies and faces. I saw an eye, a bird. Then I opened my notebook and wrote:

Ray-Ray's spirit channeled Wyatt. I can barely breathe, thinking about it.

I set my pen down and closed the notebook. Outside the window, a flock of sparrows was gathering in the early-morning grass. I felt anxious. I would normally look forward to the hearing and seeing a reunification of foster child with family, but this felt different. To see Wyatt leave with his grandparents, other people, felt painful.

Wyatt was already packed and ready to go

an hour later. I made him waffles and orange juice, and he ate in silence. I didn't want to bring up the hearing. Ernest came into the room, and I was surprised to see him turn down breakfast. He drank coffee and sat across the table from Wyatt. Both of them had their heads down, and I stood there awkwardly watching them.

It wasn't any better when I drove us to the courthouse. Nobody talked in the car. In a moment of irrational thought I wanted to steal Wyatt and drive far away, separated from everyone in Quah, away from Oklahoma. To leave this place, coasting down the interstate without a care. We passed the places Ray-Ray used to love to go: the Tastee Freez, the Smokey's BBQ. We passed the Del Rancho, old shops. Muskogee Avenue curved ahead north, and we came to a stoplight. In the rearview mirror I saw Wyatt in the back seat, staring out the window. I saw his dreamy gaze, such brilliant, drowsy eyes. A glint of sunlight illuminated his face. In that moment I saw Ray-Ray's eyes, as I had seen him so many years before in the back seat, driving north along Muskogee, and something fluttered in my heart. The car behind me was blaring its horn, and I realized the light was green. The car jumped as I hit the pedal, but neither Wyatt nor Ernest said anything. My heart was racing. I drove in silence, both hands on the wheel.

Bernice met us at the courthouse in good spirits, though I could clearly see that Ernest was upset as he sat in the lobby with his arms crossed. Wyatt and Bernice and I stood by the front door, waiting for Wyatt's grandparents to show. Ernest was looking straight ahead, irritated. The courthouse lobby was empty and pale, too quiet, with tall ceilings and photographs of elderly white men on the walls.

"I need a magazine or TV to pass the time," Ernest said.

"It's not a dentist's office," I told him. "You'll need to try to relax, Ernest."

"I can't."

"You have to try. Everything is going to be fine."

I said this more for myself than to ease Ernest's mind. I was trying to hold it together, but I could sense we were falling apart by the minute. I hoped Wyatt's grandparents wouldn't show — for Ernest's mental health, and for some measure of my own happiness. I excused myself and went into the restroom down the hall, where I splashed cold water on my face. I hadn't slept well, worried about the hearing. We had never fostered before. What a strange and profound effect Wyatt had had on us; I hadn't felt anything like it. In the mirror I saw my reflection, a face marked by lines and age. A face marked by the persistence of hope, tragedy, abandonment, and grief. I reminded myself I was a woman who maintained strength through everything.

In the bathroom, at the mirror, I waited. I summoned memories of my young motherhood: they came flooding in, like a flickering slideshow, images of Sonja, Ray-Ray, and Edgar filling the silence in the room. I saw them gathered at the dinner table, laughing and eating. I saw them sleeping in their beds. I saw them playing with their toys on sunny days outside. Thinking of the sun and the sky opening into a vast blue outside, I pictured the endless fields surrounding the kids, the still and peaceful grass. If one looked closely, there were yellow butterflies, swirling gnats, crawling insects, new life forming in nature, which I envied briefly — all those short-lived forms of life void of logic or thinking, void of emotion, guilt, or pain.

Back in the lobby, the grandparents had arrived and were talking to Bernice. I thought they were a little younger than me and Ernest, closer to Bernice's age, maybe sixty. The grandfather had white hair in a ponytail. He looked cheerful, smiling and nodding as Bernice talked. The grandmother's hair was deep black with streaks of gray. They were both tall, large of build.

When I walked up, Bernice introduced me to them. Their names were Thomas and Viv.

"How has he been?" Viv asked me.

I glanced at her, and then at Thomas. I could see the concern in their eyes.

"He's been a real joy. A real blessing," I told them, looking at Wyatt as I said this.

"He can be an angel," Viv said. "We're glad we could make the drive down."

"It was a six-hour drive," Bernice said. "Are you driving straight back?"

"Thomas doesn't like to travel anymore," Viv said, "so we'll stop and eat and then head back."

I looked to Ernest, waving him over, and we all waited for him to join us. Bernice introduced Thomas and Viv to him, and he seemed hurt, almost angry, but he was polite. The awkwardness of the moment reasserted itself. Bernice talked about Wyatt's clothes. He had dressed nicely, wearing a collared shirt and slacks. He was quiet, but he didn't look bothered or upset, which pleased me. And his grandparents were friendly and gentle with him. It was likely that the judge would release Wyatt to them.

Soon, too soon, we were called into the courtroom for the hearing. We were led in front of the bench. The judge entered in his black robe and quietly reviewed the documents. He was a short, stocky man with a large mustache. His expression was serious and never changed, not when he spoke or when he looked at anyone, including Wyatt. Bernice informed him of Wyatt's progress and his temporary placement with us.

The judge nodded, touched his chin as he silently read. He looked up from his documents at Wyatt. "Well, this looks like quite a good report, young man," he said. "How are things going in school?"

"Good," Wyatt said.

"Do you like your teachers?"

"Yes, sir."

"What's your favorite subject?"

"Probably language arts," he said. "Actually science."

The judge looked at Ernest, then at me. "He's been doing well?"

"I don't know what to say," I told him, hesitating. "He's followed our rules."

I could see the judge was waiting for more. For some reason I felt nervous. "He

338

really is so well behaved, Your Honor. He's been a joy in our home."

The judge smiled at Wyatt. All the years I stood in the courtroom with other children, all those days spent giving reports, it was all here again, yet it felt so different being a foster parent. The moment remained still, a night awaiting sunlight, some glimmer of lost hope on the horizon. Some moments remain preserved in time, remembered perfectly, and I hoped this would be true in the short time I spent with Wyatt.

It was a short hearing, of course. The judge praised Wyatt for doing well in school and showing respect in foster care. He placed him in his grandparents' custody and set a three-month review.

"Thank you, Your Honor," Wyatt said, as politely as a rehearsed line, though I knew, and certainly the judge, too, that it was sincere.

We exited to the lobby. Thomas thanked Bernice and us for taking care of Wyatt for a few days. I looked at Wyatt, and he came to hug me. I held him there, closing my eyes. Then he hugged Ernest.

"Ave atque vale," he said to us.

"What?" I said.

"It's Latin for hail and farewell."

Later, I would remember Ray-Ray using

this phrase the night before he died. At the moment, I felt too light-headed to catch it. As Wyatt and his grandparents walked out together, I put on my sunglasses and felt on the brink of collapse. I had to take Ernest's arm to brace myself as we stepped outside.

In the parking lot, Wyatt turned and looked at me one last time, a photograph frozen in the moment, timeless. He was a snapshot of Ray-Ray's spirit, looking back at me under the bright sun. He waved. I closed my eyes a moment, and when I opened them, Wyatt and his grandparents were in the car. I heard a gust of wind. I heard the roar of a plane overhead.

In that moment I had a memory of Ray-Ray falling asleep on the floor when he was little. I picked him up and carried him to bed. Another memory came: Ray-Ray sick on a rainy day, lying in his bed with a washcloth on his forehead. I removed the thermometer from his mouth and leaned down to kiss the top of his head. Ray-Ray in his pajamas. Wanting to be held. Wanting to be rocked to sleep and sung to. Wanting to sit on my lap and look at picture books. Getting out of his bed and sneaking down the hallway to crawl into bed with Ernest and me. I pretended to be asleep sometimes, letting him snuggle. Those memories flooded my mind in an instant, and I waved goodbye to him.

The car pulled out of the lot. My heart was racing. "Wait —," I breathed, and Ernest embraced me. He knew what was happening.

"Wait," I breathed again.

A year earlier, I had driven up to Calvin Hoff's place alone. I didn't want to tell anyone, not even Ernest. I didn't know what to expect. I suppose I was looking for my own personal peace or healing, but mostly I wanted closure. I needed to tell him who I was, remind him what he did. That morning I had called Calvin's sister, Madelyn Cheney, a retired nurse who attended the church near our house. We had met once, briefly, at a church supper I attended several years earlier. "He has lung cancer," she said on the phone. "It's really hard for us right now. He has in-home care."

"This is more for me than him," I told her. "For my own healing. It's been almost fifteen years since we lost Ray-Ray."

"I understand," she said. She hesitated. "He can't really have much of a conversation. It's his mind."

"This is more for me," I said again.

She was silent a moment, and then she

gave me the address.

The house was north of town on a winding gravel road that curved uphill. When I reached the house, I saw two dogs lying in the front yard. The house was brick, with a covered porch and no garage. I pulled into the dirt drive and saw a woman come to the door. When I got out, the dogs were at the fence, barking.

"They won't hurt you," the woman called from the porch.

I let myself in the front gate and the dogs were at my feet, their tails wagging hard. Somehow they never jumped up on me. They followed me to the porch, where the woman introduced herself as Ellen, the caretaker.

"Come in," she said. "Madelyn said you would be stopping by. He's resting in the back room. I should tell you his mind isn't what it used to be. He's not saying much today."

"I understand," I said, starting to have second thoughts about coming as I followed her down a dark hallway. The house was full of dimly lit rooms, warm and stuffy. Country-and-western music was playing from the back. The house held a presence of sickness, the way nursing homes feel, as if death is a shadow looming around dark corners, waiting.

When we reached the room, I saw Calvin Hoff sitting on the edge of an iron-frame bed, staring at the floor. He was wearing a white undershirt and checkered pajama pants. He looked nothing like the way I remembered him from court so long ago. He was now thin and bald, his face pale and empty from the chemotherapy.

Ellen turned off the phonograph. "He likes listening to Charlie Rich records," she said. "It's the only thing he asks for." She went over to the window and opened the blinds, brightening the room. I saw newspaper pages scattered all over the floor. Bits of dust settled in the slanted sunlight streaming in from the window.

"Calvin, this lady would like to talk for a few minutes," Ellen said to him. I waited for her to step out of the room before I moved closer to him and spoke.

"I'm Maria Echota," I told him. "My son was Ray-Ray Echota."

I waited a moment, but he didn't respond.

"I'm Maria Echota," I said again. "You shot my son Ray-Ray at a shopping mall fifteen years ago. Do you remember that? Surely you do. You remember shooting my son."

He kept staring at the floor. He scratched

at his upper lip, but he wouldn't look up at me.

"What I need to say to you," I said, "is that I want to learn how to forgive you. That's what I have wanted for a long time, to learn how to forgive you for what you did. I have thought about this for a long time."

"Charlie Rich," he said weakly. He blinked, confused. "Not the polygraph."

"I want to tell you that even though I want more than anything to forgive you, I can't," I said. "I can't. You shot my son. You killed him out of your own ignorance and bigotry. I'll never be able to forgive you for that."

He shook his head, confused. He kept scratching at his upper lip. On the dresser beside his bed were vials of pills and liquids. Magazines were stacked on the same dresser, hunting magazines, firearm magazines. I looked around the room while he sat there, silent. He was squinting at something on the floor.

I had imagined this moment very differently, with me screaming at him. I had always pictured myself hitting him repeatedly with my bare hands. The moment had finally arrived, and there I was, confronting him, ready to unleash my anger. But standing there now, I couldn't do it. I was not as angry as I had expected to be. Despite my reason for being there, despite everything, I could not help but feel sad for him.

"The revolver," he said weakly, staring into the floor.

Maybe empathy was the beginning of healing, I remember thinking. Or maybe I was unaware that time had already healed me.

September 6, that melancholy, weary afternoon lingered quietly before the evening bonfire. Back home, at lunch, the meat was cooked without a word, eaten while the sun crept in through the windows. The bread was passed to Ernest and he devoured it, crumb by crumb. I had no idea how he was able to eat. I hardly touched anything on my plate.

Late in the afternoon I tried to keep busy cleaning the house. Whatever hope I had felt lost in the moment. Sweeping the kitchen, I struggled with the situation in my mind: what would happen with Wyatt, whether I would see him again, whether I would feel Ray-Ray's spirit again. Everything would work itself out, I assured myself. I wanted to try to take my mind off things, off Wyatt and off Edgar, who had been in my thoughts a lot among everything else. I imagined the coming night, picturing the flames of the bonfire lighting up Ernest and Sonja's faces as we marked the anniversary of Ray-Ray's passing. Afterward, sitting underneath the sky in the cool breeze of the night, I would tell myself he was there with me. That everyone was there with me, including Edgar.

For me, for all of us, September 6 will always hold a strange sadness mixed with celebration.

Outside, Sonja helped Ernest gather wood for the bonfire behind the house, near the water. The wind passed over us, and the sun had gone behind the clouds, leaving a gray, oppressive afternoon. I slept on and off for a while on the couch. When I woke, I sat up and looked at my trembling hands.

Outside, the wind made it difficult for Ernest to get the bonfire going, but he had always been an expert at it, having built campfires for many years. I brought the food out, the rainbow corn and blackberries Ray-Ray always loved and the bread I'd baked, while Sonja spread blankets on the ground for us. We sat on the blankets and ate in silence, the three of us. We had our silent supper to think about Ray-Ray, our family, and what we would share. In the last light of the day, Ernest put more wood on the bonfire while Sonja and I sat together on the blanket.

"It looks good," Sonja said quietly.

"Soon it'll be dark," I told her.

Something flashed on the horizon, and we heard the distant call of an owl. The fire was warm and bright, and my breathing was shallow. We sat in silence as the sky hardened to night. I saw Sonja's eyes, harsh and gleaming.

"This is a time to think about Ray-Ray," Ernest said. "It's also a time to think about our family."

Sonja was kneeling in front of the bonfire, her head bowed. She was mysteriously still, an image of a statue in a garden. Slowly, she began to hum. When I looked at Ernest, I noticed that his eyes were watery, and I felt gratitude that he was well. I longed for the moment to last forever. I longed to lie down and roll around in the grass and let myself be pulled into a tunnel. I imagined myself crawling through the tunnel with Ernest, Sonja, and Edgar following close behind. The tunnel would be a long hallway lit with candles leading to some place far away, where the passageway ended in a reunification with Ray-Ray.

A swarm of locusts buzzed from the trees, disappearing into the dark sky. In the distance, I noticed that someone was walking toward us. I saw a figure, a man. Ernest noticed him too, then took my hand and squeezed it. The figure was difficult to see in only the light of the fire, but I could tell he was glowing and beautiful.

"Look, there," Ernest said, pointing.

Sonja opened her eyes, stopped humming, and put her hands to her face. In the stillness of the night, there was the distant sound of voices. We could see the figure emerging from the darkness and approaching us. *Listen! Do you hear? Listen.* We heard the creaking of oaks, the rustle of trees shaken alive by a gust of wind. We heard the incessant voices all around us, the voices of our people, our ancestors, all of them whispering: *Home.*

ACKNOWLEDGMENTS

Many thanks, first, to Caroline Eisenmann for the early reads, helpful comments, and important suggestions. Big thanks also to Sara Birmingham at Ecco for the strong editorial vision to help shape this book and its timeline, especially with Tsala's sections. Thanks to Caitlin Mulrooney-Lyski and everyone else at Ecco. Thanks to Brad McLelland, who suggested the title at a coffee shop in Ponca, Oklahoma. Thanks to Geary Hobson and Rilla Askew for their support. I'm indebted to Brad Morrow for publishing excerpts at *Conjunctions,* and to Claire Boyle for publishing an excerpt at *McSweeney's.* Thanks to my colleagues in the English department at New Mexico State for their support, especially Rus Bradburd, Connie Voisine, and Richard Greenfield. Thanks also to my colleagues at the Institute of American Indian Arts for their support. Some of Cherokee myths in this novel are either a product of my imagination or are based on certain myths in James Mooney's *Myths of the Cherokee* (U.S. Bureau of American Ethnology, 1897–8 Annual Report, 1902), which is a great resource for early Cherokee stories. I'm always indebted to my former teacher and mentor and friend, Stewart O'Nan. Thanks to my family for all their support. Finally, a very special thanks to the person who wanted to remain anonymous but who shared such important information to help me understand Maria's character better. *Wado* and peace.

ABOUT THE AUTHOR

Brandon Hobson is the author of the novel *Where the Dead Sit Talking,* which was a finalist for the 2018 National Book Award for Fiction and winner of the Reading the West Book Award. His other books include *Desolation of Avenues Untold* and the novella *Deep Ellum.* His work has appeared in the Pushcart Prize anthology, *The Believer,* the *Paris Review Daily, Conjunctions, NOON,* and *McSweeney's,* among other places. He is an assistant professor of creative writing at New Mexico State University and teaches in the MFA program at the Institute of American Indian Arts. Hobson is an enrolled citizen of the Cherokee Nation Tribe of Oklahoma.